The Horror of Love.
The Beauty of Death.

From the moment of conception, each new life-
form begins a journey toward death. Along the
way, living organisms seek out partners with whom
to propagate the species. Human beings, however,
may be driven by lustful passions other than
reproduction—sexual compulsions so intense that
their hungers can overcome the best of intentions
and tempt even the coldest of hearts to pump . . .
HOT BLOOD!

Praise for Previous Books in the
HOT BLOOD Series

"Outstanding . . . A daring combination of sex
and terror." —*Cemetery Dance* magazine

"One of the best . . . Rush out and buy *Hot
Blood*—but don't say we didn't warn you that
you'll be up all night reading it. . . ."
—*Fangoria* magazine

"Seek out this one (or its predecessors) for some
naughty fun. . . ." —*Booklovers*

Books Edited by Jeff Gelb and Michael Garrett

Books Edited by Jeff Gelb

Hot Blood

Crimes of Passion

Edited by Jeff Gelb and Michael Garrett

POCKET BOOKS

New York   London   Toronto   Sydney   Tokyo   Singapore

This book consists of works of fiction. Names, characters, places and incidents are products of the authors' imaginations or are used fictitiously. Any resemblance to actual events or locales or persons, living or dead, is entirely coincidental.

An *Original* Publication of POCKET BOOKS

POCKET BOOKS, a division of Simon & Schuster Inc.
1230 Avenue of the Americas, New York, NY 10020

Copyright © 1997 by Jeff Gelb and Michael Garrett

ISBN: 0-671-00949-4

First Pocket Books printing November 1997

10 9 8 7 6 5 4 3 2 1

POCKET and colophon are registered trademarks of Simon & Schuster Inc.

Cover art by Gerber Studio

Printed in the U.S.A.

Copyright Notices

To our agent, Joshua Bilmes, a hardworking, knowledgeable and friendly guy. Thanks for your belief in and support of all of our efforts. We'll make you rich yet!

CONTENTS

CONTENTS

INTRODUCTION

Welcome to the "new" *Hot Blood*!

Beginning with this, the ninth volume, we've incorporated a fresh cover design and have dropped "series" from the title. Those of you who have been with us all along already know who we are and have learned to expect erotic fiction of the highest caliber here. And those of you who are new—well, do we have a buzz for you!

If this is your first *Hot Blood*, here's what we're all about: *Hot Blood* is a continuing multiple-author collection of short stories combining elements of sex and horror. The two ingredients are "married" within each story; in other words, if either is omitted, the story collapses. There's nothing gratuitous in a *Hot Blood* story. Sex is the primary motivating factor behind the behavior of the major characters.

Sex is one of the most basic human drives, and the ultimate bond between human beings. We all think about it, practice it, talk about it, dream about it. And in *Hot Blood* we *read* about it, too.

In putting together the *Hot Blood* books, we ask the best suspense and horror writers in the world to tell us what turns them on, and simultaneously, to craft an intensely horrific story out of it. We want to keep you, the reader, happy; the *Hot Blood* books are for *your* enjoyment. You've come to expect a lot from us over the first eight volumes, and we're up for continuing the challenge. We try to balance the stories between supernatural and psychological horror, between subjects of primary interest to both men and women, young and old—we strive for a level of consistency that will assure readers an orgasm of pleasure each time a new volume hits the shelves. We encourage you to write to us in care of Pocket Books and tell us what turns *you* on. We'd like to hear from you, whether this is your first volume or your ninth.

You'll note the presence of a few tasty reprints in this volume. We've generally maintained an "all-new" story approach in *Hot Blood,* but reader demand has made us rethink this position. After all, some of your favorite authors have previously written outstanding erotic horror fiction, which has become hard to find in its original sources. This and future volumes will include a taste of historic *Hot Blood*ed fiction and a majority of new fiction.

We've always prided ourselves on including work by new writers as well—authors who have since established literary greatness. We expect no less from this volume's newcomers. At the same time we are tireless in our efforts to find established writers of significant stature who want to dip a literary limb into the *Hot Blood* waters. That's why in this, and every *Hot Blood* volume, you'll note some surprisingly familiar names, great writers who will help us expand the *Hot Blood* boundaries toward new, exciting territories.

We hope to see you again next time, with the tenth volume of *Hot Blood*. Watch for it.

Till then, *don't let the bedbugs bite* . . . unless they're friendly!

Jeff Gelb
Michael Garrett

Crimes of Passion

THE LIMITS OF FANTASY

Ramsey Campbell

As Sid Pym passed his door and walked two blocks to look in the shop window, a duck jeered harshly in the park. March frost had begun to bloom on the window, but the streetlamp made the magazine covers shine: the schoolgirl in her twenties awaiting a spanking, the two bronzed men displaying samples of their muscles to each other, the topless woman tonguing a lollipop. Sid was looking away in disgust from two large masked women flourishing whips over a trussed victim when the girl marched past behind him.

Her reflection glided from cover to cover, her feet trod on the back of the trussed man's head. Despite the jumbling of images, Sid knew her. He recognized her long blond hair, her slim, graceful legs, firm breasts, plump jutting bottom outlined by her ankle-length coat, and as she glanced in his direction, he saw that she recognized him. He had time to glimpse how she wrinkled her nose as her reflection left the shop window.

He almost started after her. She'd reacted as if he

1

was one of the men who needed those magazines, but he was one of the people who created them. He'd only come to the window to see how his work shaped up, and there it was, between a book about Nazi war crimes and an Enid Stone romance. He'd given the picture of Toby Hale and his wife Jilly a warm amber tint to go with the title *Pretty Hot,* and he thought it looked classier than most of its companions. He didn't think Toby needed to worry so much about the rising costs of production. If Sid had gone in for that sort of thing, he would have bought the magazine on the strength of the cover.

The newspapers had to admit he was good, one of the best in town. That was why the *Weekly News* wanted him to cover Enid Stone's return home, even though some of the editors seemed to dislike accepting pictures from him since word had got round that he was involved in *Pretty Hot.* Why should anyone disparage him for doing a friend a favor? It wasn't even as though he posed; he only took the photographs. There ought to be a way to let the blond girl know that, to make her respect him. He swung away from the shop window and stalked after her, telling himself that if he caught up with her he'd have it out with her. But the street was already deserted, and as he reached his building her window, in the midst of the house opposite his rooms, lit up.

He felt as if she had let him know she'd seen him before pulling the curtains—as if she'd glimpsed his relief at not having to confront her. He bruised his testicles as he groped for his keys, and that enraged him more than ever. A phone, which he recognized as his once the front door was open, had started ringing, and he dashed up the musty stairs in the dark.

It was Toby Hale on the phone. "Still free tomorrow? They're willing."

"A bit different, is it? A bit stronger?"

"What the punters want."

"I'm all for giving people what they really want," Sid declared, and took several quick breaths. The blond girl was in her bathroom now. "I'll see you at the studio," he told Toby, and fumbled the receiver into place.

What was she trying to do to him? If she had watched him come home, she must know he was in his room, even though he hadn't had time to switch on the light. Besides, this wasn't the first time she'd behaved as if the frosted glass of her bathroom window ought to stop him watching her. "Black underwear, is it now?" he said through his teeth, and bent over his bed to reach for a camera.

God, she thought a lot of herself. Each of her movements looked like a pose to Sid as he reeled her toward him with the zoom lens. Despite the way the window fragmented her, he could distinguish the curve of her bottom in black knickers and the black swellings of her breasts. Then her breasts turned flesh-colored, and she dropped the bra. She was slipping the knickers down her bare legs when the whir of rewinding announced that he'd finished the roll of Tri-X. "Got you," he whispered, and hugged the camera to himself.

When she passed beyond the frame of the window, he coaxed his curtains shut and switched the room light on. He was tempted to develop the roll now, but anticipating it made him feel so powerful in a sleepy, generalized way that he decided to wait until the morning, when he would be more awake. He took *Pretty Hot* to bed with him and scanned the article about sex magic, and an idea was raising its head in his when he fell asleep.

* * *

3

He slept late. In the morning he had to leave the Tri-X negatives and hurry to the studio. Fog slid flatly over the pavement before him, vehicles nosed through the gray, grumbling monotonously. It occurred to him as he turned along the cheap side street near the edge of town that people were less likely to notice him in the fog, though why should he care if they did?

Toby opened the street door at Sid's triple knock and preceded him up the carpetless stairs. Toby had already set up the lights and switched them on, which made the small room with its double bed and mock-leather sofa appear starker than ever. A brawny man was sitting on the sofa with a woman draped facedown across his knees, her short skirt thrown back, her black nylon knickers more or less pulled down.

Apart from the mortar-board jammed onto his head, the man looked like a wrestler or a bouncer. He glanced up as Sid entered, and the hint of a warning crossed his large, bland, reddish face as Sid appraised the woman. She was too plump for Sid's taste, her mottled buttocks too flabby. She looked bored—more so when she glanced at Sid, who disliked her at once.

"This is Sid, our snapshooter," Toby announced. "Sid, our friends are going to model for both stories."

"All right there, mate," the man said, and the woman grunted.

Sid glanced through the viewfinder, then made to adjust the woman's knickers; but he hadn't touched them when the man's hand seized his wrist. "Hands off. I'll do that. She's my wife."

"Come on, the lot of you," the woman complained. "I'm getting a cold bum."

It wouldn't be cold for long, Sid thought, and felt his penis stir unexpectedly. But the man didn't hit her, he only mimed the positions as if he were enacting a series of film stills, resting his hand on her buttocks to denote slaps. For the pair of color shots Toby could afford the man rubbed rouge on her bottom.

"That was okay, was it, Sid?" Toby said anxiously. "It'd be nice if we could shoot 'Slave of Love' tomorrow."

"Wouldn't be nice for us," the woman said, groaning as she stood up. "We've got our lives to lead, you know."

"We could make it a week today," her husband said.

"They look right for the stories, I reckon," Hale told Sid when they'd left. "I'm working on some younger models, but those two'll do for that kind of stuff. The perves who want it don't care."

Sid thought it best to agree, but as he walked home he grew angrier: How could that fat bitch have given him a tickle? Working with people like her might be one of Sid's steps to fame, but she needed him more than he needed her. "I'll retouch you, but I won't touch you," he muttered, grinning. Someone like the blond girl over the road, now—she would have been Sid's choice of a model for "Spanked and Submissive," and it wouldn't all have been faked, either.

That got his penis going. He had to stand still for a few minutes until its tip went back to sleep, and the thought of the negatives waiting in his darkroom didn't help. He would have her in his hands, he would be able to do what he liked with her. He had to put the idea out of his head before he felt safe to walk.

After the fog even the dim musty hall of the house seemed like a promise of clarity. In his darkroom he watched the form of the blond girl rise from the developing fluid, and he felt as if a fog of dissatisfaction with himself and with the session at the studio were leaving him. The photographs came clear, and for a moment he couldn't understand why the girl's body was composed of dots like a newspaper photograph enlarged beyond reason. Of course, it was the frosting on her bathroom window.

Having her in his flat without her knowing excited him, but not enough. Perhaps he needed her to be home so that he could watch her failure to realize he had her. He opened a packet of hamburgers and cooked himself whatever meal it was. The effort annoyed him, and so did the eating: chew, chew, chew. He switched on the television, and the little picture danced for him, oracular heads spoke. He kept glancing at the undeveloped frame of her window.

By the time she arrived home, the fog was spiked with drizzle. As soon as she had switched on the light, she began to remove her clothes, but before she'd taken off more than her coat she drew the curtains. Had she seen him? Was she taking pleasure in his frustration at having to imagine her undressing? But he already had her almost naked. He spread the photographs across the table, and then he lurched toward his bed to find the article about sex magic.

By themselves the photographs were only pieces of card, but what had the article said? Toby Hale had put in all the ideas he could find about images during an afternoon spent in the library. The Catholic church sometimes made an image of a demon and burned it to bring off an exorcism. . . . Someone in Illinois killed a man by letting rain fall on his photograph. . . . Here it was, the stuff Toby had found in a book about magic by someone with a degree from a university Sid had never heard of. The best spells are the ones you write yourself. Find the words that are truest to your secret soul. Focus your imagination, build up to the discharge of psychic energy. Chant the words that best express your desires. Toby was talking about doing that with your partner, but it had given Sid a better idea. He hurried to the window, his undecided penis hindering him a little, and shut the curtains tight.

As he returned to the table he felt uneasy: excited, furtive, ridiculous—he wasn't sure which was uppermost. If only this could work! You never know until you try, he thought, which was the motto on the contents page of *Pretty Hot*. He pulled the first photograph to him. Her breasts swelled in their lacy bra, her black knickers were taut over her round bottom. He wished he could see her face. He cleared his throat, and muttered almost inaudibly: "I'm going to take your knickers down. I'm going to smack your bare bum."

He sounded absurd. The whole situation was absurd. How could he expect it to work if he could barely hear himself? "By the time I've finished with you," he said loudly, "you won't be able to sit down for a week."

Too loud! Nobody could hear him, he told himself. Except that he could, and he sounded like a fool. As he glared at the photograph, he was sure that she was smiling. She had beaten him. He wouldn't put it past her to have let him take the photographs because they had absolutely no effect on her. All at once he was furious. "You've had it now!" he shouted.

His eyes were burning. The photograph flickered and appeared to stir. He thought her face turned up to him. If it did, it must be out of fear. His penis pulled eagerly at his fly. "All right, miss!" he shouted hoarsely. "Those knickers are coming down."

She seemed to jerk, and he could imagine her bending reluctantly beneath the pressure of a hand on the back of her neck. Her black knickers stretched over her bottom. Then the photograph blurred as tears tried to dampen his eyes, but he could see her more clearly than ever. By God, the tears ought to be hers. "Now then," he shouted, "you're going to get what you've been asking for!"

He seized her bare arm. She tried to pull away, shaking her head mutely, her eyes bright with apprehension. In a moment he'd trapped her legs between his thighs and pushed her across his knee, locking his left arm around her waist. Her long blond hair trailed to the floor, concealing her face. He took hold of the waistband of her knickers and drew them slowly down, gradually revealing her round creamy buttocks. When she began to wriggle, he trapped her more firmly with his arm and legs. "Let's see what this feels like," he said, and slapped her hard.

He heard it. For a moment he was sure he had. He stared about his empty flat with his hot eyes. He almost went to peer between the curtains at her window, but gazed at the photograph instead. "Oh, no, miss, you won't get away from me," he whispered, and saw her move uneasily as he closed his eyes.

He began systematically to slap her: one on the left buttock, one on the right. After a dozen of these her bottom was turning pink and he was growing hot— his face, his penis, the palm of his hand. He could feel her warm thighs squirming between his. "You like that, do you? Let's see how much you like."

Two slaps on the left, two on the right. A dozen pairs of those, then five on the same spot, five on the other. As her bottom grew red she tried to cover it with her hands, but he pinned her wrists together with his left hand and, forcing them up to the dimple above her bottom, went to work in earnest: ten on the left buttock, ten on its twin . . . She was sobbing beneath her hair, her bottom was wriggling helplessly. His room had gone. There was nothing but Sid and his victim until he came violently and unexpectedly, squealing.

He didn't see her the next day. She was gone when he wakened from a satisfied slumber, and she had drawn the curtains before he realized she was home again. She was making it easier for him to see her the way he wanted. Anticipating that during the days which followed made him feel secretly powerful, and so did Toby Hale's suggestion when Sid rang him to confirm the "Slave of Love" session. "We're short of stories for number three," Toby said. "I don't suppose you've got anything good and strong for us?"

"I might have," Sid told him.

He didn't fully realize how involving it would be until he began to write. He was dominating her not only by writing about her but also by delivering her up to the readers of the magazine. He made her into a new pupil at a boarding school for girls in their late teens. *"Your here to lern disiplin. My naime is Mr. Sidney and dont you forgett it."* She would wear kneesocks and a gymslip that revealed her uniform knickers whenever she bent down. *"Over my nee, yung lady. Im goaing to give you a speling leson." "Plese plese dont take my nickers down, Ill be a good gurl." "You didnt cawl me Mr. Sidney, thats two dozin extrar with the hare brush. . . ."* He felt as if the words were unlocking a secret aspect of himself, a core of unsuspected truth which gave him access to some kind of power. Was this what they meant by sex magic? It took him almost a week of evenings to savor writing the story, and he didn't mind not seeing her all that week; it helped him see her as he was writing her. Each night as he drifted off to sleep he imagined her lying in bed sobbing, rubbing her bottom.

At the end of the story he met her on the bus.

He was returning from town with a bagful of film.

She caught the bus just as he was lowering himself onto one of the front seats downstairs. As she boarded the bus she saw him, and immediately looked away. Even though there were empty seats, she stayed on her feet, holding on to the pole by the stairs.

Sid gazed at the curve of her bottom, defining itself and then growing blurred as her long coat swung with the movements of the bus plowing through the fog. Why wouldn't she sit down? He leaned forward impulsively, emboldened by the nights he'd spent in secret with her, and touched her arm. "Would you like to sit down, love?"

She looked down at him, and he recoiled. Her eyes were bright with loathing, and yet she looked trapped. She shook her head once, keeping her lips pressed so tight they grew pale, then she turned her back on him. He'd make her turn her back tonight, he thought, by God he would. He had to sit on his hands for the rest of the journey, but he walked behind her all the way from the bus stop to her house.

"You're not tying me up with that," the woman said. "Cut my wrists off, that would. Pajama cord or nothing, and none of your cheap stuff, neither."

"Sid, would you mind seeing if you can come up with some cord?" Toby Hale said, taking out his reptilian wallet. "I'll stay and discuss the scene."

There was sweat in his eyebrows. The woman was making him sweat because she was their only female model for the story, since Toby's wife wouldn't touch anything kinky. Sid kicked the fog as he hurried to the shops. Just let the fat bitch give him any lip.

Her husband bound her wrists and ankles to the legs of the bed. He untied her and turned her over and tied her again. He untied her and tied her wrists and ankles together behind her back, and poked his crotch at her face. Sid snapped her and snapped her, wondering how far Tony had asked them to go, and then he had to reload. "Get a bastard move on," the woman told him. "This is bloody uncomfortable, did you but know."

Sid couldn't restrain himself. "If you don't like the work, we can always get someone else."

"Can you now?" The woman's face rocked toward him on the bow of herself, and then she toppled sideways on the bed, her breasts flopping on her chest, a few pubic strands springing free of her purple knickers like the legs of a lurking spider. "Bloody get someone, then!" she cried.

Toby had to calm her and her suffused husband down while Sid muttered apologies. That night he set the frosted photograph in front of him and chanted his story over it until the girl pleaded for mercy. He no longer cared if Toby had his doubts about the story, though Sid was damned if he could see what had made him frown over it. If only Sid could find someone like the girl to model for the story . . . Even when he'd finished with her for the evening, his having been forced to apologize to Toby's models clung to him. He was glad he would be photographing Enid Stone tomorrow. Maybe it was time for him to think of moving on.

He was on his way to Enid Stone's press conference when he saw the girl again. As he emerged from his building, she was arriving home from wherever she worked, and she was on his side of the road. The slam of the front door made her flinch and dodge to the opposite pavement, but not before a streetlamp had shown him her face. Her eyes were sunken in dark rings, her mouth was shivering; her long blond hair looked dulled by the fog. She was moving awkwardly, as if it pained her to walk.

She must have female trouble, Sid decided, squirming at the notion. On his way to the bookshop his glimpse of her proved as hard to leave behind as the fog was, and he had to keep telling himself that it was nothing to do with him. The bookshop window was full of Enid Stone's books upheld by wire brackets. Maybe one day he'd see a Sid Pym exhibition in a window.

He hadn't expected Enid Stone to be so small. She looked like someone's shrunken crabby granny, impatiently suffering her hundredth birthday party. She sat in an armchair at the end of a thickly carpeted room above the bookshop, confronting a curve of reporters sitting on straight chairs. "Don't crowd me," she was telling them. "A girl's got to breathe, you know."

Sid joined the photographers who were lined up against the wall like miscreants outside a classroom. Once the reporters began to speak, having been set in motion by a man from the publishers, Enid Stone snapped at their questions, her head jerking rapidly, her eyes glittering like a bird's. "That'll do," she said abruptly. "Give a girl a chance to rest her voice. Who's going to make me beautiful?"

This was apparently meant for the photographers, since the man from the publishers beckoned them forward. The reporters were moving their chairs aside when Enid Stone raised one bony hand to halt the advance of the cameras. "Where's the one who takes the dirty pictures? Have you let him in?"

Even when several reporters and photographers turned to look at Sid, he couldn't believe she meant him. "Is that Mr. Muck? Show him the air," she ordered. "No pictures till he goes."

The line of photographers took a step forward and closed in front of Sid. As he stared at their backs, his face and ears throbbing as if from blows, the man from the publishers took hold of his arm. "I'm afraid that if Miss Stone won't have you, I must ask you to leave."

Sid trudged downstairs, unable to hear his footsteps for the extravagant carpet. He felt as if he weren't quite there. Outside, the fog was so thick that the buses had stopped running. It filled his eyes, his mind. However fast he walked, there was always as much of it waiting beyond it. Its passiveness infuriated him. He wanted to feel he was overcoming something, and by God, he would once he was home.

He grabbed the copy of the story he'd written for Toby Hale and threw it on the table. He found the photograph beside the bed and propped it against a packet of salt in front of him. The picture had grown dull with so much handling, but he hadn't the patience to develop a fresh copy just now. "My name's *Mister* Sidney and don't you forget it," he informed the photograph.

There was no response. His penis was as still as the fingerprinted glossy piece of card. The scene at the bookshop had angered him too much, that was all. He only had to relax and let his imagination take hold. "You're here to learn discipline," he said soft and slow.

The figure composed of dots seemed to shift, but it was only Sid's vision; his eyes were smarting. He imagined the figure in front of him changing, and suddenly he was afraid of seeing her as she had looked beneath the streetlamp. The memory distressed him, but why should he think of it now? He ought to be in control of how she appeared to him. Perhaps his anger at losing control would give him the power to take hold of her. "My name's Mr. Sidney," he repeated, and heard a mocking echo in his brain.

His eyes were stinging when it should be her bottom that was. He closed his eyes and saw her floating helplessly toward him. "Come here if you know what's good for you," he said quickly, and then he thought he knew how to catch her. "Please," he said in a high panicky voice, "please don't hurt me."

It worked. All at once she was sprawling across his lap. "What's my name?" he demanded, and raised his voice almost to a squeak. "Mr. Sidney," he said.

"Mr. Sidney *sir!*" he shouted, and dealt her a hefty slap. He was about to give the kind of squeal he would have loved her to emit when he heard her do so— faintly, across the road.

He blinked at the curtains as if he had wakened from a dream. It couldn't have been the girl, and if it had been, she was distracting him. He closed his eyes again and gripped them with his left hand as if that would help him trap his image of her. "What's my name?" he shouted, and slapped her again. This time there was no mistaking the cry which penetrated the fog.

Sid knocked his chair over backward in his haste to reach the window. When he threw the curtains open, he could see nothing but the deserted road boxed in by fog. The circle of lit pavement where he'd last seen the girl was bare and stark. He was staring at the fog, feeling as though it was even closer to him than it looked, when he heard a door slam. It was the front door of the building across the road. In a moment the girl appeared at the edge of the fog. She glanced up at him, and then she fled toward the park.

It was as if he'd released her by relinquishing his image of her and going to the window. He felt as though he was on the brink of realizing the extent of his secret power. Suppose there really was something to this sex magic? Suppose he had made her experience at least some of his fantasies? He couldn't believe he had reached her physically, but what would it be like for her to have her thoughts invaded by his fantasies about her? He had to know the truth, though he didn't know what he would do with it. He grabbed his coat and ran downstairs, into the fog.

Once on the pavement he stood still and held his breath. He heard his heartbeat, the cackling of ducks, the girl's heels running away from him. He advanced into the fog, trying to ensure that she didn't hear him. The bookshop window drifted by, crowded with posed figures and their victims. Ahead of him the fog parted for a moment, and the girl looked back as if she'd sensed his gaze closing around her. She saw him illuminated harshly by the fluorescent tube in the bookshop window, and at once she ran for her life.

"Don't run away," Sid called. "I won't hurt you, I only want to talk to you." Surely any other thoughts that were lurking in his mind were only words. It occurred to him that he had never heard her speak. In that case, whose sobs had he heard in his fantasies? There wasn't time for him to wonder now. She had vanished into the fog, but a change in the sound of her footsteps told him where she had taken refuge: in the park.

He ran to the nearest entrance, the one she would have used, and peered along the path. Thickly swirling rays of light from a streetlamp splayed through the railings and stubbed themselves against the fog. He held his breath, which tasted like a head cold, and heard her gravelly footsteps fleeing along the path. "We'll have to meet sooner or later, love," he called, and ran into the park.

Trees gleamed dully, wet black pillars upholding the fog. The grass on either side of the path looked weighed down by the slow passage of the murk which Sid seemed to be following. Once he heard a cry and a loud splash—a bird landing on the lake which was somewhere ahead, he supposed. He halted again, but all he could hear was the dripping of branches laden with fog.

"I told you I don't want to hurt you," he muttered. "Better wait for me, or I'll—" The chase was beginning to excite and frustrate and anger him. He left the gravel path and padded across the grass alongside it, straining his ears. When the fog solidified a hundred yards or so to his right, at first he didn't notice. Belatedly he realized that the dim pale hump was a bridge which led the path over the lake, and was just in time to stop himself striding into the water.

It wasn't deep, but the thought that the girl could have made him wet himself enraged him. He glared about, his eyes beginning to sting. "I can see you," he whispered as if the words would make it true, and then his gaze was drawn from the bridge to the shadows beneath.

At first he wasn't sure what he was seeing. He seemed to be watching an image developing in the dark water, growing clearer and more undeniable. It had sunk, and now it was rising, floating under the bridge from the opposite side. Its eyes were open, but they looked like the water. Its arms and legs were trailing limply, and so was its blond hair.

Sid shivered and stared, unable to look away. Had she jumped or fallen? The splash he'd heard a few minutes ago must have been her plunging into the lake, and yet there had been no sounds of her trying to save herself. She must have struck her head on something as she fell. She couldn't just have lain there willing herself to drown, Sid reassured himself, but if she had, how could anyone blame him? There was nobody to see him except her, and she couldn't, not with eyes like those she had now. A spasm of horror and guilt set him staggering away from the lake.

The slippery grass almost sent him sprawling more than once. When he skidded onto the path, the gravel ground like teeth, and yet he felt insubstantial, at the mercy of the blurred night, unable to control his thoughts. He fled panting through the gateway, willing himself not to slow down until he was safe in his rooms; he had to destroy the photographs before anyone saw them. But fog was gathering in his lungs, and he had a stitch in his side. He stumbled to a halt in front of the bookshop.

The light from the fluorescent tubes seemed to reach for him. He saw his face staring out from among the women bearing whips. If they or anyone else knew what he secretly imagined he'd caused . . . His buttocks clenched and unclenched at the thought he was struggling not to think. He gripped his knees and bent almost double to rid himself of the pain in his side so that he could catch his breath, and then he saw his face fit over the face of a bound victim.

It was only the stitch that had paralyzed him, he told himself, near to panic. It was only the fog which was making the photograph of the victim appear to stir, to align its position with his. "Please, please," he said wildly, his voice rising, and at once tried to take the words back. They were echoing in his mind, they wouldn't stop. He felt as if they were about to unlock a deeper aspect of himself, a power which would overwhelm him.

He didn't want this, it was contrary to everything he knew about himself. "My name is—" he began, but his pleading thoughts were louder than his voice, almost as loud as the sharp swishing which filled his ears. He was falling forward helplessly, into himself or into the window, wherever the women and pain were waiting. For a moment he managed to cling to the knowledge that the images were nothing but the covers of magazines, and then he realized fully that they were more than that, far more. They were euphemisms for what waited beyond them.

THRESHOLD

John Edward Ames

*L*adies and gentlemen, distinguished colleagues," said Oxford Professor Barry Atherton, President of the International Society of Philosophers. "It is my distinct pleasure—albeit one laced with considerable envy—to introduce a woman who, at the scandalously young age of twenty-seven, is already relegating us mature old mavens to the tomes of cracker-barrel philosophy."

Polite laughter rippled through the crowded auditorium. Kevin Sanford, sitting down front with the hoary-headed elders, was the only guest wearing blue jeans among all the dinner jackets and tuxedos. He felt belly flies of excitement stirring.

"Indeed," Atherton continued in his quaint, pedantic, veddy-veddy proper intonation, "it is not at all hyperbolic to suggest that her last few articles on the theory of consciousness have occasioned a veritable paradigm shift in the world of ideas. They have certainly advanced her beyond the status of a young Turk to the first rank of international philosophers, which her presence here tonight as keynote speaker eloquently verifies. Ladies and gentlemen, it is my sincere pleasure to present Dr. Shireen Carroll, currently occupying the prestigious William James Chair of Philosophy at the University of Michigan and this year's recipient of the ISP's Golden Quill Award for her seminal essay 'Space, Time, and the Nature of Consciousness.' ''

Kevin was among the first to come to their feet as applause crackled through the cavernous lecture hall. He watched Shireen rise from her chair at the edge of the dais and move to the podium. She looked a little nervous, but Kevin knew this amazing woman did her best work in a state of mild anxiety. His lips tilted into a grin when even this politically correct gathering—most of whom had never seen Shireen or a photo of her—loosed a collective sigh of delighted surprise at her striking good looks.

Take a good look, folks, he thought with the toe-curling elation of someone who knows a thrilling secret. That lady is a traffic hazard, and I'm the lucky mutt who sleeps with her. Evidently she did not boff her way to the top, huh?

Shireen had chosen her respectable but figure-flattering white knit dress. He liked the way the snug belt accentuated the curving sweep of her hips. Her hair was a platinum crop in the stark lighting, though from here Kevin had to imagine the smoke-colored eyes. Eyes that said come thrill me, knave, though he'd also seen them look like two pools of burning acid when she was on the warpath.

"Thank you, Professor Atherton," Shireen began, speaking without notes. "But according to your introduction, I've already eliminated the competition and solved all of life's Enduring Questions. So why don't we all just go get drunk?"

This time the laughter was heartfelt, not polite. When it subsided, Shireen added, "Professor Atherton *is* being hyperbolic, though it's quite flattering. The truth, as so often happens in the world of ideas, is that my name has been linked to perspectives developed by group endeavor. Much of my own work was directly inspired by Professors David Chalmers and Owen Flanagan."

Ahh, skip the modesty schtick, sweet love, Kevin thought. Steal from one, it's plagiarism; steal from two, it's research.

"There are legions," Shireen continued, "who clamor incessantly that the wondrous puzzle of consciousness, of subjective awareness, is no puzzle at all, much less a wonder. Thanks to a long, grinding century of Behaviorist and Positivist tunnel vision, 'consciousness' is too often perceived by science and philosophy today as the by-product of separate mechanical processes, merely the higher-order 'hum' of complex neural circuitry at work. The whole, in this view, is really just an abstract illusion, the complex sum of many separate parts. The bee *seems* to buzz in our head, this view reminds us, but in reality it's in our bonnet."

Shireen finally spotted Kevin and flashed a little grin at him before she went on with sudden forcefulness:

"Well, malarkey! Such reasoning is reductio ad absurdum masquerading as doctrine. Science does a wonderful job of describing neural-impulse transmission, for example, by looking closely at each component in the process. But mere description is not always complete explanation. The mechanical processing of a visual image is distinct from the subjective experience of seeing. Since various machines incapable of self-awareness do an impressive job of processing shape, color, even of identifying and classifying objects, why are we humans 'aware' we are doing these same tasks? This question is crucial because mechanical science cannot take us beyond it. To put it crudely, something elusive is always left intact after mechanical science has deconstructed consciousness. And that 'elusive something' that won't go away is in fact the real essence of consciousness."

Spirited applause interrupted Shireen. Kick ass and take names, chippy, Kevin thought.

"The dominant, mechanistic, 'break-it-on-down' view of human self-awareness," Shireen continued, cutting now to the vital heart of her recent work, "stems historically from the ancient Greek atomistic concept of reality, which posits that smaller units always combine to make bigger ones. But atomism is logical only when applied to solid matter. And just as matter is not the only state of our universe, some of the most valuable concepts in science are both indispensable *and* refer to realities incapable of being atomistically reduced to smaller parts—notably, space, time, and mass.

"Similarly, I and others like Chalmers and Flanagan have argued that human consciousness, too, should be viewed as just such an irreducible entity. It is *not* 'peripheral' to human functioning, *not* an accidental spin-off of neural activity. You can name all of its parts, but that will never convey its complete essence. Or in the spirit of Yeats: You cannot separate the dancer from the dance."

Applause exploded through the auditorium, loud and sustained. "Human freedom and dignity," Kevin and the rest of this select group realized all too well, had taken one hell of a battering in the Age of Anxiety. Pavlov and Skinner had replaced the inner man with a stimulus-response automaton. And few had seriously challenged them or the New Age silliness that had cropped up to fill what Kevin sardonically called "the Conrad Aiken-void" in humanity— the heartfelt need to believe that man *is* somehow central to it all, a noble piece of work, after all, not just puppets made out of meat. Shireen's essays, while precise and scientific, proved emphatically that the bee-in-the-bonnet boys were all, philosophically speaking, butt-naked under their starched lab coats.

Maybe, Kevin told himself, Shireen really *was* shifting a few paradigms in the increasingly irrelevant world of the Intelligentsia. Why not? The world's most passionate minds were often also its most passionate lovers, and damn straight Shireen could make thirty minutes in the sack more therapeutic than a week in the country.

But such thinking only robbed his brain of vital blood and made it difficult to concentrate on Shireen's keynote speech. Christ, he upbraided himself. Here the woman is, inspiring the cream of the world's philosophers with flights of stirring rhetoric, and all you can do is think about schtupping her.

Reluctantly Kevin shunted his thoughts to a more celestial plane.

"You've *never* been very impressed with my theory," Shireen complained on the first night after they returned to Ann Arbor from Oxford. "I saw all that smirking you were doing down there in the front row while I was speaking, shithead!"

"I was not—"

"Oh, yes you *were,* Kevin Sanford! Every time my work is mentioned, you get that knowing little grin on your face. What makes reality *your* private theater? Why are you so sure I'm wrong?"

Kevin was sprawled naked on the queen-size bed's sateen-quilted spread. Shireen, wearing only her lace bed jacket, sat on the edge of the bed kneading his back muscles—or at least she'd started to, he noticed with a little flush of irritation. The woman never went into deep-think mode on him until it was his turn to get a massage.

"Wrong?" he murmured, still drifting in a post-coital daze. "I never said that. Hell, even a stopped clock is right twice a day."

A moment later Kevin shouted, startled, when Shireen rained a flurry of blows on him with a pillow. "I'll stop *your* clock, mighty mouth. Now you tell me, from your smug, august position as an unemployed cosmologist, what I don't know that you evidently do."

Kevin groaned and sat up in the middle of the bed. "Look, what does Her Nips care about the warped perspectives of a thirty-five-year-old graduate-student bum? I'm just a loner with a boner, a cowboy in the boat of Ra, a fowl owl on the prowl, a—"

"You *are* a bum," she cut in. "A brilliant, infuriating, arrested-adolescent bum. Professor Oakes told me you could name your position if you'd just get off your lazy duff and finish your dissertation. Half the academics in the philosophy department take their articles to you for critique before they're submitted."

"That's right," Kevin boasted. "And the other half are unpublished."

"Mmm. So tell me, you underachieving, oversexed, laid-back genius—why so cool toward my theory of human consciousness?"

Kevin watched the twin dark spots where Shireen's plum-colored nipples dinted the lace of her jacket. "My objections can best be expressed as a formula, m'lady," he assured her solemnly. He brought his lips close to her right ear and whispered: " 'The mass of the ass, plus the angle of the dangle, equals the scream of the cream.' C'mon, fox, let's pitch whoopee!"

He lunged at her and grunted like a caveman. Shireen slapped his hand away from her tits. But his lewd "formula" forced an unwilling grin from her. "Skip the frat-boy graffiti. I'm serious. Why are you so skeptical of my theory?" she demanded.

Kevin surrendered with a martyr's groan and flopped back to the bed. "Because it places man at the center of things, that's why. But in fact, man is simply one more entity in the universe—one that rots fairly quickly, at that. There may be a higher purpose to the universe, but unlike you and your 'humanistic' peers, I don't privilege man's role in that purpose. 'The snow doesn't give a soft white damn whom it touches,' etcetera."

Kevin slyly rolled onto his hip, while he said all this, and nudged his uncoiling sex into the concave warmth of the dimple at the left base of her spine. But Shireen was mulling what he'd just said, the furrow between her eyebrows deepening in her concentration.

"Straight out of Wordsworth, nature boy," she dismissed him. "So your view decentralizes man in the universe and mine doesn't. It's just a shift in point of view. Even accepting that difference, why can't my theory still hold? Why *can't* consciousness be one of the irreducible forces in the cosmos like space or time?"

"Because that view still arrogantly privileges man and exaggerates his capacity to know himself. When 'consciousness' itself is applied to the very problem of consciousness, you are making the object of the study the same as the subject *doing* the study. Do the words *inherent bias* mean anything to you? Sweet love, we can't look under our own hoods—it's a crapshoot, at best. At worst, it's a one-way ticket to the rubber Ramada."

It fascinated Kevin, the way Shireen always listened to him as she was now, with the intensity of a cat focused on a rat. But although she always gave him a fair hearing, her ultracompetitive nature would not often concede a major point. He thought of the motto taped over her computer: *Second place is first loser.*

"You're overstating Heisenberg's Principle of Uncertainty," she finally decided. "Granted, the process of observation distorts *everything* it studies. But that doesn't render all observation null and void. We just need to compensate for the distortion."

By now Kevin's sly movements had hardened his cock and started to evoke a reflexive response from Shireen, who was beginning to move willy-nilly with his rhythms as he pressed more and more urgently into her.

"Hmm," he replied, obviously not caring a frog's fat ass, right then, about Heisenberg as he softly kissed her ear. He ran one hand around to the hard curve of her stomach and caressed it through the delicate lace. He slid the hand up and cupped one of her breasts, taking the nipple between fingers and thumb and teasing it stiff. He heard her breathing quicken as lust triggered a galvanic tickle in her loins.

"Uh-oh," Shireen said, nudging him back onto the bed. She stretched out beside him and squeezed his erection until it pulsed hard in her hand, the glans purple with hot blood. "This conversation has gone as far as it can go."

Kevin started to roll onto his side, but Shireen planted a hand on his chest and pushed him decisively onto his back. An ear-to-ear smile divided his face when he recognized her mood. Shireen was indifferent to hugging and kissing and was no big fan of foreplay, either. Although Kevin missed all that, Shireen's aggressive hunger was just compensation. At times the sex need would come over her so suddenly and forcefully that she simply took him like a shameless bitch in heat, whimpering with greedy impatience when his cock wasn't ready fast enough.

But now it was ready, so tight and swollen it leaped with each heartbeat. Shireen swung her right leg over him, settled her taut-muscled butt onto his thighs, and lined his prick up with the chamois folds of her labia. She was already wet enough to take all of him in one hard, forward-sliding plunge, her vagina opening to his thrust before the well-trained muscles closed snug as a velvet glove around his cock, gripping and releasing, gripping and releasing, milking him.

Shireen progressed from fast rocking to a hard, even faster, and more luscious plunging up and down the entire length of his erection. She power-fucked him so energetically that Kevin had to grab her tight-flexing ass while she, in turn, gripped the headboard to steady herself.

Soon his belly was slick with her drippings, and her groin slapped into it over and over with a sound like a kitten lapping milk. Kevin groaned uncontrollably, feeling his cock tense as hard as steel cable while her cunny stroked it in a maddening pleasure grip. Shireen began that low keening that always preceded her most powerful orgasms.

"I'm gonna . . . oh, Kevin, I'm gonna . . . gonna . . . I'mm gonn-nahh . . . ANHH! . . . ekss-*splode!*"

Shireen thrashed around spastically as a climax ripped through her like electric death, whip-snaking her body. She was still grinding, though the spasms were slowing, when Kevin moaned hard and thrust his hips hard off the bed, lifting Shireen high and driving his cock so deep the glans kissed her cervix when he ejaculated.

For a long time both exhausted lovers lay in a dazed, confused tangle of limbs, only slowly returning to awareness. It was toward the end of that postorgasmic lull, Kevin realized much later—after it was too late—that his free-floating mind idly formed the fatal question.

"Tell me something, chippy," he teasingly opened the debate with Shireen. "If self-awareness is as irreducible an entity as space and time, where does it go when you have one of those ballistic orgasms like that one—the *ones*—you just had? Girl, you were *out* of it. Gone. Zombified."

Clearly he was teasing her, and Shireen's first response was to tweak his cock. "Where does it 'go'? Are you getting astral on me?"

"Yeah, where does it go? What happens to it?"

"Who says it goes anywhere?"

"You did, for one. What about that slick fluff piece you sold to *New Woman* last summer? You summed up Reich's theory of the orgasm as a 'temporary escape from the tedium of cognition,' or something like that. You went on to say that we seek the release of orgasm for just that reason: release from the self. You compared it to the 'no-mindedness' of Zen meditation."

Shireen rose on one elbow beside him, frowning. "Yeah, so? If you drift near a point, big boy, feel free to make it."

"It's made! Look, you're hypothesizing that self-consciousness is, categorically speaking, as real and undeniable as space itself. Fine, very exalted. But consider this: You can easily visualize a space with nothing in it, can you not?"

Shireen snorted. "Sure. Your bank account, for example."

"Careful, your claws are showing. Now just tell me this: Can you visualize *no space?*"

Shireen's frown etched itself deeper. "Of course not. As Kant argued, space is a categorical imperative."

"Meaning space is *truly* irreducible and thus undeniable. Same thing with time—it *takes* time to refute time, so it proves itself. But how can you deny that self-awareness is definitely 'reduced' during climax?"

For Kevin all this had begun as just an amusing thought experiment. He forgot about it later that same day. But thus toying with an idea, he fired a new research obsession in Shireen: to pin down precisely where awareness "goes"—for lack of a better word—at the sexual peak. Facetious or not, she told herself, Kevin's criticism did point to a potential weakness in her theory of consciousness.

Shireen positively delighted in the attention she was getting lately for her writing. But it was her nature to *earn* her breakfast. And since Kevin must of course be wrong, she determined to discover the proof of his error.

Only wimps, she steeled herself, cringe before their critics.

"No offense, sweet love," Kevin said, his tone a hybrid of exhaustion and contrition. "But I'm working myself into a slight overbite here."

Reluctantly Shireen unwrapped her legs from Kevin's shoulders so he could sit up in bed. He made a show of cupping his jaw. Clearly, the gesture implied, even good oral sex could last too long.

"What's going on here?" he demanded. "You used to be a regular orgasmatron. Lately, I couldn't thrill you with a kick-start vibrator."

Shireen, too, sat up. Her clothes lay in a puddle at the foot of the bed. She ignored his question while she dressed, still preoccupied with the implications of yet another experimental failure.

A longtime practitioner of "directed thought" and other meditation techniques, Shireen had decided she might be able to monitor herself during sex. Her goal was to experiment with levels of awareness, to see if she could experience the "release" of sexual pleasure while also retaining her mental awareness of that release—much like those who, simultaneously, experience dying from within while also viewing it from outside their bodies.

So far, however, the effort had been a miserable failure. Dancer and the dance, she reminded herself ruefully.

Kevin knew this long silence now signified some major problem, and he suspected what it was. Shireen had never confused serious, which she definitely was, with humorless, which she definitely was not. Never, that is, he chastised himself, until he recently opened his big fucking mouth and proposed his "thought experiment."

Shireen, still deep in her thoughts, moved into the living room and sat down at the piano, warming up with some scales. Kevin followed her out. He crossed to the wet bar and poured himself a bourbon over shaved ice.

"Drink?" he called over.

She shook her head, ignoring him, watching her fingers.

"Shireen," he said quietly. She stopped playing and revolved on the bench to watch him, still saying nothing.

"You told me one time that you don't believe in pushing the learning curve for its own sake. I think you're getting carried away when you start sacrificing your—*our*—sex life on the altar of experimentation."

"Pee doodles! *You* challenged my theory, and I accepted that challenge."

"Jesus, lady! Your whole theory doesn't go kaflooey just because I—"

"A-*hah!* Now he's a True Believer! For a honking good fuck, ladies and gents, the noble cosmologist will move to a new metaphysical home. Next stop: politics."

"Piss on it," Kevin snapped, polishing off his drink and banging the glass down on the bar. He headed for the bedroom, then stopped in the doorway to look at her.

"Like I said, we can't look under our own hoods. Not like you're trying to do. The mind-body nexus is highly volatile synergy and must be respected. You are intruding Ego into space reserved for Id. You keep splicing modes, and believe me, you will sure as shit regret it."

Kevin was, by turns, pissed and then worried. As Shireen's determined quest gradually ratcheted up to an obsession that consumed her, he needed more space. He began spending more nights back in his dingy little walk-up in the student ghetto behind the football stadium.

But inadvertently, by leaving her alone more, Kevin indirectly provided the first major breakthrough in Shireen's quest. For his absence, and her present lack of any suitable surrogates, forced her to rely on an expedient she had never really fully explored before—masturbation.

She had always had an intense imagination. But Shireen was raised to believe that self-stimulation, while not exactly shameful, was certainly sad—something only lonely soldiers and inveterate losers resorted to. With one of her very first solo sessions, however, her attitude underwent a sea change.

It was all her practice lately with meditation, especially controlled imagery, that provided the breakthrough. Shireen began by setting aside plenty of time on a weekday when she didn't have to lecture. She put on some bossa nova, which always relaxed her, set a demijohn of wine on the night table, and crawled naked between her favorite satin sheets.

She used no sex toys, and in fact didn't even touch herself for quite some time. Shireen let the swaying rhythm of the music infuse her while she used systematic desensitization to relax all her muscles.

This bed, she thought, was where Kevin always fucked her so wonderfully, his lean, hard ass flexing with athletic vigor while he held both hands under her butt and lifted her to him, over and over, pounding into her until they both groaned in a sweet agony that could only be death or the glory of the rut.

Thinking all this, then seeing it on the screen of her mind, Shireen pulled one corner of the sheet taut over the silky rise of her mons veneris. Pushing against it sent a sweet, hot current of pleasure strobing through her. Her free hand slid up to her breasts and kneaded the nipples while she continued the pressure around—but not directly on—her clitoris.

Shireen held the image of Kevin riding her as she pulled the sheet aside and scissored her legs open wide. She probed three fingers into the glazed folds of her labia, teasing the little pearl out from its sheath. Shireen rubbed it a bit more directly now, her breathing beginning to quicken.

The first orgasm sneaked up on her, a sudden, welling peak that only made her excitedly go for more. In her building pleasure Shireen's long, coltish legs rose from the bed, and she bent at the knees as if Kevin really were writhing between them.

She climaxed several more times, each one a bit more intense than the one preceding it. Shireen knew she was building toward an explosive orgasm, and this time she managed to maintain focus, to hang on to self-awareness—managed to actually *will* herself attentive—even as the tidal wave of carnal pleasure threatened to overwhelm her senses.

Looking back on it later, Shireen realized that first session was only a partial success. But it gave her an exhilarating foretaste of what she was soon to grow very adept at. For a few incredible moments, her frenzied fingers managed to balance her precisely on the feather edge of that final, incapacitating climax. Somehow, her clitoris and her intellect became one, so that as her pleasure intensified, forbidden insight deepened.

For a moment, only a few heartbeats, Shireen actually monitored the initial "escape" of her own awareness. Then, frustratingly, she lost the critical balance and ruined everything—came thumping back to earth like a bird shot on the wing. Lost the insight *and* the powerful climax toward which she had been welling.

But, for that brief time, she had experienced the incredible elation of progress. She was on track toward the truth she sought.

"'In summation,'" Kevin read in the glow of a flexible Tensor lamp, "'the body, senses momentarily overloaded, virtually dies at the height of orgasmic excitation. At this peak, consciousness or self-awareness energizes to pure aura and, in effect, hovers *just* outside the body, an etheric double, until the body regains vital functioning and the self is reintegrated. That is why awareness returns only in increments after powerful orgasms, never all at once—very much like blood returning to a "dead" limb. We may thus accurately say the self is temporarily displaced during orgasm, but it is *not* demonstrably eliminated or reduced.'"

Kevin dropped Shireen's rough draft back onto the

dining room table and looked up at her. Those smoke-colored eyes of hers scintillated with the ecstasy of intellectual triumph. But he shuddered inwardly at the shocking change in her appearance since he'd last seen her a week ago. The haggard shadows under those eyes, the oily, lopsided clump of her hair—Shireen, who usually showered twice a day, now looked like she'd spent several rough nights in detox.

"Well?" she demanded. "All subjective, undocumented bullshit, right?"

That new tone, too, Kevin noticed—as if she felt a huge, bottomless contempt for him and anyone else who dared dispute her. Shireen had always taken strong stands, but this ride-it-till-it-crashes arrogance was new and alarming.

"It's not bullshit at all," he told her truthfully. "It's brilliant. Look, I got goose bumps reading it. But Jesus, lady. Have you looked at yourself in a mirror lately?"

"I've been doing a lot of things with myself lately," she assured him.

"I see that. And David Oakes told me you canceled your Friday lectures? You *never* cancel classes."

"Oh, spare me the fallen-woman spiel. Do you comprehend what I've accomplished here? *Do* you? I am sure as hell not the only person capable of this—based on my report, my experiences can be replicated, verified. This will stick a Skinner box right up the Behaviorist butt!"

"Shireen," Kevin said, concern lending him new patience, "this is all fascinating, but you're carrying on like you've found a cure for AIDS. Calm down and—"

"Fuck AIDS, you simpering, bleeding-heart wuss! You're just jealous. I proved you wrong."

"Listen to yourself, would you? I don't care if I'm wrong. Fine, you're right. Okay? You're missing the point here. This . . . stuff you're fooling around with is obviously dangerous, it—"

"Prove it!"

"You are proving it for me, right now. The way you look, the way you sound. This isn't you, Shireen. That 'hovering' business you keep raving about—don't you understand? That has *got* to be a vulnerable and unstable time for the self. Judging from your description, at that moment the self has been torn loose from its usual moorings. What if you push it out too far, somehow lock it out? Maybe it could drift off and never return, like some astronaut sucked out of his capsule into the endless maw of outer space."

Shireen gathered up the pages of her essay, her face hardening. "You know what? You obviously don't know dick about my work. As usual, you're spouting a priori bullshit and *I* am describing empirical research."

"Em*pi*rical? You diddled yourself, for Christ sakes!"

Shireen smacked the table hard. "That's why you're so bent out of shape, isn't it, you 'sensitive' hypocrite? How dare I cut off your God-given ration of pussy?"

"Take the pine cone out of your ass, I—"

"God, did I delude myself," Shireen fumed, her throat swelling shut from anger. "You're nothing but a glib little ectomorphic bookworm! Get out of my apartment, nowhere man, or I dial 911."

Kevin's jaw fell open in astonishment. "Just like that?"

"You got it in one, Cosmo," Shireen informed him. She crossed to the door and opened it for him.

"See you in the funny papers," Kevin muttered on his way out. But just before she slammed the door on him, Kevin recovered from his shell-shock long enough to feel a resurgence of coppery-tasting fear.

He caught her arm by the wrist and added, his voice

rising in his urgency: "Shireen, for Christ sakes *please* don't go on with this!"

Kevin was wrong . . . oh, so hopelessly, blindly, wonderfully wrong, Shireen soon discovered.

At first, immediately after he left her place for the last time, she had felt guilty for her treatment of him. But even then the forbidden knowledge loomed in the back of her mind, her silent secret: *With what you've taught yourself, girl, you'll never need or want a sexual partner again. This isn't virtual reality, it's ultimate reality.*

This, Shireen repeated, writhing between the satin sheets. *This* . . . it was Wednesday, just past three P.M., and she had skipped yet another lecture to enjoy another "afternoon delight," as she now termed her exciting sessions of autoeroticism.

Her right middle finger was in fast motion, teasing the slick nubbin of her clitoris up from its hood. Warmth like the sudden glow of a toaster coil moved up into her lower belly. Faster, two fingers now, and Shireen's heels began to rumple the sheets as more blood engorged her clitty, exciting her. It was swollen so hard it felt like a small penis.

This . . . oh, *this* . . . and now Shireen was soaring toward that final, incapacitating peak. She gave in to pleasure, but also held on to awareness, balanced on that fine, feather edge between Thanatos and lust oblivion. Soon Shireen was literally "beside herself," watching the pretty girl on the bed drive herself to an ecstasy. She felt the sensation of weightless flight and the exhilarating rush of timeless, limitless motion.

This . . . oh, God, *this*. . . .

"We've not only done every known test, Mr. Sanford," the internist assured him. "We even made a few up. Tests for toxins, viruses, any parasites—all negative. Her CAT scan is normal so far as organic functioning. So are her body reflexes and pupillary response to light and darkness. It's extremely baffling—if you tickle her feet, for example, her toes will curl. She requires no life-support system except IV feeding, yet brain-wave activity is virtually nonexistent. Such cases are not unheard of, but this is the first I've seen. Her family is absolutely devastated."

"Yes," Kevin said tonelessly. "I'm sure they must be."

It had been six weeks since Shireen gave him the boot, riding the high of her experimental triumph. And now look at the great thinker—turned into the very thing she had passionately claimed human beings were not—mere puppets of meat. A medical Maxicart sat beside the bed, recording the vital functions that were no longer vital—just functions. And where, Kevin wondered, his flesh crawling against his shirt, was the *rest* of Shireen?

"I hear," the medico volunteered politely, discreetly glancing at his watch, "that she was—ahh, is—quite renowned in philosophy?"

Kevin nodded. Looking at the wan, expressionless face on that pillow made him feel like he was trying to swallow a nail sideways. God, couldn't they at least somehow shut her eyes—no longer eyes, just two gray buttons stuck to a headpiece filled with straw.

"Yeah, she was," he finally managed to answer, not bothering with the hypocrisy of the present tense. "She was always one for staying ahead of the curve."

The force field of her will radiated out of her, expanded away from her like a hot spirit wind howling over a dark wasteland. The thoughts, the desires, the shameful and hopeful secrets of countless minds surrounded her now in an incoherent white noise, got mixed with hers, and now her mind was a field of oscillating waves mixed with so many others in a wild, tumbling rush of images and thoughts, and then those, too, rushed off in the shrieking, empty vastness, and Shireen's mind shut down to a long, silent, eternal scream.

THE GREAT WHITE LIGHT

Greg Kihn

In the summer of '67 things happened that had never happened before.

If you were there, you know. If you weren't—it might be hard to imagine some of the weird shit that can happen in a rarefied atmosphere of sex, drugs, and rock and roll such as the world has never seen. Me? I was there.

I drove cross-country with my buddy Weasel that summer, all the way from Baltimore, Maryland, in a turquoise VW Micro-Bus. After a long and arduous journey we arrived at our destination—the teeming neighborhood of Haight-Ashbury.

We went immediately to the address of our friend, Fuzzy Bill. Bill was a housepainter who had offered us a summer's work helping repaint the infamous Avalon Ballroom. We'd worked for Bill before, slopping paint on suburban split-levels around Baltimore, but this was different. The Avalon was the Taj Mahal of hippiedom.

"It's gonna be like painting the Sistine Chapel," Weasel said. "Only better, 'cause there's chicks."

Fuzzy Bill had become our personal saint. We figured it was the kind of thing that could put a guy in the housepainting hall of fame. We brought along all our best brushes.

Bill lived with Strange Rollo in a row house on Haight Street. From what I'd managed to glean from a few stoned-out, late-night phone calls, the place was a "chick farm" in the classic sense of the word.

"There's people crashing everywhere, man, chicks like you wouldn't believe," Bill gushed through the phone lines. To two horny nineteen-year-olds, it seemed like heaven. California was definitely the promised land.

Weasel's older brother Chucky said we were both crazy, and all we'd find on the West Coast was a case of the clap. We didn't care. I could count my sexual experiences on one hand, and Wease, on two fingers. Any advancement in that department was okay by us, even if it carried the promise of a visit to the clinic.

Anyway, Chucky, only a few years older than us and just back from Vietnam, was already out of the loop. Things were happening fast. Our hair was getting too long for the Baltimore scene.

Strange Rollo answered the door barefoot, his eyes bloodshot. We stood there for a few seconds gaping at each other before Rollo said, "Hey . . . It's the guys from Baltimore."

"How're ya doin', man?" Weasel asked.

"I'm doin' O and K," he said after sticking his head out the door and looking up and down the block. "Why don't you guys come on in and smoke a joint?"

Weasel looked at me and beamed. "Well, Jake, I guess we finally made it to good old 'Frisco."

Rollo winced. "Rule number one—never call it 'Frisco, kid. It's San Francisco. People hate that."

The house had been decorated from junk stores, all funky old stuff. It smelled of pot smoke, incense, and mildew. Rollo took his seat on a faded couch between two of the cutest girls I'd seen since leaving Baltimore, both of them with long hair, wearing short cutoffs and semitransparent Indian shirts. Their nipples shone through the gauzelike material like nature's beacons. Me and Wease sat on two overstuffed easy chairs opposite them and tried not to stare.

Between the chairs was a low table cluttered with dope-smoking paraphernalia, some record albums, a few underground newspapers, and a sleeping cat.

Rollo said, "This is Lazy Lisa and Suze. The cat's name is Howlin' Wolf."

The girls nodded. I could tell that all three of them were stoned. The cat was catatonic. Suze got up to put on a record while Rollo busied himself rolling a joint from a carved wooden stash box.

"We just drove all the way out here from Baltimore," Weasel said. "Can you believe that?"

"Really?" said Lazy Lisa, her eyes pink and wondrous. "Isn't that on the other side of the country?"

Wease answered her with a nod and a goofy smile. "Took us three weeks. I'm amazed we actually got here—almost got busted a couple of times, and some townsfolk hassled us while we were campin', that happened a lot, ran out of money, and the damn bus kept breakin' down, but . . ." Weasel raised his arms and looked around the room. "Here we are."

Lisa looked bored, she wasn't really listening anymore. Rollo lit the joint, took a hit, and handed it to me.

"Where's Fuzzy Bill?" I asked.

"I haven't seen him for a couple days."

"Is he around?"

Rollo nodded. "Oh, yeah, I'm sure he's around. You might find him in the park tomorrow. There's a concert, I think."

I toked and passed the burning weed to Weasel, who began sucking on it noisily.

"But he still lives here, right?"

Rollo closed his eyes. "His stuff is here, but Bill lives everywhere, man."

The album *Electric Music for the Mind and Body* by Country Joe and the Fish began to play. Suze closed her eyes and began to sway.

"This is a great album, man," Rollo said reverently as the sinuous guitar of Barry Melton began to unwind around us. The electric organ sounded other-worldly.

Suze sat on the floor and shuffled through some album covers. There were several fruit crates full of records and more scattered around the room. Bill had an excellent collection.

Weasel held smoke in his lungs and talked in a constricted voice. "Have you seen Freeman?"

Rollo thought for a moment and said, "Freeman? Yeah, man. He works with a band now. They gig around here and there."

"Freeman's in a band?" I asked.

"Well, he's not really in it, he rolls joints for 'em." Weasel laughed. "Are you kiddin' me?"

"Nope. All he does, day and night, is roll joints. That's his job."

Weasel whistled. "Beats paintin' houses."

Rollo continued. "The way I heard it, some dealer put up a ton of money, and all they do is play music and smoke dope." He took the joint. "You should go over there sometime, it's cool."

After a short, appreciative silence, Weasel said, "We need a place to crash. Is it okay if we crash here? Bill said we could."

Rollo rolled his head. "I guess so." He thought for a moment, then pointed to the hallway. "Why don't you stay in Bill's room till he gets back? I don't think he'd mind."

"We won't touch any of his stuff, promise," Weasel replied.

"You better not, he's touchy about that. And if you happen to find his secret stash, for God's sake, don't smoke it."

Weasel raised his hand in a Boy Scout salute. "We would never do that. Honest. We just need some space to crash is all. Is anything goin' on tonight?"

Lazy Lisa came out of her daze and smiled seductively. "Big Brother's at the Avalon, wanna go?"

"Sure," I said, blushing slightly.

"But we need a ride," she said. "Does your bus still work?"

We nodded vigorously.

"Okay, we'll be back here in a couple hours to get you guys." Lisa stood, stretching her lithe body, and I got my second good look at her. She was slim, tanned, and exotic in a way Baltimore girls never were.

"I gotta go meet somebody," she said. "You comin'?" she asked Suze.

They left suddenly, and their peculiar flowery scent lingered in my nose.

Weasel beamed. "We've only been here half an hour, and we already got a date with two chicks to go to the Avalon," he said. "Plus we got a place to crash and we're smokin' killer dope. Not bad for two boys from the 'Big B' on their first day."

Rollo responded with a grunt. "You guys are hopeless. Rule number two—around here you gotta act cool, not like a couple of bumpkins. Meeting chicks and goin' to the Avalon happens all the time."

Weasel interrupted. "What about those two chicks, man? What's the scoop, they got boyfriends?"

Rollo laughed. "Dozens of 'em, you know. . . ."

"Dozens? What do you mean?"

"Well, things are different out here in California, boys. There's this new thing that's happenin' called *free love*. Most of the chicks around here are very open about stuff like that."

"I've heard about that," Weasel whispered reverently, "but I never thought I'd live to actually see it."

Rollo smirked. "There's a revolution goin' on, man. We're all part of it."

"Where do they live?"

Rollo leaned forward and spoke in low, confidential tones. "Let me tell ya something about those two. They're really into acid, I mean *really* into it. They live in this commune over on Filbert Street where a lot of weird shit goes on."

"What do you mean?"

"I mean, like, weird shit, you know? They do a lot of acid there. The main guy is on a real strange trip. He thinks he's God."

Rollo paused to suck on the joint. He continued, after exhaling and coughing mightily. "He makes this killer stuff called White Mist. It's pure lysergic acid diethylamide, puts Owlsley's to shame. What I heard is that he's some heavy chemist who flipped out and went underground. He's got this lab down in the basement, and he makes it right there in the house."

I whistled low. "An unlimited supply. Christ, that sounds kinda scary."

"Yeah," Rollo replied, "and when you do *that much acid,* it makes you *strange,* you know what I mean?"

I nodded. "Yeah. I've only done it once, and my face hurt from smiling for two days."

Weasel shook his head. "I've never done it. I've been waitin' for the right time and place."

Rollo raised an eyebrow. "Hey, man, don't get me wrong, acid's heavy. I've done it a couple of times myself, but . . ." His voice trailed off.

"They all do it together?" Weasel asked.

Rollo nodded. "Yep, all of 'em, there must be a dozen or so, gettin' crazy behind all that high-test LSD every night. Havin' orgies 'n shit. Man, it's too much."

"Orgies?"

"That whole house is floatin' half the time. They say they got people levitatin' over there, leavin' their bodies 'n shit. It's a real intense scene, man."

"Orgies?"

"People go there and wind up never comin' down long enough to leave. Those two chicks? They scare me sometimes. They get real high and start wantin' to hump."

"Are you serious?"

Rollo nodded. "They fuck like rabbits, those two. But they only do it on acid. Have you ever had sex while you were trippin'?"

"No," we replied in unison.

Rollo leaned forward and dropped his voice again. "It's incredible. You feel like you're literally comin' your brains out. And the time distortion makes it seem like hours. I can't describe it, but it's like your bodies meld together and you become one being for a while, you know, like, *the beast with two backs.*"

Rollo leaned back and smiled, his voice modulated upward. "I've done it with both of 'em together."

"Holy shit. That's unbelievable," Weasel said.

Rollo relit the joint, took another hit, and handed it back to me. "It's pretty intense, man. The only problem is—while you're fuckin' 'em, they start talkin' about Sebastion, like they're tryin' to recruit you to come over and join their family."

"Sebastion's their leader?"

"Right, he's the guy who makes the acid. He's a very freaky person, got hair down to here, and crazy eyes. Likes to wear Indian clothes, acts like a fuckin' guru. I see him all the time at the ballrooms. But listen, what I said about him being a famous chemist, though, nobody's supposed to know about that, so don't say anything about it, okay?"

I nodded, unable to erase the mental image of Lisa and Suze, naked, taking turns riding me while I tripped my ass off.

Rollo continued. "You'll probably run into him at the Avalon tonight, especially if you're with those two." Rollo raised a finger. "But be careful, man, they might dose you."

The Avalon pulsed with sound and light. Amoebas danced on the wall behind the stage, and people dressed in colorful clothes bathed in the ear-shattering music.

Lisa and Suze got lost in the crowd as soon as we were inside, and I saw them a few minutes later dancing in front of the stage as if in a trance.

"Hey, there's Freeman!" Weasel shouted above the music.

I recognized Freeman from across the room, and we made our way over to say hello.

"Great to see you guys!" he gushed. "Welcome to San Francisco."

"We just got here; we're crashin' at Fuzzy Bill's."

"Is he around?" Freeman asked. "He was supposed to meet me a couple of days ago and I haven't seen him."

"He's disappeared," Weasel said.

"What happened to him?" Freeman asked. "I was hopin' I'd see him tonight. We're thinkin' of opening up a head shop together, and I wanted him to come down and look at a storefront I found."

"It's not like Bill to drop out of sight like this."

"Maybe he went to Mexico," Weasel offered. "He was always talkin' about it. Maybe he just up and split."

"Nah, he'd tell me. I know he's got a new chick—I think he said her name was Cassandra, maybe he's with her. I saw her once, she's unbelievable. Maybe we should ask around. A lot of people here know Bill."

Music played and Freeman melted back into the crowd.

We found Lisa and Suze hanging out in front of the stage while James Gurley of Big Brother finger-picked his electric guitar. Some freaky-looking people suddenly surrounded us and started hugging Lisa and Suze.

"These are my friends from the commune," Lisa said. Without bothering with names, they all shook hands or hugged.

A tall man with shoulder-length blond hair and piercing blue eyes stepped forward. He appeared a little older than the rest of them.

"I'm Sebastion," he said. "We're having a party after the gig. You can come if you want."

On Sebastion's arm was the prettiest girl I had ever seen in my life. Her face was absolutely perfect—lips, nose, and chin exquisitely matched. Everything just so. Her sparkling eyes reflected the light show. I was captivated.

Sebastion noticed my interest and said, "This is Cassandra."

I recognized the name and smiled. "Hi, I'm Jake. Do you know a friend of mine named Fuzzy Bill?"

Cassandra's face, though flawless, showed no emotion. "No," she said.

There was something mysterious about her, and for some reason I didn't believe what she said about Bill. Sebastion gave Lazy Lisa and Suze a Bodhi-Bag of wine and they began to squeeze the yellow fluid into their mouths.

"You guys want some?" Lisa asked.

I shook my head. "I'm strictly a beer man."

Weasel said nothing and took the bag. He squirted some wine down his throat and laughed. "That tickles."

Lisa grabbed his arm and said, "Let's dance."

As the night wore on, Weasel began to act strangely.

While he was dancing, he began to make wider, longer, more exaggerated movements, until he was leaping across the floor like a maniac. I'd known Weasel for years, and I'd never seen him dance like that.

That's when I knew the wine had been dosed. When the music ended, Weasel began laughing hysterically. Weasel was tripping his ass off.

"How do you feel?" I asked.

"I feel great! Wonderful! Everything is so beautiful. . . ."

Cassandra, who had been talking to Lisa and Suze, slid next to me and said, "Your friend is really enjoying himself."

My heart accelerated in her presence. "Yeah, but I think you guys dosed him. Look, I don't know if that was such a good idea, he's never done acid before, he might have a bummer."

"Not with us," Cassandra said. "Nobody ever has a bummer with us."

"Yeah? Well, I don't know." I realized I was staring at Cassandra. Her beauty was distracting. "I mean, he didn't have any choice in the matter. You think that's right?"

"Sure." She smiled. "He's having a beautiful experience. Look at him."

I watched Weasel dancing with Suze, even though the music had stopped. He smiled expansively.

"Well, he seems to be having a good time," I admitted.

Lazy Lisa produced the leather bladder of acid-laced wine and offered it to me. "Why don't you join us?"

I shifted on my feet, suddenly nervous now. "I don't know, I'm not really in the mood tonight. Why don't we just smoke pot?"

"Forget pot, this is special. Come on, drink some electric wine, you'll love it," Cassandra said seductively.

She took the bag from Lisa and squeezed a long stream of wine down her slender throat. "See? There's nothing to be afraid of. Why don't you have just a little. It's the best thing you've ever felt."

Suddenly I was nervous. I shook my head. "That's okay, I'll pass."

"Don't be a party pooper." Cassandra's eyes sparkled and I gazed into them like a deer stares into a car's headlights. "Drink some and then come with me to the party," she said softly, her full lips wetly forming each syllable. "We could spend some time together."

"Together?" I stammered.

"Just the two of us, Jake, all alone in my magic bedroom. What do you say?"

I wondered what her game was. Was it some of that free love Rollo mentioned, or was it something more? The question faded as Cassandra touched my arm, gently sliding her fingers up and down.

I sighed, and felt my will ebbing away. "I really wasn't planning on tripping tonight."

Cassandra stepped forward and kissed me. As her tongue played with mine, I feared she would feel the obscene hammering of my heart right through my shirt. And I was getting hard.

"Trip with me," she whispered. "You'll never be the same again. It'll blow your mind."

My mind flooded with images of riding Cassandra, our bodies glistening with passion juice, hallucinating that my dick was ten feet long. What would it feel like when I came?

The choice was clear: Cassandra and incredible acid sex or go back to Bill's place alone. I looked at Cassandra again, drinking in the possibilities. My eyes wandered down her throat, to her open peasant blouse, to the smooth, full cleavage below. What was I so afraid of? Cassandra was worth it, I reasoned.

"Okay, but first I gotta go do something. I'll be right back."

I located Freeman in a corner talking to some freaks. "I see you found Cassandra," he said.

"Are you sure? She said she didn't know Bill."

"That's bullshit, he was with her the last time I saw him."

"Maybe it's a different Cassandra."

Freeman shook his head. "I wouldn't forget a face like that. That's definitely her."

"You think she's lying?"

Freeman shrugged. "Who the fuck knows? All I'm sayin' is I saw her with Bill. If she's lyin' about it, I guess she's got her own reasons. Are you going to their party? I hear things get pretty wild over there."

I blushed and nodded. "I guess the little head is doin' the thinkin' for the big head."

"I don't blame ya, man, she's the best lookin' chick in the Haight. But, be careful, those acid freaks are crazy."

I drove Weasel and the three girls to a house on Filbert Street; a large, run-down, semi-Victorian in the middle of a quiet block. Sebastion was already there, sitting cross-legged on the floor at the center of a circle of people.

Cassandra, looking more beautiful than ever, led us into the circle. "These are my new friends," she said. "They'd like to join us."

Sebastion raised his hands. "Welcome to this house."

Cassandra had insisted that I swallow some of the acid-laced wine on the way over, and I was beginning to feel warm and fuzzy. I'd taken as little as I could, making it look like more. Cassandra had been pretty damn insistent about it, and I hated myself for giving in. LSD scared me, and I wasn't really keen on tripping. But the promise of sex with her overwhelmed everything.

"Please share what we have," Sebastion said, an electric smile painted across his face. He waved his hand at a low table spread with fruit, pastries, wine, and cheese. There were also some rolled joints.

"Thanks, man."

We ate, drank, and smoked, and felt the acid comin' on.

Later I watched Weasel crawl across the hardwood floor, examining the grain of the boards. Lazy Lisa frantically looked through his scalp.

"I saw something," she explained to me when I asked.

"What did you see?"

"I saw something burrowing around in his scalp. I think it was some kind of centipede."

Weasel screamed and jumped to his feet. "A centipede? Where? In my brain?"

"Relax," Cassandra said. "You're tripping, everything is all right, you're with us."

Her delicate face and tone of voice reassured. She had a strange blankness about her, a Mona Lisa quality. She neither smiled nor frowned. Her cool beatific beauty gave no indication of what was going on inside.

I found it hypnotic. I noticed that she changed subtly from moment to moment, like a multifaceted crystal turning on a string. Viewed from different angles, she mirrored different aspects of what went on around her. The first time I saw her she looked dark—auburn hair and olive skin. Now she appeared almost Nordic, her hair noticeably lighter and her skin paler.

Cassandra was a little spooky. If she hadn't been such a knockout, I would have bolted. But I stayed and stayed, the acid steeping into my brain.

The more I searched her features, the more I saw reflected my own desire. I was tripping pretty good now. Colors and sounds were intense. I thought of the cosmos and watched the heave and fall of Cassandra's perfect breasts. Everything was moving.

Weasel, who had ingested even more LSD over the course of the evening, was becoming psychotic. "There's acid in everything here," he said during a short lucid period. "I can taste it, man. It's in the fruit, the juice, it's even on the toilet seat."

"How many mikes do you think we absorbed?"

Weasel drooled. "This shit isn't measured in mikes, it's on a whole 'nother level."

"I hope this turns out to be a good trip."

Weasel laughed, short and nasal. "That's funny," he said. "There are no good trips or bad trips, Jake, there's only *the* trip. Everything else is inside you."

Weasel was not known for his philosophic bent, and hearing him talk like this struck me as odd. "You okay, man?"

"Yeah," Weasel said a few moments later. "Never been better, Jakey old boy. Except . . . this red air . . . is kinda hard to breath."

My face twisted into an involuntary smile. "The

air's not red, man, it's clear . . . but I think there's stuff swirling in it."

Weasel bit at the air, then chewed a mouthful and licked his lips. "Hmm, I can taste it. I'm starting to see things differently now. There's a lot of light in here."

Cassandra touched us both on the arms. We looked into her liquid eyes and sighed. As long as she was around, everything would be all right.

"It's the Great White Light," she said.

I looked around with sudden chemical paranoia. "Where did everybody go?" It seemed that a moment ago the room was full of music and laughing people. Now it was silent and only the five of us remained— Cassandra, Weasel, Lisa, Suze, and me.

The ceiling seemed impossibly high.

"They all went away," she said softly, "to different parts of the house. The house is huge, you want to see? I can show you."

"Don't leave me!" Weasel shouted. "For God's sake don't leave me here. They'll get me!"

"Hey, Wease, nobody's gonna get you," I said reassuringly.

Cassandra put a cool, dry hand on his cheek and looked into his eyes. "Everything's all right. Don't worry. You have the power to do anything you want. You can change the universe if you want."

"I can?"

"Yes," she whispered. "I think you know what I mean. Don't you?"

"Yeah."

"Why don't you take off your clothes?"

Lisa and Suze began to unbutton Weasel's shirt. Like a pair of earthy seductresses, they ran their fingers across his chest.

"You want to fuck us?" Lisa purred in Weasel's ear.

I watched, wide-eyed, as they removed the rest of his clothes, then their own. Lisa mounted him and began to undulate, pulling herself up and down his chest, kissing his torso with her pussy lips. I saw the glowing, iridescent trail of her juices.

She reached down and maneuvered his shaft into her. Weasel moaned. Suze straddled his face and lowered herself onto his questing tongue.

I felt myself getting hard. Cassandra gently rubbed the bulge in my jeans. "Look at them. They're making the beast with two backs, or maybe I should say, the beast with *three* backs. It's pure, natural sex. We should do it, too, Jake. Let's go upstairs."

Cassandra's room was a pleasure palace. There were Indian-print bedspreads hanging on the walls, candles and incense burning, and a huge bed.

"Lay down," she commanded, and I did.

She undressed me, and my nakedness felt wonderful on the smooth sheets. The psychedelic sensations rippled from my skin to my brain and back again, setting up a feedback loop of numbing rapture.

When she kissed me, I felt my soul being sucked into her mouth. Our tongues seemed the size of pythons, entwining passionately.

I'd never been this high in my life. I was melting in and out of reality, hallucinating in unpredictable spurts. Cassandra knelt over me and took my dick in her mouth. The sensations were overwhelming.

She slipped off her dress and mounted me. We began to copulate, gently at first, then progressively harder. I pushed deeper into her until I felt the tip of my penis disappear into what seemed like another dimension. It was a very odd sensation. I was confused, but too horny to stop.

She rode me endlessly, the throes of our passion so

intense that for the moment everything else ceased to exist. I could feel myself melting into her as wave after wave of ecstasy swept over me.

"We are the beast with two backs," she whispered into my ear. "We are one. Give me your seed."

"Huh?"

"Fuck me!" she screamed, and grabbed my buttocks. We bucked and writhed for what seemed like hours. The LSD coursed through my system with the wild tidal pounding of my own pulse. I floated through space—the head of my dick a swollen navigator through the void. My entire being seemed perched there, waiting.

Cassandra's face dissolved and all I could feel were the wet, hungry lips of her vagina, devouring me. I closed my eyes, and when I opened them again a strange thing happened.

I saw the bed six feet below us.

"Holy shit!" I whispered, suddenly afraid. "We're floating." My voice sounded far away and I clung to her like a drowning man.

"Yes, that's right. The beast can float, my love," she cooed. "The beast can do anything. Now shut up and fuck." She constricted her vaginal muscles and massaged my aching rod like an oily hand. I lost myself in her again.

We pumped vigorously, suspended in the nothingness. "I think I'm gonna come," I said at last.

Then I exploded in her, gushing an impossible stream of jism. I felt the very essence of me drain through the end of my dick and into her. She drank it in. My soul, my intellect, my memories, all flowed out in the river of semen.

I climaxed in waves, losing a little bit more of myself in every load of ejaculate. It scared me, but as the increasingly pleasurable sensations took control, I forgot why I was afraid.

When it was over, we gently floated back down to the bed and I passed out.

When I next opened my eyes, Sebastion was in the room. I covered my groin and said, "Hey, what are you doing here?"

Cassandra got up from the bed and kissed Sebastion. I was confused.

"He's not ready yet, is he?" Sebastion asked.

"Ready for what?" I wanted to know.

Sebastion sat on the bed and put his hand on my leg. Incredibly, my boner was still going strong, throbbing even.

"You're going to go on an incredible journey tonight," he said. "You will see things as they *really are,* my friend. You will behold a new world. In the meantime, why don't you and Cassandra make the beast with two backs again? Call my name when you're ready."

"Ready for what?" I asked again as he departed.

"Ready to change," he said as the door closed.

Even though I was frightened, Cassandra expertly aroused me yet again and we had more sex. We floated, making the beast. But as each new height of ecstasy came, I lost more of myself, until I forgot who I was and what I was doing there.

Later I felt restless, and when Cassandra left the room for a moment, I decided to explore. The LSD was making me anxious and I had to move. I wandered until I came to a narrow staircase leading up. At the top was a door and I opened it.

Inside, I saw a couple of people lying on mattresses. I stepped closer, alarmed that they weren't moving. Then I noticed a head of fuzzy black hair and looked closer. It was Bill. My memory, and why I had come here to begin with, returned in a rush.

I rolled him over. He seemed completely limp, but warm and still alive. I looked into his eyes and gasped.

Bill's eyes were completely white—his pupils were gone. I cradled him in my arms, horrified.

"Bill! Can you hear me, man? What happened?"

Bill's mouth bubbled as he tried to speak. "Beast," he mumbled. ". . . with two backs . . . I went into the light . . ."

"Leave him alone," Cassandra's voice came from behind. "He's resting.

"But his eyes . . ." I stammered.

"His eyes are fine, that's just a hallucination. You're tripping, remember?"

When I released Bill, he flopped back onto the mattress like a dead fish.

Cassandra's voice was like bitter honey. "Let's go back to the room now. You're naked, you know."

I looked down at my body—my penis stood out like an elephant's trunk. The acid was causing some wild visual distortions.

Weasel screamed from somewhere in the house.

"It's Wease!" I shouted. "I gotta help him!" I dashed from the room before Cassandra could react.

I ran down endless corridors, looking in doors. The psychedelic experience was making me lose perspective. I caught bits and pieces of weird scenes as I moved from room to room. People looked up from what they were doing and smiled, but the smiles were evil.

In one room a naked young couple seemed to be smeared in blood. In another I saw demons dancing to the music of the Grateful Dead. A woman appeared in the hall in front of me, the top of her head removed. She absently twirled strands of her brain around her finger and giggled.

I'm tripping, none of this is real, my mind reasoned.

Cassandra was right, I *was* seeing things as they really were, and it wasn't what I'd expected. Things weren't beautiful at all, they were grotesque. The smiles of the people I interrupted were full of sharp teeth. They looked at me with carnivorous blood-lust.

Weasel screamed again and I ran in the direction of the sound.

The hallway became distorted. It seemed to stretch to infinity, and my legs felt as if they were underwater. Somewhere behind, I heard people coming after me.

I stumbled down a flight of stairs and burst into a room I hadn't seen before. Sebastion was there, standing over Weasel. He looked up, surprised. He had an eyedropper in his hand.

"What are you doing?" I shouted.

Weasel screamed again, blinking and clawing at his face. "He put the White Mist in my eyes!" he sobbed. "My God! I'm starting to fade!"

Cassandra and several others crowded into the room. They stood and stared at me, and I was suddenly aware of my nakedness.

And something else.

I felt less disoriented. The acid was wearing off.

"What the hell are you doing?" I shouted.

Sebastion raised a hand. "It's quite all right. You see, I've produced an absolutely pure, liquid form of the Mist. Its effects are best experienced when applied directly to the cornea."

"But he doesn't want that!" I shouted. "Look at him!"

Weasel rolled on the floor, moaning. His hands were over his eyes.

Sebastion shrugged. "Any second now he'll become one with the Great White Light. The beast with two backs has taken him there. Ride the beast, see the light."

While I watched, Weasel began to levitate off the floor. He rose to a height of two feet and hovered there, floating on nothing.

"Jesus Christ," I muttered. "Who *are* you people?"

Sebastion smiled. "We're travelers, my friend. You're a traveler, too. The light is our guide through the darkness. The beast with two backs is our beast of burden."

I backed away, but Cassandra and her flock moved between me and the door.

"The light loves you," Sebastion said. "It loves us all."

Weasel floated in the air, his head back and his not-quite-shoulder-length hair hanging down. I waved my hand above and below him. Nothing. Weasel rolled his head and looked at me.

"The light," he said. "The Great White Light. It's here. I have to go now, Jake. Say good-bye to everybody for me, okay?"

He opened his eyes and smiled at me, and I shuddered and shrank back. His eyes were all white, just like Bill's, completely devoid of pupil, iris, and cornea.

"He's seeing God," Sebastion whispered. "Ride the beast, see the light. Kinda nice how that works, isn't it?"

I wanted to run, I wanted to jump out the window and take off down the street and get as far away from this place as possible. Sebastion put a soft hand on my shoulder and peered into my face. "You want me to explain it all to you?"

I looked at the window. It was a huge curved-glass monstrosity looking out onto a yard on the side of the house. I was surprised to see that it was daytime already. How long had I been tripping?

Sun sparkled through the glass. Just a few feet away, Filbert Street teemed, wild and free. I calculated how many steps it would take me to get close enough to dive out through the glass.

It seemed a mile away.

Sebastion noticed me looking at the window and

said, "Don't even think about it, friend. The glass is thick and the fall is steep. You'd never make it."

"Tell me how this is happening," I asked.

"The Great White Light is God," Sebastion said. "Who would have thought that God would be attainable through advanced chemistry? You see, the light itself is intelligent, it talks to me, it tells me what to do.

"I discovered it about a year ago, experimenting with different forms of LSD. I'm a chemist by profession, a pioneer in my field, actually. I read about Leary and Alpert's work and decided to run my own set of tests.

"I realized that additional mind-altering properties could be caused by a quirk in the formula, so I tinkered with it. It's really quite simple—just your basic $C_{20}H_{25}N_3O$ with a twist."

Cassandra and her friends drew closer and I tensed. I was crashing from the acid and my face was sore. But the sun was up now, a new day had begun, and I was coming down.

Sebastion smiled and showed rows of tiny, pearl-white teeth. He continued talking, calmly and persuasively. "Souls pass in and out of the light all the time. People are born, people die. But occasionally the light wants to see a new soul, one that's not scheduled to pass.

"I found that the eyedropper-application method of my new liquid form of the Mist, coupled with a chemical the brain secretes during sex, brings a person face-to-face with the light without having to go through the long spiritual journey. Sex triggers it, you see, and the acid accelerates the process. With just one exposure, the light shows itself to whomever I choose."

I tried to swallow, but my mouth was as dry as ashes.

"What do you want with me and Wease?"

Sebastion chuckled. "I should think that's obvious. Once the acid gets into your bloodstream, it knows everything about you. You ride the beast with two backs, then you're part of it. The light has already chosen you."

"What makes their eyes turn white?"

"That's the first of a series of unusual side effects. There are others that come as the process continues. I can only describe it as a metamorphosis."

I was suddenly angry. "That's not right, man. Weasel never tripped before. You blew his mind. Why don't you drop it in *your* own eyes?"

Sebastion laughed. "I've done it *hundreds* of times. Hell, I perfected it. *The light itself* guided me, had me make further modifications of the formula. It was working through me to perfect itself, to find a way to tap directly into the ocean of human souls. I have gone far, far beyond this larval stage."

I watched Weasel hover in space. His body convulsed in little spasms, like a sleeping dog. *I'm still tripping,* I thought. None of this is real.

"You have sex with somebody who already has the light in them," Sebastion continued, "and you change. You walk again on the earthly plane, but you're not the same as before. Those who are absorbed by the light go on to a higher plane."

Cassandra touched my hand and I jumped. "It's a great honor," she said.

"Looks like your friend is merging nicely," Sebastion said. He gently placed his hand upon Weasel's chest and slowly guided him to the ground. "He's already there."

"Is that what happened to Fuzzy Bill?"

"Bill went fast—the light really wanted him. You see, some of us possess souls that just seem to yearn for realization. Bill was like that, a very evolved human being, it was his destiny. The rest of us have looked into the light and returned. Bill's metamorphosis will be complete soon. He'll be back to carry out the wishes of the light, to bring in more souls."

"Like me and Wease," I said.

"Yes, like you and Wease."

Cassandra held my hand tightly. "Think about it, Jake. It's the light of God. Most people only see it when they die."

"After you merge, what happens to you?" I asked, trying to postpone the inevitable now, trying to keep them talking. When the explanations ended, I had a pretty good idea that it was my turn to see the light.

"We change," Sebastion said softly.

"You look the same to me," I replied.

"Look again."

I gazed around the room.

"Remember what I said before, about seeing things the way they really are?" Cassandra's voice was soothing. "Use your other eyes, Jake, use the eyes of your soul."

I squinted, watching her face.

It began to ripple. The muscles flexed and thickened. I gasped and tried to pull away.

Her face was melting. I looked around in a panic—all their faces were melting. I found myself standing in the middle of a circle of faceless people. They had no eyes, nose or mouth, just a smooth unbroken plane of skin stretched over their expressionless skulls.

All except Sebastion. He held up the eyedropper and said, "Now it's your turn. Join us and never suffer the harsh pain of reality again."

"But I like reality!" I shouted, my head suddenly clear.

They encircled me. I tried to fight them off, but it

was no use. They held me down, and their fingers forced my eyes open, while Sebastion reloaded the eyedropper with the Mist. He stepped up and held it over my left eye.

"Ride the beast, see the light, and know God."

I couldn't blink, so I was forced to watch as the clear fluid fell in a perfect droplet directly onto my pupil. I screamed. I pushed a palm against my watering eye and felt a strange numbness wash over me.

Incredible visions exploded from my left eye, followed by an intense white light. Then the face of God revealed itself to me, but it was not God at all. *It was the devil.* I could feel the evil emanating from it, reaching out for me.

Panic and adrenaline exploded in my body, and I somehow managed to jerk free from their grasp. I dived for the window.

The glass was as thick as Sebastion had said, and the fall was just as bad, but I was determined to survive. My naked body crashed through the barrier like a steel arrow. Miraculously I landed in a roll and tumbled into some shrubbery, which broke my fall. In a heartbeat I was on my feet again, naked and bleeding. I could feel the morning sun on my face, and its golden rays gave me hope.

My left eye pulsed and squirmed in its socket. I was half blind and tripping, but somehow my fear overcame these handicaps.

Above me Sebastion shouted, "You won't get far, pilgrim. They're already on their way. *And the light is already in you!"*

His voice faded as I sprinted across the yard. I saw two of the faceless creatures coming around the side of the house. They looked unnatural and hideous in the light of day.

I made a mad dash for the fence, and the two

moved to cut me off. I zigzagged like a halfback and accelerated past their outstretched arms. Two steps later I was at the fence. It stood before me, a twelve-foot-high redwood barrier to freedom.

Without thinking, I vaulted it.

The street was bright and open. People who were strolling in the fresh morning air looked up to see a naked man running. I rocketed between them and vanished around the corner, leaving a trail of blood droplets.

The creatures kept coming.

My feet pounded the pavement like leather pistons as I raced through the streets, my dick bouncing up and down comically. It whapped against my stomach, making a sound like tiny hands clapping. People stopped and gaped as I flashed past.

When the cops found me wandering around in the woods of the Panhandle, I was a raving lunatic. Lacerated and incoherent, I babbled about the faceless creatures who were after me.

The doctor who injected the thorazine told me I had torn out my own eye and packed the wound with mud. He said they had to pry the loose eyeball out of my hand with a screwdriver. I wondered why.

I came down a week later. The only thing I can remember about the hospital was how it smelled. I gradually regained my memory. The police called my parents, who called Weasel's parents, and Chucky.

That's when the shit hit the fan. Chucky led a team of cops into the house on Filbert Street. The scene they found defied logic. The police report said they found people *floating in air*. By the time anyone could decide what to do, the bodies gently settled to the floor. The government confiscated Sebastion's lab and all notes containing his formulae.

But Sebastion and Cassandra were not in the house at the time of the bust. The king and queen of LSD simply vanished into the hippie underground.

Someone in my therapy group heard that they'd hooked up with a guy named Charlie in the desert near L.A. A place called the Spann Ranch.

And later, when the cops came for Charlie, Sebastion and Cassandra slipped away again. What happened to them is anybody's guess. I'm sure they're out there somewhere, pulling souls.

The glass eye took some getting used to, but now I can manipulate it pretty well. For a while in the seventies I wore an eye patch, like the Hathaway shirt man, but I grew out of it. Women dug it, but the "Jake the Pirate" jokes were getting on my nerves.

Poor Weasel has been vegged out these past thirty years, but I still drop by now and then to see him. I gaze into his blank, lifeless eyes and remember Cassandra.

My own therapy is ongoing and I manage to live a reasonable life. The flashbacks have almost gone away completely.

But sometimes at night, when I close my eye, I can still see it. The great white light.

And I find myself floating. . . .

HOT EYES, COLD EYES

Lawrence Block

Some days were easy. She would go to work and return home without once feeling the invasion of men's eyes. She might take her lunch and eat it in the park. She might stop on the way home at the library for a book, at the deli for a barbecued chicken, at the cleaner's, at the drugstore. On those days she could move coolly and crisply through space and time, untouched by the stares of men.

Doubtless they looked at her on those days, as on the more difficult days. She was the sort men looked at, and she had learned that early on—when her legs first began to lengthen and take shape, when her breasts began to bud. Later, as the legs grew longer and the breasts fuller, and as her face lost its youthful plumpness and was sculpted by time into beauty, the stares increased. She was attractive, she was beautiful, she was—curious phrase—easy on the eyes. So men looked at her, and on the easy days she didn't seem to notice, didn't let their rude stares penetrate the invisible shield that guarded her.

But this was not one of those days.

It started in the morning. She was waiting for the bus when she first felt the heat of a man's eyes upon her. At first she willed herself to ignore the feeling, wished the bus would come and whisk her away from it, but the bus did not come and she could not ignore what she felt and, inevitably, she turned from the street to look at the source of the feeling.

There was a man leaning against a red brick building not twenty yards from her. He was perhaps thirty-five, unshaven, and his clothes looked as though he'd slept in them. When she turned to glance at him his lips curled lightly, and his eyes, red-rimmed and glassy, moved first to her face, then drifted insolently the length of her body. She could feel their heat; it leaped from the eyes to her breasts and loins like an electric charge bridging a gap.

He placed his hand deliberately upon his crotch and rubbed himself. His smile widened.

She turned from him, drew a breath, let it out, wished the bus would come. Even now, with her back to him, she could feel the embrace of his eyes. They were like hot hands upon her buttocks and the backs of her thighs.

The bus came, neither early nor late, and she mounted the steps and dropped her fare in the box. The usual driver, a middle-aged fatherly type, gave her his usual smile and wished her the usual good morning. His eyes were an innocent watery blue behind thick-lensed spectacles.

Was it only her imagination that his eyes swept her body all the while? But she could feel them on her breasts, could feel too her own nipples hardening in response to their palpable touch.

She walked the length of the aisle to the first available seat. Male eyes tracked her every step of the way.

* * *

The day went on like that. This did not surprise her, although she had hoped it would be otherwise, had prayed during the bus ride that eyes would cease to bother her when she left the bus. She had learned, though, that once a day began in this fashion its pattern was set, unchangeable.

Was it something she did? Did she invite their hungry stares? She certainly didn't do anything with the intention of provoking male lust. Her dress was conservative enough, her makeup subtle and unremarkable. Did she swing her hips when she walked? Did she wet her lips and pout like a sullen sexpot? She was positive she did nothing of the sort, and it often seemed to her that she could cloak herself in a nun's habit and the results would be the same. Men's eyes would lift the black skirts and strip away the veil.

At the office building where she worked, the elevator starter glanced at her legs, then favored her with a knowing, wet-lipped smile. One of the office boys, a rabbity youth with unfortunate skin, stared at her breasts, then flushed scarlet when she caught him at it. Two older men gazed at her from the water cooler. One leaned over to murmur something to the other. They both chuckled and went on looking at her.

She went to her desk and tried to concentrate on her work. It was difficult, because intermittently she felt eyes brushing her body, moving across her like searchlight beams scanning the yard in a prison movie. There were moments when she wanted to scream, moments when she wanted to spin around in her chair and hurl something. But she remained in control of herself and did none of these things. She had survived days of this sort often enough in the past. She would survive this one as well.

The weather was good, but today she spent her lunch hour at her desk rather than risk the park. Several times during the afternoon the sensation of being watched was unbearable and she retreated to the ladies room. She endured the final hours a minute at a time, and finally it was five o'clock and she straightened her desk and left.

The descent on the elevator was unbearable. She bore it. The bus ride home, the walk from the bus stop to her apartment building, were unendurable. She endured them.

In her apartment, with the door locked and bolted, she stripped off her clothes and hurled them into a corner of the room as if they were unclean, as if the day had irrevocably soiled them. She stayed a long while under the shower, washed her hair, blow-dried it, then returned to her bedroom and stood nude before the full-length mirror on the closet door. She studied herself at some length, and intermittently her hands would move to cup a breast or trace the swell of a thigh, not to arouse but to assess, to chart the dimensions of her physical self.

And now? A meal alone? A few hours with a book? A lazy night in front of the television set?

She closed her eyes, and at once she felt other eyes upon her, felt them as she had been feeling them all day. She knew that she was alone, that now no one was watching her, but this knowledge did nothing to dispel the feeling.

She sighed.

She would not, could not, stay home tonight.

When she left the building, stepping out into the cool of dusk, her appearance was very different. Her tawny hair, which she'd worn pinned up earlier, hung free. Her makeup was overdone, with an excess of mascara and a deep blush of rouge in the hollows of her cheeks. During the day she'd worn no scent beyond a touch of Jean Naté applied after her morning shower; now she'd dashed on an abundance of the perfume she wore only on nights like this one, a strident scent redolent of musk. Her dress was close-fitting and revealing, the skirt slit oriental-fashion high on one thigh, the neckline low to display her decolletage. She strode purposefully on her high-heeled shoes, her buttocks swaying as she walked.

She looked sluttish and she knew it, and gloried in the knowledge. She'd checked the mirror carefully before leaving the apartment and she had liked what she saw. Now, walking down the street with her handbag bouncing against her swinging hip, she could feel the heat building up within her flesh. She could also feel the eyes of the men she passed, men who sat on stoops or loitered in doorways, men walking with purpose who stopped for a glance in her direction. But there was a difference. Now she relished those glances. She fed on the heat in those eyes, and the fire within herself burned hotter in response.

A car slowed. The driver leaned across the seat, called to her. She missed the words but felt the touch of his eyes. A pulse throbbed insistently throughout her entire body now. She was frightened—of her own feelings, of the real dangers she faced—but at the same time she was alive, gloriously alive, as she had not been in far too long. Before she had walked through the day. Now the blood was singing in her veins.

She passed several bars before finding the cocktail lounge she wanted. The interior was dimly lit, the floor soft with carpeting. An overactive air conditioner had lowered the temperature to an almost uncomfortable level. She walked bravely into the room. There were several empty tables along the wall but she passed them by, walking her swivel-hipped walk to the bar and taking a stool at the far end.

The cold air was stimulating against her warm skin. The bartender gave her a minute, then ambled over and leaned against the bar in front of her. He looked at once knowing and disinterested, his heavy lids shading his dark brown eyes and giving them a sleepy look.

"Stinger," she said.

While he was building the drink she drew her handbag into her lap and groped within it for her billfold. She found a ten and set it on top of the bar, then fumbled reflexively within her bag for another moment, checking its contents. The bartender placed the drink on the bar in front of her, took her money, returned with her change. She looked at her drink, then at her reflection in the back bar mirror.

Men were watching her.

She could tell, she could always tell. Their gazes fell on her and warmed the skin where they touched her. Odd, she thought, how the same sensation that had been so disturbing and unpleasant all day long was so desirable and exciting now.

She raised her glass, sipped her drink. The combined flavor of cognac and creme de menthe was at once warm and cold upon her lips and tongue. She swallowed, sipped again.

"That a stinger?"

He was at her elbow and she flicked her eyes in his direction while continuing to face forward. A small man, stockily built, balding, tanned, with a dusting of freckles across his high forehead. He wore a navy blue Quiana shirt open at the throat, and his dark chest hair was beginning to go gray.

"Drink up," he suggested. "Let me buy you another."

She turned now, looked levelly at him. He had small eyes. Their whites showed a tracery of blue veins at their outer corners. The irises were a very dark brown, an unreadable color, and the black pupils, hugely dilated in the bar's dim interior, covered most of the irises.

"I haven't seen you here," he said, hoisting himself onto the seat beside her. "I usually drop in around this time, have a couple, see my friends. Not new in the neighborhood, are you?"

Calculating eyes, she thought. Curiously passionless eyes, for all their cool intensity. Worst of all, they were small eyes, almost beady eyes.

"I don't want company," she said.

"Hey, how do you know you don't like me if you don't give me a chance?" He was grinning, but there was no humor in it. "You don't even know my name, lady. How can you despise a total stranger?"

"Please leave me alone."

"What are you, Greta Garbo?" He got up from his stool, took a half step away from her, gave her a glare and a curled lip. "You want to drink alone," he said, "why don't you just buy a bottle and take it home with you? You can take it to bed and suck on it, honey."

He had ruined the bar for her. She scooped up her change, left her drink unfinished. Two blocks down and one block over she found a second cocktail lounge virtually indistinguishable from the first one. Perhaps the lighting was a little softer, the background music the slightest bit lower in pitch. Again she passed up the row of tables and seated herself at the bar. Again she ordered a stinger and let it rest on the bar top for a moment before taking the first exquisite sip.

Again she felt male eyes upon her, and again they gave her the same hot-cold sensation as the combination of brandy and creme de menthe.

This time when a man approached her she sensed his presence for a long moment before he spoke. She studied him out of the corner of her eye. He was tall and lean, she noted, and there was a self-contained air about him, a sense of considerable self-assurance. She wanted to turn, to look directly into his eyes, but instead she raised her glass to her lips and waited for him to make a move.

"You're a few minutes late," he said.

She turned, looked at him. There was a weathered, raw-boned look to him that matched the western-style clothes he wore—the faded chambray shirt, the skin-tight denim jeans. Without glancing down she knew he'd be wearing boots and that they would be good ones.

"I'm late?"

He nodded. "I've been waiting for you for close to an hour. Of course it wasn't until you walked in that I knew it was you I was waiting for, but one look was all it took. My name's Harley."

She made up a name. He seemed satisfied with it, using it when he asked her if he could buy her a drink.

"I'm not done with this one yet," she said.

"Then why don't you just finish it and come for a walk in the moonlight?"

"Where would we walk?"

"My apartment's just a block and a half from here."

"You don't waste time."

"I told you I waited close to an hour for you. I figure the rest of the evening's too precious to waste."

She had been unwilling to look directly into his eyes but she did so now and she was not disappointed. His eyes were large and well-spaced, blue in color, a light blue of a shade that often struck her as cold and forbidding. But his eyes were anything but cold. On the contrary, they burned with passionate intensity.

She knew, looking into them, that he was a danger-ous man. He was strong, he was direct and he was dangerous. She could tell all this in a few seconds, merely by meeting his relentless gaze.

Well, that was fine. Danger, after all, was an inextricable part of it.

She pushed her glass aside, scooped up her change. "I don't really want the rest of this," she said.

"I didn't think you did. I think I know what you really want."

"I think you probably do."

He took her arm, tucked it under his own. They left the lounge, and on the way out she could feel other eyes on her, envious eyes. She drew closer to him and swung her hips so that her buttocks bumped into his lean flank. Her purse slapped against her other hip. Then they were out the door and heading down the street.

She felt excitement mixed with fear, an emotional combination not unlike her stinger. The fear, like the danger, was part of it.

His apartment consisted of two sparsely furnished rooms three flights up from street level. They walked wordlessly to the bedroom and undressed. She laid her clothes across a wooden chair, set her handbag on the floor at the side of the platform bed. She got onto the bed and he joined her and they embraced. He smelled faintly of leather and tobacco and male perspiration, and even with her eyes shut she could see his blue eyes burning in the darkness.

She wasn't surprised when his hands gripped her shoulders and eased her downward on the bed. She had been expecting this and welcomed it. She swung her head, letting her long hair brush across his flat abdomen, and then she moved to accept him. He tangled his fingers in her hair, hurting her in a not unpleasant way. She inhaled his musk as her mouth embraced him, and in her own fashion she matched his strength with strength of her own, teasing, taunting, heightening his passion and then cooling it down just short of culmination. His breathing grew ragged and muscles worked in his legs and abdomen.

At length he let go of her hair. She moved upward on the bed to join him and he rolled her over onto her back and covered her, his mouth seeking hers, his flesh burying itself in her flesh. She locked her thighs around his hips. He pounded at her loins, hammering her, hurting her with the brute force of his masculinity.

How strong he was, and how insistent. Once again she thought what a dangerous man he was, and what a dangerous game she was playing. The thought served only to spur her own passion on, to build her fire higher and hotter.

She felt her body preparing itself for orgasm, felt the urge growing to abandon herself, to lose control utterly. But a portion of herself remained remote, aloof, and she let her arm hang over the side of the bed and reached for her purse, groped within it.

And found the knife.

Now she could relax, now she could give up, now she could surrender to what she felt. She opened her eyes, stared upward. His own eyes were closed as he thrust furiously at her. *Open your eyes,* she urged him silently. *Open them, open them, look at me—*

And it seemed that his eyes did open to meet hers, even as they climaxed together, even as she centered the knife over his back and plunged it unerringly into his heart.

Afterward, in her own apartment, she put his eyes in the box with the others.

A REAL WOMAN

Mike W. Barr

The transfer to Tirton wasn't as bad as I thought. Tirton was smaller than Cleveland, it had the feeling of a real community, but was still large enough to have the attractions of a big city. That made it fine for both Nancy and me. She could make some new girlfriends, and so could I.

Understand, I really love her. It's just that, you know, women like sex, but men *need* it. At least, men like me do. The smallness of Tirton might make it difficult, but nothing is impossible, not when a man's got the itch.

But I promised myself that for the first few weeks I wouldn't scratch, and I kept that promise. Fifteen days qualifies.

And it was pretty easy, since Nancy was setting up the house, and I was hammering the local office into shape. Tirton was good for Nancy, the little lines under her eyes lost their hold, and some of the sparkle came back to her brown eyes. She almost looked like the girl I married again.

Because it took a while for Nancy to unpack the

kitchen stuff—and because she'd forgotten what little she knew about cooking after she discovered the Crock Pot, though she tries hard, I'll give her that—we ate out a lot. It was all expense account, which was fine, and it gave me a chance to check out the local spots to see which ones were right to bring clients to. I was looking for that, but I was looking for something else, too. And Nancy knew it, or thought she did, which is why I stayed on good behavior. Besides, nothing this town had to show me was any better than I could have gotten at home.

Until that night. The place on the edge of town had a new owner and was trying hard to go with the flow, to be a family place and appeal to the college crowd as well. One big room was the main dining room, and another part of it was a dance floor, all set up with a live band, even on a Thursday. They were trying hard. And from where I sat, they had succeeded.

She was the most gorgeous woman I had seen in Tirton. Okay, that's not saying much. Let's say this: Even in Hollywood she would have turned heads. She was above average height, with broad shoulders and some meat on her, which I like. Models are great for magazines, but I like a little substance. Her hair was coal-black and it actually had blue highlights. I wondered if that was her natural color; I found out later that it was. Her blue eyes matched the highlights, and her nose was small but good and straight, not a pug. Her mouth was broad and full. She wore a red dress that coated her from shoulders to knee; that doesn't sound sexy, I know, you had to see how it fit. She was dancing with some college kids, but something about her told me she wasn't with them, even though she couldn't have been much older than them. But even on a dance floor filled with college girls she stood out. The college girls were cute, but they were all in short skirts and tight tops cut down to here. Not that I mind that at all, but next to my target, they looked like little girls trying on their mothers' clothes. She was dancing to just some dumb karaoke tune, but the way she was moving made me realize she was following some internal rhythm of her own. And I had to be part of it.

I didn't think she was aware of anyone else in the room, but she suddenly looked at me and smiled, a 500-watter with a momentary flash of small, gleaming teeth. Then she was back dancing to her own beat.

I almost made a move then and there, until I remembered Nancy. I paid the check and took her home, wondering what I was going to do. Frankly, the last few weeks had been nice, if a little dull. I thought I hadn't made up my mind until I realized I'd paid cash and took the receipt, instead of using my credit card. Once again, my dick had made my mind up for me.

Nancy had been having trouble sleeping since the move, so I poured some milk in a pan. While it was warming I rummaged around in the unpacked bathroom stuff and found the bottle of happy pills the doctor had prescribed the last time she caught me. They'd expired, but Nancy kept them anyway, bless her heart.

I snapped one in half and crushed it with a spoon in the bottom of her mug, then poured the milk in. I thought for a moment, then I crushed the second half and dumped it in. No sense in half measures.

She was watching the news in the living room; I took it in to her on a saucer with a napkin and a cookie. That got me points, I'll tell you; we moved over to the couch and she sat with her head on my shoulder, sipping her milk. The smell of her hair was all around me; it was nice, and I almost changed my mind. But by the time the lottery numbers came on, she was gone.

I laid her on the bed, pulled the covers over her, and got down to business.

The place was still open—it wasn't late—I took a quick look around to see if any of the few people in town I'd met were there; none of them were. The hostess looked at me and raised her brows, asking if I'd forgotten something. But she didn't know me and I had paid cash to keep it that way. I shook my head and went into the bar. She was still there, thank God. I took a barstool while I planned my move.

I wasn't sure how I was going to approach her. Not that I cared what the college crowd thought, but I didn't want to look like a dork in front of them, not to her. But she solved that problem. She glided over to the bar, stood at the railing for a moment and took a breath, which made her look even better to me. She had a light sheen of perspiration on her forehead which looked great; I imagined the glow it gave to the rest of her soft, golden body.

She took a compact from her purse and gave her face the once-over. I don't like a woman to be too vain, but I couldn't blame her. If I had a face like that, I'd want a look at it, too, now and then.

"Don't bother, you don't need it," I said.

She looked at me, not with the sudden realization that a stranger had made contact, but acknowledging a prior awareness, as if she knew I'd say something. I imagine every man—every real man—she met made some kind of remark to her, if only to have been noticed by her for one moment.

Then she smiled. It was as if all the lights had come on in the room, but it also seemed more intimate.

"Thanks, Handsome," she said. Something in her voice capitalized it. Her voice was low and soft; something in it reminded me of a moonlit pool on a warm, fragrant night. "Do you know your way around a dance floor?"

"Only to something slow," I replied. I lifted my drink, and realized I'd forgotten to take off my wedding ring. It had been a long time. I put down the drink slowly and moved my left hand behind me, hoping she hadn't seen. To this day I don't know whether or not she had; if she had, it didn't slow her down much.

"My very thought," she said. She extended her hand, and I took it. It was warm and smooth and supple.

On the way to the dance floor my right hand was against the small of her back, and enjoying every second of it. I had my left hand in my pants pocket, working my wedding ring off.

She was a terrific dancer. She let me do the steering, but provided just enough resistance to make it interesting. The dance floor lights flowed over her onyx hair, giving it the luster of thick fur. For the most part she kept her eyes closed, a small smile on her face, as if enjoying a pleasant dream. The weight and texture of her against me got me stiffer than a fireplace poker, and hotter.

When it was over, I noticed we were the only couple left on the floor. I don't know how long we'd danced, but the waiters had cleaned up and the band looked like it wanted to go home. She took my arm as I escorted her off the dance floor, then turned to face me as we reached the bar. My arms were around her warm softness, and her hands were flat on my chest, making me glad my personal gym was the first thing I'd unpacked.

I thought this was it. Her lips pursed as she rose to meet me. And she kissed me on the cheek.

I must have looked every bit as startled as I felt, because she suddenly laughed, at once startled, apologetic, and sympathetic. "Thanks for the dance, Handsome," she said. I was standing there like a log as one of the college girls—a redhead in a patent-leather dress—walked up to her, glared at me, put her arms around my partner and kissed her. And my partner kissed back. "Let's go, Samantha," she said when their mouths parted.

Okay, I'd fallen for it. Let's yank the hetero's dick. But as she and the redhead walked away, with the most beautiful motion I'd ever seen, she turned and gave me another of those killer smiles.

"See you again, Handsome," she said, and there was genuine longing in the caress of her voice.

I felt like that damn asshole prince in "Cinderella." "How?" I asked. "What's your name?"

She was out the door; I didn't even think she'd heard me. But then her voice drifted back, soft and sweet. "Marissa," it said.

I sat down—which was tough enough with what that dress of hers had done to me—and took a deep breath.

Usually I drove home with the windows down, to wash away any perfume that wasn't Nancy's. Not this time.

I told Nancy I really liked the food at that place; we went back once for dinner, and I took guys from the office there twice for lunch. But there was no sign of Marissa, and I didn't want to start asking about her, not yet. Then I got the brainstorm of taking clients to some of the local college spots. They liked fantasizing about the coeds, and I could keep an eye out for Marissa. But no luck.

Nancy was delighted—for the wrong reason, of course, but she couldn't have known that. She was just happy that I was spending so much time at home and was paying so much attention to her. But what was the point of sleeping with any other woman, once I'd had Marissa in my arms, once I'd felt the nearly electric shock of her running through my arms around her, straight down to my crotch? I slept with Nancy, sure—you have to keep in practice—and she seemed happier than ever with the sex. I didn't tell her that in my mind—and in my dick—she had black hair with cobalt highlights, and was named Marissa.

And my mind was the only place I saw Marissa. Not until I'd given up looking, of course. One night I'd taken Nancy, a client from out of town, and his wife to the local theater to show that we weren't just a backwater town. We'd just been seated when I got a whiff of that perfume.

I said I'd given up looking. As though I ever could. Catching her scent again made me realize neither it nor she had ever really left my mind, they'd just gone under my skin, like a fever that's never really cured.

I was on the aisle. Marissa wafted within a foot as she walked toward the back, close enough for me to touch her, and with more than my hands. But she didn't look at me; I didn't know if she'd seen me or not. I excused myself and made for the lobby. No one there, but her perfume lingered, luring me on. I headed out toward the parking lot. But she was gone.

Then I heard the music of her laugh from behind me. I turned, she was walking toward me from the kiosk of a very confused parking attendant. She was wearing a charcoal gray jacket and skirt that looked as though it belonged in a corporate boardroom, except she wasn't wearing anything under the jacket and about an inch of midriff peeked between the bottom of the jacket and the waist of her skirt. "This is a theater, Handsome, I thought you'd be playing hard-to-get," she said, as though we'd last parted five minutes ago. Her smile seemed to provide the lighting for the lot.

"I'm an amateur," I said as I approached her, "next to you." I realized I was taking in little sharp breaths, like a bloodhound. I was seeking her scent.

I gathered the soft, yielding weight of her in my arms and went to kiss her. But I got her palm instead. "Not here," she whispered. "It wouldn't be right." A car horn trilled behind me. Marissa's head swiveled to one side as she looked behind me. I didn't want her having anyone else's attention, so I did a one-eighty on my feet and looked where she had.

A boyish brunette sat behind the wheel of a sports car, her glance somehow directing the indignant beeps right at me.

"I have to go," said Marissa. My hands stayed where they were. She struggled against me; I liked that, I imagined her on top. But I had to get her attention, so I took my best shot.

"Haven't you ever had a man?" I asked.

"Never," she said. I guess my surprise showed, and she smiled. "Only women. Women who have never had a man."

"Then you're not a woman at all," I said, "you're just a girl."

There was a flash in the depths of those cobalt eyes; I liked that, too. Anger was better than indifference. I released her and grinned, adding a little contempt.

"Whenever you're ready to be a real woman," I said, "just call."

She didn't say anything, she just marched off with a cute little indignant tilt to her chin. Not all women are beautiful when they're angry—Nancy sure wasn't—but Marissa was. When she hopped in the sports car, the brunette began saying something harsh. I heard Marissa say, "That's enough, Vicky—" but the rest was lost over the engine's roar.

I returned to the theater as the curtain rose, making some lame apology that I put over strictly due to personal charm. And why not? I felt great. For the next couple of hours people moved on the stage before me, but I barely saw them. I knew I'd encounter Marissa again, and I knew I'd be more than just another lover. I'd be her first, her first real lover. And I'd make her a real woman.

It's funny how having a specific goal in mind changes your outlook. I'd never believed it in business school, which is probably one of the reasons I'd flunked out. After my first meeting with Marissa, I was afraid I'd never see her again. And if I had seen her again, all I wanted to do was fuck her, which I guess was specific, but was hardly a brilliant plan.

But after our meeting in the parking lot it was all clear to me. I knew I'd see her again, and I knew what I'd finally do. I'd popped my share of virgins—Nancy was one—but Marissa would be special. I remembered how stiff she'd made me, and I almost envied her. But I'd be gentle.

I was on to her now. She wanted me to find her, not for sex, at least, not immediately. She wasn't just a cockteaser—if that was the case, she'd have been all over me with her hands and that terrific mouth—but I wasn't sure what she did want. If it was just the attentions of a male, she could have that from anything in pants, and gladly. If it was to make her lez girlfriends jealous, couldn't she have just played them one off against the other?

No, she wanted me, but on her terms. She wanted it, of course, she just was afraid to admit it to herself. Which was fine with me. One thing I learned in business school is let the other party think she's getting what she wants, as long as you get yours.

I didn't see Marissa for a couple of weeks. I can honestly say I wasn't looking for her, because I knew she was seeking me; leading me on. It was an odd feeling, knowing I was the pursued and not the pursuer; kind of like the situation women had been in since the dawn of time, I guess. Not that it mattered, as long as I got what I wanted. So I didn't look for her, even though I really was, deep down. I guess that's Zen or something.

The next time was when I was heading home from taking a client out. It had been daylight when I'd parked the car, but it was night now, and the working girls were out in force, waiting in front of the parking deck like an all-girl smorgasbord. There was nearly every type of woman you could ask for; I was surprised a place like Tirton had that much variety. Not that I planned on anything for myself; I was in training for Marissa, with an occasional squirt into Nancy just to keep the top of my head from blowing off.

Cars drifted by the girls as the drivers looked over the merchandise and the merchandise looked back, drifting like moths around a light. A couple of the girls with a little more ambition were scanning ahead—that was when they saw me, and began moving toward me. I could tell they liked what they saw. Not that they'd say otherwise, but I could see something beyond the usual avarice in their eyes. Like I said, I try to stay in shape.

"Hey, baby," said one of them as I crossed the street, "got a date?"

I was going to reply, "Sure, October thirteenth," but never got it out. I'd only started when I noticed movement to my right. Walking toward the parking deck from the sidewalk at right angles to mine was a silhouette I'd seen in every other waking moment and in every second of my dreams.

"Hi, Handsome." She smiled, as though it was a pleasant coincidence. "Going my way?"

Her greeting wasn't that much different from the hooker's, but it sounded like the difference between hamburger and filet mignon. She was wearing a gray wool dress that clung to her body like my thoughts. Some of the working girls glared at Marissa, like they thought she was competition (like they'd ever been in her league!), others watched, uncertain what a woman like her was doing in a neighborhood like that. It occurred to me that maybe I could put a slight scare into her, make her happy there was a real man around.

"You may be glad I am," I said, jerking a thumb to my left. "This neighborhood is a little rough."

She turned the corner without missing a beat, nailing me with another of her smiles. The cold weather made her perfume even stronger as it washed over me, going straight to my crotch. "I like things a little rough," she replied.

We'd see about that. Most women are put off by hookers, so I followed, a couple of steps behind her, waiting for her to need me. Some of the johns in the cars turned as Marissa approached, looking at her the way I look at a hundred-foot yacht. Then some of the hookers saw their customers checking out something else, and they turned. Then they got a look at Marissa, every one of them, as though their heads were all attached to the same string.

Then they parted before her, like an ocean meeting the bow of an aircraft carrier. I can't describe the emotion I saw in their eyes, like dread and fear and respect, each one alternately bubbling to the top, like Ping-Pong balls at a Bingo game.

Marissa walked past them like they were statues and entered the parking deck, but I approached one of the pack. She was shaking her head, dazed, like coming out from gas or a drug.

"What did you see?" I asked. "What was it?"

She shook her head some more. "It was her eyes." Then she said it again.

I left her and went into the parking deck. Marissa was getting into a little red Corvette, the door held for her by a slim blonde with a pageboy and a great ass.

"I thought you'd never come," Marissa said. Whether she meant the double entendre I still don't know.

"What did you do to those women?" I asked her. I realized I sounded like some dumb kid who'd just seen his first woman sawn in half. I looked into Marissa's eyes; they were cool and blue and beautiful as always, but not threatening. At least, not to me.

"Women don't like me," she said with a fake pout.

"Some women do," said her companion, who had flowed into the driver's seat. "The right kind." Marissa chuckled throatily, turned to her, and the two kissed as if I wasn't there. And a few seconds later I wasn't.

I drove home at about eighty miles per hour, confused and mad at myself, at women, at the world. Nancy looked up at me as I entered the house, her face afraid.

She started to ask me what was wrong. I didn't give her the chance, I slammed her against me and stuck my tongue halfway down her throat. My hands ran over her thin body as I told myself she wasn't who she was.

I practically shoved her into the bedroom and tore off the frumpy housecoat she was wearing, my hands seeking something new in her small breasts, her thin body. She'd have to do.

I think she liked it. I was well inside her and working my way to the big bang when she suddenly went stiff, too, but in a different way. She was cold as well, and her brown eyes looked at once hurt and disgusted.

Then I realized why. I had screamed "Marissa."

She struggled, but I held on to her long enough to shoot my wad. Then I left, pulling my clothes on, leaving her sobbing on the phone to her fucking mother.

A contact I'd made in the DMV had traced the license plate of the car Marissa drove off in the second time I saw her, so I knew where she lived. I drove there, keeping a lid on my anger—the last thing I needed was to get stopped—and found the address. It was a two-story house at the edge of town, surrounded by a high-security fence and far enough away from the neighbors for some solitude without being totally isolated.

I drove up to the gate and pressed the button on the security console. After a second a female voice came through, not Marissa's: "Yes?"

"Tell Marissa I—" I never finished. The hum of an electric motor filled the still night air, concealed gears caught, and the gate opened.

I drove up to the carport, got out of the car, and stepped toward the house. Then I remembered. I went back to the car, took out the spare tire, and removed the package I'd hidden there a while ago. I had it professionally wrapped where I bought it, with red satin paper and lots of bows.

I walked toward the house, wondering what to expect. The door opened, and the boyish brunette, Vicky, walked toward the street. Then she saw me.

She stopped still and looked at me, as if she had been seeking a life preserver or an anchor, and she wasn't sure which one I was. From the cast to her green eyes and her pug nose, I wasn't sure which one she wanted. "What do you want?" she asked. Then she caught herself. "Oh, right."

"Right," I nodded. I didn't want a scene, I just wanted Marissa, and no hundred lesbos were going to stop me. But Vicky put a hand on my chest as I tried to pass her, and I turned to look at her, expecting hostility.

Instead, I saw fear. "You ought to stay away from her," said Vicky, "take it from me."

"What is she," I asked, trying to keep it light, "some kind of vampire?"

"All a vampire takes is blood," she replied. Then she walked off, and I entered the house without knocking.

Inside was a living room with a broad staircase leading upstairs. The whole place was decorated in good taste, lots of earth tones and pastels.

And in the center of the main wall, a huge painting of Marissa.

A couple of girls I'd seen in Marissa's entourage were watching television as I entered, sitting next to each other, but not touching. They looked up at me and spoke before I could. "She's upstairs."

I crossed between them and the television as I approached the stairs. They were watching a video-tape of a third girl making love to Marissa.

The house smelled just like her; I got stiff just by breathing. I climbed the stairs; the hallway branched off to either side. Somehow I knew which way to go.

I didn't knock. Her room was the equivalent of a separate apartment; I entered a kind of foyer, with pictures and books and the smell of heaven in the air. From the doorway came her voice. "Stephanie?"

I didn't say anything, I just stood there and waited. After a few seconds Marissa came to the doorway. She didn't seem surprised to see me, but she never did. She smiled. "I knew it would come to this," she said. "Hi, Handsome." She was wearing a long blue dress that looked like ocean water running over her superb body; something iridescent in it rippled as she walked toward me. "Care for a drink?"

"No," I said. She knew what I wanted. I threw down the package on the couch. Through the open door I could see her bed. I approached her and grabbed her, my hands flowing over her, feeling the yielding firmness of her stomach, her ass, her breasts. I looked straight into her eyes, trying to see what others had seen there, when I heard the door open and she looked past me.

I turned, to see another girl standing there, looking disappointed. Stephanie. "Sorry, honey," said Marissa. "I'm afraid you've been bumped." During this she stood close to me, her crotch against mine, getting me even stiffer and keeping me that way.

I heard the door close; all I saw was Marissa's smile. "Had enough?" she asked.

"Not yet," I said.

Her hands moved lower over me, unzipping my pants, stroking me. She was getting hot, too. I could sense the lust rising in her, but something else, as well.

Just before she kissed me, I finally saw the full depths of her eyes. I couldn't turn away.

Then Marissa was gone after helping me prepare, promising to return very soon.

I sit here, awaiting her. The night air is cool against my bare shoulders. I wear the teddy which I bought for her, but which now fits me well. I turn my head, trying to grow accustomed to the thick, soft weight of hair against my neck.

Marissa enters, looking like my every dream in a bra and garter belt. No panties. She approaches me, bends over me. Our lipsticked mouths fuse, her tongue caresses mine.

The old urge rises within me, but in a strange new

form, an increasing heat, yes, but a softening rather than a stiffness. I pull away, uncertainly. Marissa looks down, her blue eyes smile.

"Don't worry, Beautiful," she says, and her cool, probing fingers find the heartbeat beneath my left breast. "I'll be worth it."

For God's sake, Marissa, you'd better be.

MADAME BABYLON

Brian Hodge

*F*or every turned cheek, a hand to stroke it; for every pursed mouth, another to kiss it; for every bared back, a whip to stripe it . . . for every desire, fulfillment, and for every act of every kind, eyes to watch it.

These, the unwritten credos of exhibitionist and voyeur.

If it could be done, Kraaft wanted to watch it; if it could be done by Shawn, so much the better.

He had an image fixed in mind, from last year; couldn't get it out of his head; spent time with it every day, like a painting bought for a desperate sum, then hoarded from all other eyes.

Shawn's was one of the better-developed abdomens he'd seen, daily workouts augmenting what had been genetically blessed already. He'd always enjoyed pressing his cheek against it, and running a hand over the golden-olive skin, so warm, so silken on the surface, the muscles beneath hard and taut in their intricate contour of ripple and curve. Her flaring hipbones were magnificent petals; her shallow navel was both oyster and pearl.

Kraaft no longer recalled the faces of her lovers from that weekend afternoon—they were as interchangeable as his students at the university, and often drawn from the same pool—only that there had been four of them. It had been September and still warm, the breeze blowing through the bedroom windows sticky, the blunt tips of her honey-colored hair clinging to her throat. From chest to mons a copious musk of sweat and saliva and semen coated her skin with a milky glaze. She'd drawn an unhurried fingertip up through the slick and put it to her lips, while looking at him across the room and smiling, nothing in her green eyes to connote anything other than lust and free will. Certainly not coercion.

He returned to the memory of this the way men in wars clutch photos of home, reminders of what once was real.

Nine months later, and she was gone without so much as a phone call or note. There'd been no foul play here, not with an emptied closet left behind to plunge him into doubt, second-guessing each act to which she'd agreed and every cock that wasn't his. Combing recollection for any hint she'd not been enjoying herself as much as he after all.

This could not be the end.

To Kraaft there was nothing inherently sacred about marriage.

But he missed her terribly, and broken vows deserved at least an explanation, if nothing else.

The first true lead came during high summer, while the campus readied for its brief hibernation before resuming with the fall term. When Kraaft came home each afternoon and checked the voice mail accounts, he teetered between eagerness and dread; the hope of news was often all that got him through the day. Nights took stronger stuff.

He'd sprinkled personals ads throughout possible destinations Shawn might've had. While she could've gone anywhere, he'd begun with the most likely metro areas. Chicago first, ninety miles to the east. Milwaukee and Indianapolis and St. Louis, the next nearest cities of any size. More. He'd composed ads directed at her, others for those who may have come to know Shawn in all her passions, for while she might conceivably have quit herself of thcm, he'd believe that when he saw it. Hungers, once roused, were like dragons: easier to awaken than put to sleep again. Any addict would tell you as much.

His ads had gone into papers catering to adherents of, if not the expressly forbidden, then at least the widely reviled. Such pulp stock media made sex lives easier, saving time and effort, a cutting of the chase altogether. Vanilla sex needed no networking. Vanilla sex was a closed system—one cock, one cunt, one position, ideally a marriage license, and all of polite Protestant society bestowcd its hands-off blessing. Skew the equation's components too far out of balance, though, and how easy to find yourself contemplating the new horizons of underground self-help.

Personals ads were part catalog shopping, part messages in bottles, but weeding through his voice mail messages in each city availed Kraaft of the ugly truth: They drew more than their share of pranksters, predators, and dolts. The honestly mistaken were the least of his troubles.

Callers who claimed to have filmed her. Callers who claimed to love her, warning him from the search. Callers who claimed to have loaned her money, demanding of him repayment. Callers who assured him there could be no reunion unless they first repented of their sodomite ways. Callers who claimed to have dismembered her. Callers who claimed to *be* Shawn, then made demands—money usually, but not always; one pretender said there was somebody he'd first have to kill.

Of course it was a sick world. The astonishing thing was the *degree*.

Finally, then, hope, a single ray from a black sun:

"I know her—the one from your ad? I met her a few months ago and that was it, but I could check around, maybe." The voice was nearly sexless but ultimately female. "The offer's only good if you're who I think you are, maybe she mentioned you once or twice. You teach college? Sociology?"

At last, a response that didn't reek of lies. From Chicago, no less. Very heartening—if Shawn hadn't deep down wanted to be found, why, then, had she stayed so close to home?

"So how do I know I can trust you?" was the first thing she said. "How do I know if I help you, you're not planning on just shooting her in the head when you find her?"

"Shooting her in the *head*? . . ."

"Like you've never heard of that happening. It's what men do best. Track something down and kill it. Why should their wives be exempt?"

Her name was Maggie and she appeared nearly as sexless as her voice. She wore no makeup, and her tangerine hair had been shaved to cross-hatched stubble on the sides of her head, chopped longer at the crown. Her face, squared; her clothes, shapeless; her nails gnawed to the quick. He counted nine silver rings up one ear.

"Because Shawn must've left you with a different impression of me," he said. "Otherwise you never would've answered the ad in the first place."

Around them, the clink of forks on dense white plates, the rattle of sweaty water glasses. Diner noises. The place had been her edict, public and neutral. A few strides down Lincoln Avenue and he could stand before the Biograph Theater, where six decades ago John Dillinger and his big swinging dick had exercised their final lapse in judgment.

"Any other reason you would've called?" he asked.

"That's a rhetorical one, right? If you're dropping ads into *Back Door Chicago,* you have to know you won't be hearing from people out of the goodness of their hearts."

Kraaft slipped a hundred-dollar bill from his wallet, split Franklin's face down the middle before pressing half into the ring left by her water glass. It soaked through, clung to the tabletop like a wet leaf.

"Just like you have to know I'm not paying for attitude."

His voice and steadiness of hand . . . for a moment he felt they were someone else's. Someone who hadn't rehearsed conversations in his head, writing his script in advance. He tried to regard it as no different than any classroom lecture.

Maggie peeled the sodden half-bill from the table and began blotting it between napkins. "Okay, I'm thinking. . . ."

While she blotted, his gaze began to wander, sifting those he found watch-worthy from the rest, settling on a couple in a booth. The woman was East Indian, perhaps twenty, perhaps a student. Her lips were generous and softly brown; he watched them pucker around the tip of a straw, watched the shallow dimpling of her cheeks. The leap was a given, imagining how she'd look with her friend, mouth widening to accommodate. The palpitations of her throat were teasing, would caress flesh like the beating of a bird's heart. Her hair, silk spun from obsidian, would sweep down to tickle the sensitized balls. He imagined the urgent coaxing of her hands.

"Hey," Maggie said sharply. "Didn't anyone ever

teach you it's rude to look at other women when you're with one already?"

He was too startled to do anything but shrug an apology, then pressed on about Shawn.

"It's too early now to do anything anyway," Maggie said. "I just wanted to meet you first. You want me to earn the other half of that hundred, you'll have to wait until tonight."

"You haven't even told me how you met her."

"Like I feel like sitting here, telling you my business? I don't think so." She tucked the damp half-bill into a pocket. "But tell *me* something, Professor. You loved her, right?"

Kraaft said that he did.

"Then how could you do it? And don't pretend you don't know what I'm talking about—Shawn told me, I *know*. How does a man sit there and get off on watching the woman he loves fuck other men? Groups of them, even. How does a man ask her to do that in the first place?"

He considered outright refusal; if she wouldn't tell him her business, what right had she to expect it from him? On the other hand, he wasn't keen on Maggie's harboring mistaken impressions.

"There was no gun to anybody's head," he said. "You think Shawn couldn't've said no anytime she wanted? You don't credit her with much, do you, implying she had no will of her own."

"Well, obviously she did. She took off and now here you are." Maggie's smile was smug. "Would you fuck her after everyone else was through?"

"Yes."

"Slip and slide around in whatever the others had left," she said, and now he began to wonder what was going on; this had gone beyond idle cruelty. "When you kissed her, could you taste another man's cum?"

"Is there a point to this?"

"*Could* you?"

Kraaft felt himself sucked in; with an unsettling twist of loins realized not only that Maggie might've been enjoying this for its own sake, but so was he—revelations to a total stranger.

"Sometimes," he whispered, "it would be on her breath."

"But it wasn't a gangbang every time, it couldn't be. It *was* just the two of you sometimes, wasn't it?"

Kraaft nodded. "Most of the time, in fact."

"Those must've been pretty dull in comparison. How'd you get through them?"

"I—" He frowned. "I pretended to be somebody else."

"No shit," Maggie said, with abrupt and crushing judgment. "You must really hate yourself."

She stood then, telling him when and where to meet her later, and as she left he decided against arguing; it would've done no good to cause a scene.

While finishing his coffee he returned to the Indian woman—what else might her splendid mouth inspire? But when her friend made her burst out laughing, her teeth were nothing as he'd imagined—yellowed as old ivory, with darker stains and snaggled spaces. Her gaze met Kraaft's, and instantly self-conscious she clapped a hand over her mouth, then a moment later began to choke, as though laid low by his unexpected revulsion.

It had to have been written all over his face.

Kraaft considered checking into a hotel but knew he'd have no patience to while away the hours there. He instead remained in the broil of late summer and the throb and crash that was Chicago, that was anyplace of comparable size. He'd always found a morbid fascination with it, its barbarism far removed from small-town university life. It encouraged the deviant because the deviant was so easily overlooked here, its incubation nurtured behind endless facades of pace and purpose.

Beside its Great Lake, Chicago drowsed and rumbled around him like a leviathan, slow to rouse, but when it did, its demands could be insatiable. Its residents had about them all that civilization could offer, yet still died by the helpless scores. Last summer's worst heat wave had burnt hundreds in their skins. Winters were crueler still. In January he'd read of an old woman, unseen for days, discovered in the frosty gloom of her apartment, kneeling in prayer and frozen into two inches of ice from a burst water pipe. A statue, in the temple of the satanic mill.

Its casual brutality aside, the city's distractions had been antidotal whenever life in academia approached the intolerable. Faculty duties paid a dynamite wage, but the living was gilded with sameness, each semester beginning with an audience of glazed and indifferent eyes, challenging him to make them react, for whatever benefit that would be; they were sheep, shorn of the futures enjoyed by their parents, and they knew it. To the banana republic squabbles in his department there was no end, nor of exhortations to publish or perish, careers absurdly furthered by wordy masturbation read only by the few, the proud, the stagnant. *Here* was higher learning.

While this life laid no direct claim on Shawn, its touch could hardly be escaped. She taught dance to girls, pubescent and younger. Nearly all were brought by their mothers—faculty wives, often. Seeds of great talent lay in few, if any, but that was no loss. The sad part was seeing them begin with the pure joy of the dance, then watching their feet grow heavier and their shoulders droop, as the nattering moms pecked the joy right out of them.

Two-career couples, here were their lives, well-paying prisons they might've become.

Bodies, then—hers, his, and others'. Bodies would be their escape, new geometries of limb and loin their frontier to explore. It was never hard to find willing men; impossible to find any who could exhaust her. Shawn made love with a dancer's grace, turning orgy into poetry, and poetry into flesh. Watching her with others was like discovering her all over again, each familiar swirl of tongue and thrust of hips made new to him by this radical change in perspective. He could feel her grind against him even though he was across the room. Seeing her greed for what strangers offered became prolonged and exquisite torture. It had gone on just long enough for Kraaft to forget who'd suggested it in the first place.

And now that she'd left, he could think of only two reasons: It had become too much for her. Or it was no longer enough.

He met Maggie late that night in a midtown bar, just the sort of place he'd expected her to be a regular—from the street, not very inviting, and once inside, not very reassuring. Her drink of choice appeared to be green. He didn't ask.

"Did you bring money?" she said, and he told her he had. "How much?"

"This wouldn't be a pre-robbery inventory, would it?"

"Well, that's that, I guess you're just too smart for stupid me." Late hours certainly hadn't diminished her charm. "I'm just making sure *I* don't look like a dipshit, bringing somebody around asking questions but he can't tip for answers. Just see how far you get with goodwill and IOUs."

"We're meeting somebody else here?"

"Downstairs."

"And what's downstairs?"

"Fucking King Tut's tomb, would you just chill awhile? Like, keep your mouth shut and your wallet open? You might as well start practicing now."

As Kraaft watched the clock behind the bar, Maggie twice got up to confer with the bartender, coming back fuming each time.

"Couldn't help but notice," he said, "you carry a lot of weight around here."

"You're so observant, how come you didn't notice your wife packing a suitcase?" Maggie slumped in her chair and began nibbling her fingernails, worrying at them until it seemed that anything would be better than the click of her teeth. "She, um, she said you teach college. Sociology? Isn't that it?"

"My main course is Collective Political Violence. Looking at riots, revolutions, coups."

Her interest perked up. "Those who can't do, teach, right?"

"Excuse me?"

"Like you never had the urge to throw a bomb. God, it's so obvious now that I know this." She'd forgotten about her nails. "Look at you, that stumpy little ponytail, that grotty little goatee. You're too young to have done the sixties, but you're too old to make those look really fashionable. So you talk about riots and revolutions and wish you'd been there, right?"

"You can tell all that, from the most superficial details. Amazing. Although it's a pity you never learned any better than that romantic notion that anything substantial was accomplished in the sixties." Clearly she'd learned cultural history from music videos. "But if you want to talk haircuts, fine, what about yours? What's with the waffle-iron look?"

"Oh, go build a bomb and get it over with, why

don't you," and she said no more until the bartender called her over. After speaking with him a moment, she motioned for Kraaft to follow her toward the back, through the smoky crush.

They were buzzed through one door that led them to another, manned by a pair of bull-necked giants who were flipping coins to determine who got a bruising punch on the shoulder. Both nodded at Maggie, ignoring Kraaft completely. The hallway reeked of sour armpits.

"Slow night, Magpie?" said one doorman. "Can't stay away?"

"What's up with this?" said the other. "Either you're with a guy, or that's the hairiest dyke I seen you with yet."

She barely slowed while elbowing past them. "Hit each other a little harder, why don't you. Maybe you'll break the skin and the steroids'll run out."

Kraaft followed, and heard behind him the wet smack of a huge fist on flesh, a grunt. A pause. A smack and another grunt.

Her path led back around to yet another door, no wider than a broom closet's. When she opened it, out drifted muffled music and the voices of an appreciative crowd. Kraaft could see nothing but a steep narrow stairway. Evidently an employee's back route, it led down into a warren of tiny rooms, not much bigger than phone booths and lacking doors, dingy with scabbed paint under the harsh light of bare bulbs. Each stall was furnished with a folding metal chair and a cracked mirror. Inside some of the empties, clothing hung on nails. In one his eyes met the flat, unblinking gaze of a woman in a garter belt who slumped splay-legged in her chair while dragging off a joint. In the next a muscular kid buckled a leather cuff-and-strap contraption around the base of his swaying cock.

"You like to watch," Maggie said, "well, now's your chance."

They slid out from backstage and along a side wall, ignored by an audience of thirty, forty. Onstage, cuffed at the wrists and ankles, a man leaned face-first into an X of wooden beams. Someone else—Kraaft couldn't discern gender because of angle and obstructions—knelt at the feet of the rack, busily fellating the man. Under low lighting, a corseted woman withdrew the coils of a whip from a bowl, then lit its length from a taper. It came alive then, a bright serpent. Each time she lashed the man, more gently than one might expect, it left across his back a long trace of flame that flickered blue, then went out as he shuddered.

"She calls herself Brandy Infernal," Maggie said. "Like she ever burned anything more expensive than rubbing alcohol."

Kraaft could only stare as the man writhed under conjoined assaults of whip and mouth and flame. Gradually, senses returned. He understood in his gut before the picture was clear in his head.

"She performed here," he said. "Shawn performed here."

"Getting that Ph.D. must've been a whiz for you."

He felt more left out than betrayed, Shawn having forsaken his eyes for those of strangers. It thrilled him and enraged him, left him with a deeper ache than any he'd known before. On that stage. Up there. She'd opened herself there and he'd missed it.

Maggie tugged at his arm. "See that guy over there? That guy who looks like he'd steal bread from an Ethiopian? He manages the downstairs. Whatever I say, go along with it, okay?"

The manager was thin-faced and balding, tufts of wiry hair bristling from either side of his shiny domed head. He appeared to regard Maggie as he might a stepdaughter on the verge of being disowned. They stood in the doorway of his cubbyhole office and argued, although not viciously, and too softly for Kraaft to make much of it. Finally Maggie turned to point at him.

"I really hate that it's come to this, Skeeter, but since you never would tell *me* where she went, then meet her husband. Maybe you'll tell him, instead."

"Husband." Skeeter scowled while checking him out. "Why would I even tell this moke to duck when I spit?"

"Well, *look* at him, Skeeter, you don't think he can afford to hire enough lawyers to give you more headaches than Tylenol ever heard of?"

"I don't take Tylenol for headaches, I have 'em shot in the back of the skull."

"Gimme a break, you manage a hardcore tittie bar, not Murder, Incorporated."

Skeeter gave her a warning look, wagged a finger. "You don't think I'm a fucking connected man, you think again."

"Yeah, connected to the point of being disposable if you don't keep this place low profile. This isn't Bangkok, y'know."

Finally, something that Skeeter seemed to take seriously. He gave Kraaft another appraisal, then stepped back into the privacy of his claustrophobic office. Maggie and Kraaft followed, shutting the door on the music.

"Lawyers," Skeeter said. "That right? What the fuck *for,* you mind telling me?"

"A civil suit." It was the first thing out of Kraaft's mouth. "Alienation of affection between husband and wife."

Skeeter guffawed. "If that was your wife, she didn't need any alienating from *me*. Wasn't *my* snoot buried between her legs. You want someone to sue, sue

Carrot Top here." He gave Maggie a look beyond disbelief. "Fucking psycho-cooze, what kind of game are you running, you bring this—"

There was obviously so much she'd neglected to tell him that Kraaft wasn't sure how to proceed. Not that it mattered now, not after Maggie slapped Skeeter across the face, hard as she could.

"You don't call *me* that!" she cried. "Nobody calls me a name like that!"

Fiery-cheeked, Skeeter was swift to retaliate; one hand raked over his desktop and found a letter opener. He jabbed at her once, missing by a clumsy foot, and then her hand shot back at his face, spritzing it with pepper spray. The dagger was dropped, Skeeter's hands slapping over his eyes, and he screamed. How he screamed. He groped blindly for the phone, but Kraaft beat him to it, hopes of finding Shawn melting away as Skeeter fell back across his desk, and Kraaft whacked the receiver against his brow. Again, again, until the man was beaten over that threshold where survival pins its hopes on silence rather than shrieks.

The battered head thrashed before him at waist level, mouth wide enough to count fillings, eyes poached and bloody. He gripped it by either side, levering a thumbnail into each crimped eyelid.

"You don't understand," he said, and this was news to himself as well, nothing he'd admitted until now. "If I don't go home with Shawn, I might as well not go at all."

"Oh, God, oh, God," Maggie was murmuring, backing away from the desk, fingernail at her teeth. "Oh, God . . ."

Just as Kraaft thought she'd be no more help, Maggie lunged forward and threw herself over Skeeter's knees to stop his kicking. His arms still roved free, but as feebly as the legs of a stepped-on roach.

"Where did she go?" Kraaft asked, but heard nothing sensible in reply. He pushed his thumbs deeper into the hot, teary folds of eyelid, listening to himself repeat the question. Himself, yet not; another man, really. Another man buried deeply beneath the layers of civility and diplomas.

Sentences begun, never finished; words bitten off between syllables. Kraaft eased some of the pressure. When something like coherence emerged, it meant nothing to him. Just talk overheard, Skeeter said, heard last week, or month; the whore below, it was Shawn now. The whore below—this was all he knew, nothing more.

The whore below. While the phrase meant nothing to Kraaft, he caught the recognition flickering across Maggie's face. There, then gone, and still his thumbs were in another man's eyes.

The injustice of it overwhelmed him—all that this man, this Skeeter, this parasite, had seen of Shawn, to *his* exclusion. Here was the agony: All that these eyes had taken in of her, to their owner it was only commerce. To the poetry he was blind already.

Beneath Kraaft's thumbs the eyeballs felt hard as peach pits. But he knew better; stood back and watched as that other man deep within gouged hard enough to find the softness at their core.

It was a start.

Dawn must've been near before she said much, after giving out with a duffel bag half-packed. She sat beside it on the floor, and watched the door as if any moment expecting its implosion.

"Why fucking bother?" Maggie said. "They'll come, sooner or later, somebody'll come and that's it.

Skeeter wasn't kidding about being connected. He had bosses." She hugged her knees with both arms. *"You* they don't know, *you* can go back to your house and play like it never happened. *Me* they know. *Me* they'll kill."

From his pockets, a key ring. He removed one, tossed it across the room. It clattered on scuffed wood near her work boot.

"The front door," he said. "I can draw you a map."

"I never hurt anybody before," she whispered. "Not even the ones who deserved it."

"But you'll lie, won't you. You knew Shawn a lot better than you let on."

Maggie rocked back and forth, a fetus who'd learned to sit. Outside the window, the sudden metallic hurricane of an El train, subsiding as swiftly as it had come. Like violence, like lust.

"Yeah, so?" she said. "The first thing I tell you is that I . . . maybe loved her? I don't think so."

The story came in fits and starts. Kraaft rarely needed to prompt, just waited and let it find its way out of her. For a few weeks she and Shawn had performed together, onstage, at that club for basement voyeurs. It was where they'd met, Shawn having apparently answered a personals ad, performers wanted, and knowing what it really meant.

"She told me she didn't have any experience with women, but you meet a lot of them like that. Curious. Even if they only try it once. All they need's some time, and . . ." Maggie shook her head. "But you know how, maybe once or twice in your life if you're lucky, you find someone and even if they're a lot younger, or totally inexperienced, it doesn't matter? You still feel like a beginner with them, like a kid? Like they can swallow you whole, and . . . you want them to? That's how it was with Shawn. When her tongue would hit me . . ."

Maggie trembled. And he waited for more, starving for it. The door waited as well, to admit the violence seeking them out. Yet he had to hear more. Shawn with another woman was like no Shawn he'd ever known. If Maggie stopped now, she might never speak to him again.

"And she left you, too," he said.

Maggie nodded.

"You don't know why?"

"She never gave me the chance to ask."

"If you felt this way about her, why answer my ad, why bring me here at all?"

"I knew she wasn't back with you. I'd call the studio where she taught, so I knew she hadn't gone home. I thought Skeeter might know where she was, like maybe because she looked as good as she did they might have her somewhere doing movies, but he wouldn't tell me shit. He's a prick like that. I thought if you showed up, you could afford to buy it out of him. Or he'd give it up if he thought her husband was gonna complicate things for him."

"Did she ever tell you"—each slow word was another notch of dread cut into his heart—"why she left *me?*"

"Are you sure you want to hear this?" Maggie asked. "Like I said, Shawn never made any secret of what you two were doing. But I think she was starting to feel she liked it too much. You know, here's this heavy kink she's into, but it's totally against everything her family and everyone else taught her to be, and wherever she goes back home, and everybody she sees, she's thinking, oh, God, if they only knew. If they only knew . . .

"That whole life, you know what she told me it was? A skin that she had to shed while she still could, and she just didn't have the heart to tell you." Atop her knees, Maggie's hands turned to fists. "So I have her for six weeks, and one day she's gone, and I'm left thinking, well, what the fuck does this make me? Just one more skin?"

Kraaft wandered to the window, saw El tracks and power lines and the backs of brick buildings as seedy as this one. Feeling very far from a home and a life that would take him back, never knowing what a sham he was. These weren't him and maybe never had been; maybe they'd only been the path of least resistance.

It occurred to him that the studies he found most fascinating were those of humanity at its worst. Sweeping change that was not pretty, indiscriminate tides that sought to topple empires. Riots, revolutions, coups . . . these began with mere sparks but developed momentums and wills of their own, making puppets of people, slaves to the whole. Single cells in the body politic, they were freed to indulge urges buried so deep within, they might never have known such drives were there at all.

Show me the worst, Kraaft had all along been saying; I have this need to see it. Show me the worst of hate, and love, and the destinations where they lead.

"What'd that mean, 'the whore below'?" he asked, ready now to hear it. "That meant something to you."

But Maggie was up and around again, boots clomping across the floor as she salvaged her remaining possessions worth stuffing into the duffel, apparently planning to abandon the rest. She pointed at an orange crate a few steps from him; on it sat a kiln-fired mug, its clay like serpent's coils. "Grab that, will you?"

He looked at her without moving.

"Like I want to stay here tempting fate any longer? I don't think so." She pointed again, impatient, as though jabbing at an elevator button. "I never think

I'll mind dying very much. But then I remember how much I hate pain."

He checked them into a hotel downtown, with hundreds of rooms and a parking garage, twenty-four-hour room service and laundry. No one ever need set foot outside, if he didn't want to.

In the bathroom Maggie colored her hair, ridding herself of the screaming tangerine and going with black, instead. Giving herself glum looks in each mirror. "I look like everybody else now," she'd say. "Let the sides grow in a little, take out the earrings, and they'll never recognize me. Because *I* sure don't."

"You don't have to stay," he told her, and offered to buy her a ticket—bus or train or plane, her choice—anywhere she wanted. Family? Did she have family somewhere? Maggie only looked at him, as though envying him a certain redemptive ignorance.

At least so long as he had her, Kraaft realized, he could pretend he wasn't as desolately alone as he really was.

" 'The whore below,' " he tried again. "What does that mean?"

"Just one of those things I heard somebody talking about once or twice. Not recently, maybe a year or two or longer. Way before Shawn ever showed up. One of those urban legends, was my take on it. Like albino alligators in the sewers. But I never knew anyone who was supposed to *be* it." She curled her upper lip in disgust. "True or not, I hate the name. It's got a real claim-staking ring to it, you know it had to be a man who came up with that one."

And when she told him what it was, or her understanding of it, her words fell on incredulous ears. This went beyond all limits of rationality. It was a fevered erotic dream gone grandly perverse; a nightmare conjured for the propaganda of puritans; a drug-induced vision of a licentious paradise, the Garden of Hedon.

It was too good to be true.

"There can't be anything to it," he said. But didn't denying its possibility also mean denying any hope of Shawn's reclamation? "It's insane."

"Get off campus a little more, Professor. Plenty of places and things out there could give you a whole new appreciation of insane."

While insane, he amended, didn't necessarily mean impossible.

The whore below.

Armed with this, Maggie said there were people she could talk to, acquaintances she could ask. But she didn't want him along, so he was forced to play it her way. Nocturnal already, she came in around dawn most mornings, and always he would awaken, his slumber never deep to begin with anymore, and he never had to ask if there was news, nor even see her face to know there wasn't.

Days. One week. Two. She was using him and Kraaft knew it; if she'd had anyplace else to stay, she'd already be there, cutting him away like a sixth toe. She was using him to finance her own search for Shawn, and he knew it, and knew that she knew that he knew. They could almost joke about it, compulsive to obsessive.

"If I could," Maggie said, "I'd cook her down and shoot her into my arm."

The morning she didn't come back, he was willing to give her the benefit of the doubt. Surely Maggie wouldn't find Shawn, then be so cruelly ungrateful as to withhold the news. Keep Shawn all to herself and leave him sitting in his hotel room. More likely, then, her recent past had finally caught up with her. He daily combed the *Tribune* and *Sun-Times* for news of her body turning up, with name or without, but found no matches. Best to stay put, then, so she'd know where to find him, or when she came back for her clothes. As a rational man, it was vital that he not lose sight of these things.

Days. Two weeks. Three. Twice the hotel informed him a credit card was at its limit; he would give them another and it was clout enough. Sometimes he would call home, in case Maggie had tried him there, and listen to the answering machine until he realized the tape was full, much of it taken over by his department chairman, concerning scheduled courses with no professor. As yet untenured, Kraaft supposed he never would be.

He took to leaving the hotel, needing things like toothpaste and razor blades, and sometimes he'd find himself miles away with no recollection of the journey there.

On a dozen billboards he saw the same ad for a health club, staring at it because the near-topless woman it featured had the same muscled abdomen as Shawn. Thirty feet tall and perfect, she loomed over Chicago, unattainable as grace.

Shawn's mouth he saw in ads at bus stops, wet and glossy and poised over a wine bottle. Her thighs he recognized at an El train station, and they'd never looked sleeker; he tried smashing the glass covering the picture so he could lay a hand upon the image, but it was really plastic, and he was quickly rousted by a transit cop. They'd cut her up and strewn pieces for miles, and wouldn't even let him touch one.

Except for that, Kraaft decided he'd never been happier, and went out sometimes to gloat, the watchful eye in rush hour's hurricane. He saw thousands in a day, desperate to get from here to there and breathing poison to do it; those who looked joyful he could count on two hands. Freed of ambitions, he could see so much more clearly now. Virtually none wanted to be where they were at any given time, but dared not deny the civilizing machines they'd created, which now rode them into the ground. Scowling, they shoved each other out of the way so they could get home and dream for a few hours of people whose love for them was as perfect as the flesh that contained it.

And when Maggie at last returned, in the birth of autumn's bluster, it was by daylight, as if she had no more secrets left. She was waiting for him in the room, boots on the bed.

"Where to find her," Maggie said. "I wrote it down for you. Like a map. Over there on the dresser."

He picked the paper up. "La Salle Street Station? . . ."

"Who'd've guessed, huh?"

"Thank you," he said.

"Like I'm doing this because I think it'll make you happy? Not on your life. No, I *want* you to see her. I *want* you to see what she is now, motherfucker. I *want* you to see what you woke up in her." Maggie swung herself off the bed, for a moment looking as though she intended to hit him. "I felt sorry for you, kind of. What stopped me is, I just can't understand you. Pretending to be someone else when you have this beautiful, sensual creature all to yourself. Much less the rest. Who really brings themselves to fuck in front of other people unless they need the money?"

"You really don't see," he said, "how someone can do it for love?"

She was biting on a thumbnail, and spat the fleck at him. "I never felt like *I* had the luxury of choosing." Maggie walked past him, toward the duffel that sat packed and waiting, and slapped him on the chest, very hard, a mockery of camaraderie. "I stayed down there with her for . . . I'm not sure how long it was.

Because I thought I could . . . could get her to . . . oh, fuck it.

"She's yours now," Maggie said. "Take a number."

He waited until late at night, for rush hour's antithesis to leave La Salle Station as empty as he was likely to find it. With trains so few and far between, the place seemed to hold its breath in profound unease, as if sensing its incompleteness, that without the commuting hordes it was nothing but an absurd edifice, a ruin in the making.

Hollow, solitary, Kraaft's clicking footsteps rode upon the hush. He was watched—an eye here, a pair there—but by none that mattered. They saw; they didn't comprehend.

He paused at the edge of the platform, then leaped off to the tracks below, taking care to stay clear of the third rail. With a crunching of grit and pebbles of glass, he walked into the deeper darkness of the tunnel Maggie had specified, let it swallow him in its blackened gullet.

Thirty paces, forty—he was getting close; took out a butane lighter and flared a yellow ball of illumination so he didn't miss the notch along the wall. There. He stepped up onto the concrete pad, to the metal door. Only the knob shone in his light, worn clean by frequent hands, greasy to the touch.

But how readily it turned. You'd think the city would keep it locked; perhaps they once did, while now there was newer design.

He found stairs on the other side, followed where they led. Lower landings presented other doors, but Maggie's map made it clear: Those were not for him.

Every level further felt like greater descent into mystery, and damn whatever prosaic origins behind this labyrinth of cellars and caves, forgotten passageways and shelters built in times when everyone feared a holocaust of atoms. All cities, Kraaft supposed, had such nether regions, abandoned to become the inversion of the daylight world, where refuse and rejects found their level in a night that the sun never reached.

Prior travelers had left their marks, painted names and glyphs as vivid now as the day of their spraying; beside the door that Maggie's map indicated, he spotted an especially intricate one, curves and loops and slashes, undecipherable in its weird beauty. He wondered if there was any connection with what lay on the other side, or if its meaning would die with its artist.

Beyond the door, then, other corridors, other bends; the brick walls weren't as dry as he'd hoped, but this close to the Chicago River, seepage was inevitable. With fingertips he brushed them, found a cool slick film that was nearly organic. Beyond the limits of his light, red reflecting pinpricks watched, then turned to flee. Rats inherited every kingdom eventually.

A glow beckoned ahead, defining itself every few steps closer. Kraaft wondered if the palpable arousal that had begun to steal over him was born solely of anticipation, or if it was a power beyond him that anyone—even those with no idea what lay ahead—would feel pulling them forward by the loins. He walked into it as he might walk into smoke that thickened until at last he would find the fire.

The very walls seemed to ripple and stir, and the air itself to moan. There *was* great power here; it impelled and caressed and engulfed; it twined its way to the root of impulse; it stroked and lured and enticed. He'd know Shawn anywhere, just hadn't expected to recognize her in advance of his eyes. He finished the walk in reverence for the immensities of deity and desire.

The chamber was sepulchral, lit by the glow of

softly hissing lanterns that draped the rest in undulating shadow. The throaty alto of Shawn's groan greeted him, as well as an earthier rhythm, the meaty slapping of sweat-slick thighs.

She lay on her back atop layers of mattresses, and while most of her was obscured by her lover, bracing himself on rigid forearms, the familiar curve of hip and side-swell of breast were the same. Her fingers clutched at thick shoulders; her ankles were high, hooked together behind the man's back. The soles of her feet were black with grime. Kraaft could plainly see her open cleft and the shaft of cock, pained and spellbound by the way it glistened.

Scattered about were more than a dozen others of both sexes, awaiting a turn or come to watch. Others paid no attention at all, content to breathe the musty air and absorb. Of his entrance, few took notice at all.

"What's your pleasure, sir?"

To his right, a paunchy man slouched in a chair padded with quilts. When he turned up the fuel on his lamp, Kraaft could see that the man was older than he'd expected, with a close beard gone gray, and hair combed straight back. It had been a very long time since its last washing.

"What's your part in . . . in this?" Kraaft asked him.

"Don't know as I have one. I just get a kick saying that whenever someone finds his way here." He rummaged through a box at his side, came up with a sandwich. "What brings you, anyway? Dream? Intuition? Recommendation? I've heard everything."

"I'm her husband."

A humoring smile crossed the man's face, broad and heavily lined. "Heard that one, too."

Kraaft slipped a picture from its wallet sleeve, and the man nodded at it in the lantern glow, offering his hand and giving his name as Hiram. When Kraaft's hand was his own again, he lifted it to his nose; it smelled of anchovies. It returned to his wallet and began counting out greenbacks.

"I want . . . I have to . . ." He looked toward Shawn again, saw the heels of her feet slamming down on the small of the faceless man's back. Saw the pale globes of her bottom straining up and down off the mattress. His hand shook. "I can pay."

"Put that away, do I look like anybody's pimp to you? Pay. Christ almighty." An aggrieved chuckle sounded in his throat, but he waved Kraaft down beside him. With no place to sit, squatting sufficed. "I guess the sun's still coming up in the east, is it?"

"You've been down here that long?"

"Probably four months since I've last been topside. When the trains get scarce, like now"—he pointed overhead—"that's another night. I've just been . . . here. Hard to turn your back and walk away from a miracle."

"Miracle?" said Kraaft, and if he couldn't quite articulate its nature, he knew he'd felt it already.

"In that time, by my guess, she's had more than six thousand lovers."

"Oh, my God," Kraaft breathed, fearing he might be ill, for the first time swamped by the true enormity of her being torn from him. Separation he could withstand, because reunion would end it; sharing her with others had been aphrodisiacal, because afterward they all went home. But such numbers as these went beyond conceiving. "Six thousand, that's . . . impossible."

Hiram shook a bottle and upended it, drizzled jets of liquid onto his sandwich. "Unnatural maybe, but not impossible." He showed Kraaft the bottle. "Fish sauce, what you smelled a minute ago. The Roman army carried fish sauce everywhere it went. Keeps you

116

from getting sick in new places, even if you drink the water. You look like you could use some."

Kraaft pushed it away.

"Suit yourself," Hiram said. "It's all she does, just about. Round the clock. She hardly sleeps. People bring food, and she *will* eat, but it's not a driving need."

"Somebody explained it to me, but I don't think I believed it, not rationally." He tried to continue but couldn't hold on to his thoughts.

"That's your problem, trying to make something rational of it. Life's a lot richer when you can get past the rational."

"How did *you* manage it?"

"Brokered some investments a few years ago for other people's money, and got convicted on it. And disappeared when it came time to *do* time." He shook his head as if at some monumental absurdity. "I don't miss it. That world. Philosophers, I've decided, are more the creations of what they've given up than what they've learned."

Around them a minute trembling, as the rumble of a train's arrival overhead conducted down through bones of iron, skins of concrete. A pause, while it disgorged cargo and took on new, then it rumbled along again. Kraaft imagined all the tracks leading away from the transit system's heart, the complex geometries they made across the face of Chicago. Conduits of power, weren't they modern versions of the ley lines of the ancients?

Hiram flipped one hand overhead after the departed train. "You know, they build these places, mile after mile of packing in as much as they can. Stacking it up to the sky. Breeding like rats to fill everything up. Then they piss and moan how the place'll be the death of them, drive them crazy, squeeze the juice out of them. But still arrogant enough to think they're lords of it all. Never even consider they might've made something that came alive."

To one who'd studied the living madness of crowds, the notion was hardly alien. Cities had long seemed to demand their murders, their savage tributes of spilled blood. Why, then, shouldn't they demand finer pleasures, as well?

" 'They' build them, you said. Not 'we'?"

Hiram turned on him with a grimace. "You side with who you want."

Shawn's lover finished with grunts and a groan, for a moment lying slack atop her before backing out from between her upraised knees. In the interim while the next skinned on a condom, Kraaft ached with yearning as he finally saw her whole, naked, eclipsing any extreme he could've brought her to on his own. He saw now that her sex had been shaved; how childlike and vulnerable it seemed.

Her arms raised to welcome the next, and when the man's hands went to her hips she turned onto one side. He straddled her thigh, while Shawn lifted her other leg, bracing it high up against his shoulder. Kraaft stared transfixed by the arching of her lower spine, a moist furrow between two ridges of muscle. They soon found their rhythm, deep in the rolling of her hips.

When Kraaft gasped, he wasn't the only one. It hit different watchers at different times, like the first ecstatic plunge into union, enfolding from without rather than bursting from within. It surged through one and all, then surged beyond, while a warm glow settled in Kraaft's loins.

"Oh, my God," he whispered again. Hiram mopped his brow and nodded. "Is it like that every time?"

"More or less."

"How far away can it be felt?"

"Who knows. But then, it's not strictly a human agency that's . . . sanctioned this."

"Shawn's not the first, is she?"

"First that *I've* seen. But no."

"What happened to the earlier ones?"

Hiram averted his eyes. "Well, you don't just quit one day and go back home, do you?" And this was all he would say.

"Have you? . . ." Kraaft said, and nodded toward her.

Shamefaced, Hiram shook his head. "Do yourself a favor. Shoot yourself before your prostate gets big as a lemon." He nodded at Shawn as well. "Are *you?*"

"Disease," Kraaft murmured. "She must be riddled with disease by now."

"You'd think so, wouldn't you?"

But it wouldn't matter. Even if she burned with it, perhaps he could know no greater ecstasy than to immolate himself on the pyre of her, let it ravage him to worm and bone.

"Go ahead," whispered Hiram. "Do it for me."

Hiram or not, there'd never been any choice but that he would. Their marriage had hardly been conventional, and if this marked its end, then let the end come in ceremony. Let it mean something, even if it killed him. Let it feed a greater hunger.

With loosened clothing, Kraaft took his place among the semicircle to wait. With his eyes he drank her in, as she in her exaltation drank pleasures for an id of millions.

Cities, he reflected, had in their dawn been places of great sexuality. A Roman, an Athenian, a Babylonian could scarcely turn around without confronting another fertility icon, or an unabashed depiction of genitalia and what they were for. Temple prostitutes made love as the proxies of deities lacking flesh rather than appetites. He felt cheated, then, that the puritans to follow had seen to the burying of all this, the driving of it under wraps and shadow, until all that was left, really, was the teasing gloss of image.

Billboards. They had billboards.

This close, from so few feet away, it was difficult to miss Shawn's bruises, purple mottlings against livid skin.

He had never been one to invest faith in the pipe dreams of anarchists; opportunists would swarm to fill any void. But cities, he allowed, were always of two minds. Above ground the servants of the empire strained beneath yokes of state, of faith, of ambition emptied of all but the vainest of acquisitions. While far below their watch, anarchy gnawed at the seams of the straitjacket to spill its redeeming violence, here a trickle, there a torrent.

And down here, among the lowest, surely some epiphany had been achieved, orgasm as magick on an epic scale. Or was this but a pipe dream of his own, dreamed in one more galley of slaves?

Kraaft watched as she took another, and another after that, tiring of waiting for his turn. Had he no rights here at all? He seized her present lover by the hair; yanked him up and off her, and slung him into the wall. Others rose to their feet and there was a brief scuffle, until Kraaft grabbed one of the lanterns and used it to brain the nearest and threaten the rest into surrender. They backed into deeper shadow, cowed and beaten with arms raised to protect their skulls, but unable to bring themselves to leave.

On the mattresses Kraaft knelt between her outstretched legs, and for the first time in half a year laid hands upon her belly. He looked her over now that no more illusions could come between, to see what demand had wrung from her. Her shoulders, bruised;

her ribs, scraped; her fathomless green eyes were threaded with blood.

"Do you even recognize me?" he whispered.

Somewhere within was the Shawn he'd known, and she seemed to rise as though from the bottom of a lake. And when she smiled, her teeth appeared to have lengthened, until he realized that, no, her gums were just receding.

"How could I forget?" she said. "No matter how hard I tried."

His hands trembled as they roamed across her, and she warmed beneath his touch. When one fingertip dipped into the tiny crevice of her navel, she cooed, and he knew that no one had cared enough to realize she'd liked that, too; not one out of six thousand. He stroked the tender skin behind her knees, and everyone there could feel what it did for her. He massaged her temples. He kissed her eyelids.

From now on he would be all that she needed, and they would feed the beast together, until their flesh rotted and their bones were rattled apart by the passage of trains above.

Not even death would part them now; the revolution within him had gone too far for that.

After all these years of pretense he was himself, and no one else. He could prove it.

He had witnesses.

SEXUAL PREDATOR

Stephen Solomita

*T*he creep did everything but drool when I walked into the bar. The bar was in Malcolm, Nebraska, maybe five miles from the Lincoln airport, and my first thought was that the creep came with the plastic-covered bar stools and the Budweiser sign over the cash register and the bartender's phony smile. In his late thirties and trying to look twenty, the creep's waist and jowls were rapidly thickening while his coarse black hair was so thin he had it parted an inch above his left ear and swept over the top of his skull. He wore a green-gold polyester shirt open to his diaphragm and a gold chain that nestled in chest hair thick enough to appear matted. Like he'd missed his appointment at the groomer's.

Once upon a time, the creep's features had proba-bly been strong. But his chin had gone fleshy and the large pores on his nose had reddened. Only his eyes were sharp. They carefully undressed me as I walked past him to a stool.

Mostly, I hate the creeps and the creep looks they've been giving me ever since I developed something to look at. Unless I'm in a certain mood like the one I was in that night. Then I think about how far I can degrade them, how badly I can humiliate them before they show a speck of pride. If they ever do.

I let my skirt ride up a few inches as I hoisted myself onto the stool, and the creep let loose with an audible sigh. "Absolut," I told the bartender, "on the rocks with an olive."

The bartender was a decade-and-a-half younger than the creep and handsome in a perky, Midwestern way. I flashed him a smile the creep would have given his left testicle to receive. "What's your name?" I asked him.

"Jimmy."

I stretched out my hand and we shook. "Carmen," I told him.

Jimmy turned his back and took a bottle of Absolut from the shelf. "I haven't seen you before," he said. "You from around here?"

"Uh-uh." I could see the creep in the mirror behind the bar. I don't know where he'd been off to when I came in, but he was standing about ten feet away. Looking at me like a dog eyeing a steak on its master's plate. "I flew in this morning for a sales conference in Lincoln. Tomorrow morning, I'll be gone." I paused long enough to let Jimmy lay a cocktail napkin on the bar in front of me. "I guess you could call it a one-night stand."

Jimmy grinned, winked, then strode off toward a trio of customers at the far end of the bar. I picked up my glass and licked at an ice cube floating above the rim. The creep shifted his weight from side to side. For a minute I thought he was going to break into a dance, but then he took off for the men's room. I watched the door close behind him, knowing he'd return as soon as he fabricated an opening line.

Sure enough, I barely had time to unbutton the top buttons on my blouse before he reappeared. This time he came plowing back, head down, nostrils flared, like a bull at a red cape. He took a seat two stools away from me and signaled to Jimmy, who was pulling bottles of beer from a cooler. "Slow night," he said to my reflection in the mirror.

I didn't bother responding. In fact, I felt rather insulted. I was pressing thirty, but I had to be worth more than *slow night.* Even to a creep.

The creep's heels found the rung of the bar stool. Again, he signaled to Jimmy. Then he looked over his shoulder and repeated, "Slow night."

I leaned forward and his eyes flashed down to my breasts. Meanwhile, he still hadn't been able to meet my eyes.

"Too slow for a fast guy like you, right?"

He thought it over for a minute, then said, "Let's just say I'm used to better."

"You want to hear something amazing?" I waited for him to nod. "That's just what I said to myself when I walked through the door and saw you standing there. I said to myself, 'There's a guy who's used to better.' "

It was a critical moment. If he had any guts, if he wasn't a desperate jerk still nursing memories of high school glory as he advanced into a coarse, ignorant middle-age, he'd shrug his shoulders and live to fight another day. It's happened before, many times, but that's the price you pay when you've got an itch for something very specific. An itch only a creep can scratch.

Very slowly he unhooked his heels and swiveled to face me. "I been to a lotta places," he told me in a very serious voice.

"So has a truck."

Jimmy's arrival gave the creep some time to think it over. "You havin' the same?" he asked.

"Yeah, the same."

The same turned out to be a bottle of domestic beer, no glass. As the creep brought it to his mouth, several drops of condensed moisture dropped from the bottle to land in his chest hair. Trying not to puke, I finished my drink, then raised my glass to Jimmy.

"The same?" Jimmy asked.

"I never repeat myself." I flashed him another hot smile. "This time I'll take it with a cocktail onion."

Jimmy was a smart kid, smart enough to know the creep was going to keep on coming back and I was going to vanish on the following morning. Instead of flirting, he said, "Hey, did you meet Eddie?" He gestured to the creep. "Eddie, this is Carmen. Carmen, Eddie."

The creep managed a pathetically grateful smile. He saluted me with his beer bottle. "Pleased to meet you, Carmen."

"Why?" I asked.

"Because," he said, as if he'd rehearsed the line before the urinal in the men's room, "you're so beautiful."

Very slowly, very deliberately, I let my eyes run from the top of his head down over his soft chin, flabby chest and hanging gut. Then I shook my head and turned back to my drink. "Better make it a double, Jimmy."

Jimmy rolled his eyes and shrugged. He'd done his best for the creep and now he was off the hook. The creep said, "Hey, don't take it the wrong way. I didn't mean nothin'."

"Why does this not come as a surprise to me?"

Jimmy used my remark as an exit line, moving off down the bar to rinse a dozen glasses standing next to a small sink. I picked the onion out of my vodka and let it sit on my tongue for a minute before biting down hard. "So, Eddie, what does a man who's been to a lot of places do in Malcolm, Nebraska?"

He blushed, scratched his chin. "I work for a trucking company. Midwestern Express."

"And what do you do there?"

"I'm a driver." He paused, then added, "Hey, things ain't always like they seem."

Again, I let my eyes run over his body. "I guess I'd have to disagree with that, Eddie. Sometimes, like tonight, things are *exactly* what they seem." Then I crossed my legs, flashing a glimpse of my thighs and panties along the way. The creep's eyes shot down to my crotch, and his whole body quivered. For a minute, I thought he was going to fall off the stool.

We went on that way for the better part of an hour. The creep just would not give up, no matter how little encouragement I gave him. Along the way, he drank two more beers. I don't know how hard he'd been going at it before I arrived, but he was definitely sloppy by the time he finished. Definitely sloppy and still trying to impress. He'd already told me about the Corvette he used to own, the condo where he used to live, and the nightclubs, far from Malcolm, where he once reigned supreme. He'd described his high school wrestling prowess, the injury to his knee that kept him from a college scholarship, and the homecoming queen he'd taken to the prom.

I slashed at him with my words, while I raised his temperature with my body. The signals weren't just mixed, they were coming from opposite sides of the universe. I leaned back against the bar and thrust my breasts at his face while I told him just how pathetic his small-town act really was. I steepled my fingers and pushed them down between my knees while I described his polyester shirt and gold chain as gangster-wannabe chic.

"You have to come up with some better lies," I finally told him, though I had no intention of letting him go. "Some little thing to hold my interest, before I finish my drink and go back to the motel. So far, I haven't noticed anything more exciting than the paperwork sitting in my briefcase."

The creep scratched at his five o'clock shadow. He looked down at his scuffed penny loafers and cocked his head as if listening for suggestions. "Lemme ask you a question, Carmen." He raised his head to look me directly in the eye, then half-whispered, his voice an octave lower than it had been, "You ever hear of Johnny Calabrcse?"

"Is that your gangster-wannabe voice? The one that goes with the shirt and the chain?"

"I'm serious here."

"Ohhhhh. Well, sorry, but I just never heard of Johnny Caballero. Maybe I should try to get around a little more."

"Calabrese," he said, leaning close enough for me to taste his sour breath. "Johnny Calabrese. You tellin' me you never heard of him?"

"You want it in writing? I've never heard of him."

The creep shook his head in disgust. "Johnny Calabrese was the boss of Tallahassee. You musta heard of him. The feds sentenced Calabrese to life without parole a couple of years ago. His whole crew went away."

"The boss of Tallahassee." I shook my head in wonder. "So what's the boss of Tallahassee got to do with a truck driver from Malcolm?"

He took another look at my breasts, probably for inspiration, then said, "I put Johnny Calabrese away." When I didn't react, he added, "I was Johnny's accountant and I testified against him, so they put me in the witness protection program. That's why I'm livin' in the sticks."

"Uh-huh. And before I went into sales and had my sex-change operation, I was the King of Thailand." My laughter cut into the creep like a razor blade. His eyes squeezed shut and his mouth drew up into a little pout. Before he could burst into tears, I laid a manicured fingernail on his lower lip and shook my head. "You don't have to make up any more stories to impress me, Eddie. I've decided that you're fine just the way you are. In fact, I think you're going to be absolutely perfect." Then I let my finger trail down along his throat to hook his gold chain. "Will you trust me, Eddie?" I asked. "Because if you trust me, if you trust me completely, I'll take you to a place you've never been. A place far away from Malcolm, Nebraska."

The creep wriggled on the bar stool and his hand dropped in a very predictable arc toward his crotch. I grabbed it halfway down and laid it on his knee. "I didn't tell you to do that, Eddie. Not doing anything I don't tell you to do is one part of the deal. The other part is you do whatever I *do* tell you to do. And you do it without hesitation. Understand?"

"Yeah," he said, his voice wary, "I get it."

"Do you really, Eddie? Do you really want to play? Do you really trust me?"

This time he actually thought about it. I could see the wheels turning behind his dark eyes. Finally he said, "Whatta ya wanna do?"

I shook my head and started to swivel away from him. "Wrong answer, Eddie."

"Okay, okay. Whatever you want."

"Anything?"

"Anything."

I turned back to him, my legs well apart, and

smiled. "Ready for a little practice?" I waited for him to nod, then said, "I want you to run the fingertips of your right hand very lightly along the inside of my right thigh. You think you can do that?"

I didn't waste any time getting the creep out of the bar. The truth, though I maintained my ice princess demeanor, was that I was hot enough to melt wax. As for the creep, he was just perfect. When I told him to get into my rental car, to leave his Trans Am in the parking lot, he obeyed without protest. When I told him to unbutton my blouse and unhook my bra without touching my breasts, he did it so carefully I wanted to pat him on the head. Finally I pushed him against the seat and dropped my hand to his crotch and squeezed, gently at first, then hard enough to make him gasp.

"Do you still trust me, Eddie?" We were stopped at a traffic light. Outside, it was raining lightly.

"Yes, yes. I trust you."

"Do you want to go where I want to take you?" I squeezed a little harder.

Please," he said, "please don't hurt me."

Naturally, the creep's apartment was small and tacky, not unlike the creep himself. And, naturally, he offered to fix me a drink. I refused and ordered him into the bedroom where he walked directly to a brass bed set against the far wall, then hesitated.

"Turn around," I demanded. "And leave your hands at your sides."

I kissed him for the first time, his mouth, his chin, his throat, then stepped away. "Take off your clothes," I told him, "and lie down on the bed."

Now that he had me alone in his bedroom, the creep might have attempted to reestablish his macho self-image. I was prepared for that. But as far as I could tell, he never even thought about it. Instead, he flipped off his loafers and his fingers dropped to his belt buckle as if he'd been waiting all along for my command. When he finally stood naked in front of me, I wondered if he had any sense of how ridiculous he looked with his erection half-obscured by his drooping gut. His mouth was hanging open and he was panting as he stripped the covers off the bed and laid down; his eyes, when he finally looked up at me, were imploring.

"Soon, Eddie. I promise." I took four crimson scarves from my bag and sat down next to him. "These scarves," I told the creep, "are made of silk. They seem flimsy, but silk is a very strong fabric. I want to tie your wrists and ankles to the slats on the headboard and the footboard. Once I do that, you'll be helpless. Do you understand?" I ran the tip of a finger along the length of his cock, then in a little circle over the head. "Do you agree?"

"You're not gonna . . ." His voice trailed off. As if even that little bit of rebellion was beyond him.

"I'm going to take you to heaven, Eddie. I'm going to take you to a place you've never been. A place you've always wanted to go."

He raised his arms over his head and spread his legs to make it easier. I tied his wrists and ankles quickly, giving him less than an inch of slack. Then I stood and slowly undressed. In my late teens and early twenties, I worked as a model. I never made the runway, but I did a lot of catalog work. My specialty was lingerie, and I still had the body to prove it.

When I finally stood naked before the creep, hands on hips, legs slightly apart, the creep groaned with pleasure and began to rub his soft ass against the cotton sheet. Then I took the narrow, double-edged knife from my purse, and his eyes opened to the size of dinner plates.

"Don't bother struggling," I whispered as I sat next

to him on the bed. "There's no turning back now. You have to go on with it." I leaned forward to let my breasts graze his lips, then straightened. "What's going to happen now, Eddie, is that you're going to perform for me. You're going to perform until I tell you to stop. If you don't . . ." I scraped the edge of the knife over the hair on his chest, clearing off a small patch just above his right nipple. Then I licked the exposed flesh.

"Please," he said, "don't hurt me."

"I'm not going to hurt you, Eddie," I again explained. "Only a fool hurts the animal that pulls the load. Pain is for quitters. And you're not a quitter, right?"

Before he could answer, I began to work his body with my hands and mouth. I started at his throat and moved downward, licking, biting, kissing, pinching. Until he was again the creep he'd been on the ride to the apartment; until he was again ready and eager to prove his worth. Then I swung over his hips and quickly took him deep inside.

I wanted to scream with the pleasure of it, to abandon myself completely to the sensations rushing through my body, to obey the imperatives of the flesh. Unfortunately, the creep was ready to explode. His geek eyes were squeezed together, his little creep hands curled into fists, his creep teeth clenched as if in pain. I brought myself under control with a long, deep breath before jabbing the point of the knife a quarter inch into his chest.

"Oh, God, please . . ."

I responded by jabbing him again, then again. "By now," I told him, "you're probably getting the point." The pun may have gone over his head, but as I began to slowly rotate my hips, the essence of the message filtered through and he finally began to concentrate.

Once he got the hang of it, the creep was okay. Not

the best, maybe, but pretty good. I took him (and myself) toward one peak after another, only to bring him back down, to make him begin all over again. Along the way, I told him just what a creep asshole he was and how much I truly despised him and his pitiful creep ego. I told him that he was nothing and would never be anything, that he was no more than an elaborate vibrator with which I was masturbating.

The creep loved it, as I'd been certain he would. When I ridiculed him, he responded by pounding into me. When I touched his throat with the point of the knife, he lay back and whimpered in fear.

I didn't let myself go until the very end, until the two of us were slick with sweat and I felt like I was riding a greased pig. Then I told the creep, "Show time, Eddie," before dropping down into my body. For a few minutes, I gave up all control. I surrendered to the rising crest of a great wave that I knew would eventually engulf me. From a distance, I could hear the creep's screams above my own, hear the wet slap of our bodies coming together. Then I was simply gone.

When I finally came back to myself, the creep's head was thrown back on the pillow and his eyes were closed. He was panting like a dog in a desert.

"Wake up," I told him. "Wake up, Eddie."

His eyes slowly opened. "That was unbelievable," he told me.

"You were very good," I admitted. "The best."

The gratitude that flowed into his creep eyes was thick enough to touch. In a few minutes, with a little effort, I knew I could have him reprimed and ready to go. But I had a plane to catch, a private plane flying from an airport a hundred miles from Malcolm, Nebraska.

I laid the point of the dagger against the creep's

throat and told him, "I have a greeting for you, one you should have heard long before tonight."

"Please," he said. Then he repeated the word twice: "Please, please." He tried to smile as he begged. Tried and failed. "I gave you what you wanted, didn't I?"

Instead of answering, I got off the bed, laid the knife on the table a few inches from his hand, then dressed and brushed out my hair. I was all business, now, my concentration focused on the end game. The creep continued to plead as I worked, his voice rising as he struggled with the scarves that bound him.

"I told you, Eddie," I said as I returned the brush to my purse, "that silk is a strong fabric." My voice was as cold and calm as I could make it. "I told you that you'd be helpless. Why are you surprised?"

With no ready answer, the creep finally shut up. I retrieved the knife and walked to the head of the bed. The creep's breath was coming in short sharp gasps, as it had been just before we finished. His eyes were so wide open, his irises looked as if they were lying in a bucket of white paint. "Johnny Calabrese," I told him as I raised the knife above my head, "says to tell you that he'll see you in hell." Then I brought the knife down with all the force at my command.

I was almost out the door when I decided to take a last look, to fix the scene in my memory. The creep was frozen in place. Trying, I guessed, not to look at the knife buried in the mattress an inch from his flabby throat. Or to think about how long he was going to have to lay in those urine-fouled sheets before he broke loose. I wanted to make some parting comment, something brilliant I could repeat to my lover when I got back home. Instead, unable to contain myself, I burst out laughing at the comic scene. This was one night the poor pitiful creep was going to carry into the grave.

It was still raining and a good deal colder when I finally left the building. I was tempted to go back to the creep's apartment and wait it out, but I was afraid he'd break loose and try to rebuild his image by exacting a little revenge. In that case, I'd have to really hurt him and I didn't want to hurt him. No, what I wanted was for the creep to remain in the best of health until I tracked down a hood named Johnny Calabrese and discovered exactly what he'd be willing to pay for the whereabouts of a creep named Eddie.

LOVING DELIA

Melanie Tem

*D*elia's small fingers had wandered the soft folds and tunnels between her legs. Her labia felt pink. Her clitoris was like a berry.

When her mother had come in to kiss her good night, Delia had stopped touching herself and given the touching to him. He lived inside her. Maybe he had always lived inside her, but that night—his fingertips sliding into places of herself she didn't dare touch, her arms safely around her mother's neck—she'd been aware of him for the first time.

Now she was an old woman, beautiful, the object of his intense desire, and dying.

He was there, stroking the inside of her thigh, when she heard and then understood the news. While they tried to tell her, he kissed her, distracted her, protected her.

First, her daughter, having spoken to the doctor on the phone while Delia herself kept busy baking bread: "No, you talk to him. *You* talk to him. The dough's ready to be kneaded." Her daughter coming into the kitchen and just standing there. Not touching. He knew Delia would have liked her daughter to rest her hands on her shoulders or take her in her arms. But then the younger woman would have known he was there, and Delia would have stiffened and pulled away to get on with her kneading, to keep him secret, captive, hers alone.

Her daughter took a breath and said, "Mom." The name sounded, as always, stiff and artificial; Delia and her daughter had never quite known how to address each other. He and Delia, though, had countless little names for each other, some affectionate and others bitter but all of them fundamentally terms of endearment. Now that it fell to the daughter to say to the mother, "You have cancer," she began with, "Mom," and it wasn't the right name, "let's go in the living room and sit down."

Delia glanced into her daughter's face. Not for very long. Not ever for very long, but with such sharp openness that it startled them both and shocked him. He and Delia often gazed into each other's eyes for long, long periods of time, but he'd seldom known her to look directly at anybody else. Then she floured her hands again and said testily, "Wait'll I get this dough set to rise. You can just wait."

"It's cancer, Mom. You have cancer." The daughter had to say that to the mother. Recognizing it as a gift she dared not accept, Delia passed it hastily along to him.

He'd been there when her mother died. Delia was sixteen, and he had been obsessed with her small young breasts. Once, when her daughter had asked, Delia had said she didn't remember being terribly upset—"after all, I was almost grown"—and he'd treasured the secret knowledge she'd given him of her desolation. "I don't remember," she'd declared. "It was a long time ago." Rebuffed, her daughter hadn't asked again.

He was there at the oncologist's office, through whose tinted tall eleventh-floor windows they watched clouds, black and gold, teardrop-shaped, and separate from each other, puff across the mountains and plains. Delia joked about the size of her bust: "If you can even find them to examine, Doctor."

Youthful, the doctor blushed, and found it even harder to tell her what he had to tell her, what he told people day after day. "I'll take good care of you. I won't allow the pain to get bad. This thing will get you in the end, but until then I'll see to it that you can live your life."

Not easily embarrassed, her daughter had blushed, too. The joke had not been intended to put the doctor or the daughter at ease. It was not for the sake of politeness, though to anyone but him Delia would have insisted it was.

Caged beneath her breasts, he still found them lovely, small and sagging now, so soft. "Thank you, Doctor," she said. While she and her daughter waited outside for the cab to take them home, he held his breath like the black and gold breeze that blew over them both and waited to be let out. But he was not. They talked about the weather, about what they would each fix for their separate dinners.

He'd been there when she was a very young woman and the world seemed to offer itself before her. She'd danced. She'd loved to dance, and he'd danced with her, closer than any other partner. She'd loved pretty clothes. She'd had many suitors; they sat out on the front porch swing, walked in the park, danced. She, her father's favorite, ran off with the one her father most disliked, and it was years before she and her father spoke again. He went along, keeping her company as her husband did not.

He'd been ready to sacrifice himself in order to serve her, to run loose and tell her father when the marriage started to go bad. When the handsome and exciting husband didn't come home nights. When she had to send someone to fetch him, or go herself, from the whorehouses down along the river. When there was no money.

She wouldn't let him out. She would talk to no one but him. From inside his cage he touched her while she cried, and he was aroused to painful tenderness by the drifting of her hair across his fingertips, but the bars kept him from putting his arms around her.

Once she said to him with teeth and fists clenched, as if it were his fault, "Life's not fair. Life didn't keep its promises to me." He tried to tell her how sorry he was. He pledged to make it up to her. He pressed himself into her wherever she would let him, his tongue to the back of her mouth, his fingertips among her ribs and around the inward swelling of her breasts, his flank along the corridor of her vagina before it ever opened to anyone else in the world.

Then something else was inside her, crowding him, threatening to displace him. Naive, he didn't know what it was, and he cowered. Only when she'd called her aunt who ran a pharmacy, took the morning-long train ride there and the afternoon-long ride back, and swallowed the bitter contents of the small brown bottle did she allow him to understand. By morning the baby was gone, flushed away with Delia's tears and bitter brown vomit and with his thin ejaculate sprayed into her hurting hidden places.

It was their secret; Delia never told anybody else. But when she lay in her bed in the evening after work, waiting for the whoring husband and then not waiting anymore, she loved the infant who would never be born as much as her mother who had died, which was more than Delia would ever love anyone alive.

He was under the sheet with her on the hospital gurney, waiting for the needle biopsy. The woman on the gurney ahead of them was weeping, steadily and almost without sound. Delia didn't cry. He cried.

Her daughter said, "I love you."

Startled and offended, frightened, Delia knew this was only because she was sick. "I *know,*" she snapped.

Her daughter couldn't find a place to sit or stand where Delia would know she was there from flat on her back on the gurney at such an awkward height. Not awkward for transporting, but awkward for looking at each other.

Delia knew perfectly well that she was there. She felt her daughter's yearning to speak to her about what was happening to them both, even to touch her, and she cringed away into his arms. She was more beautiful to him than she had ever been; he kissed the nape of her neck. She spoke only to him. "I'm scared," she told him, peevish as a child, and his heart, going out to her, encountered hers. Both of them caged, their tender exposed surfaces brushed back and forth across each other with every beat, calming Delia, arousing him.

He'd been with her when she allowed herself to be courted again, by a man distant and difficult but steady. They sat on the porch together in the twilight. They held hands, the man's fingertips playing distantly along the lines of Delia's palm. They kissed, lips steadily touching, lingering until the proffered intimacy had softened into a gentle distance between them.

The suitor made him both frightened and curious: If she could love this man, maybe she wouldn't need him anymore. Maybe she would let him go. He thought he and Delia might not have lives apart from each other; he also thought they might.

Delia never mentioned him to her new husband. He was affronted, both by Delia's slight and by the fact that her husband couldn't tell he was there. In their marriage bed. Mouth on Delia's nipple before her husband's was, hand cupped under her chin keeping her face just slightly turned away. Stretched taut inside her to receive her husband's entry and to repel him.

Delia's babies were born dead. One, two, three, and the doctors didn't know why; a fourth Delia didn't tell anyone except him. She knew why. The dead babies, the bloody tissue in the toilet bowl were her punishment. For drinking from the bitter brown bottle. For being intimate with the wrong man. For being such a bad child that her mother had left her. For loving anyone.

After the fourth dead child, she refused for many months to have relations with her husband and turned instead to him. Every night and often during the day she came inside to him, slipped between the bars of his cage, and took him to her. He was helpless with adoration of her. All the time he quivered in anticipation and fear; fervently as he loved Delia, he was also afraid of her. She hurt him sometimes, clutching him in her fierce passion, moving his mouth and hands and penis where she wanted them. She pinched his scrotum. She called him foul, erotic names. She pledged herself to him again and again, and he emptied himself into her, and she pushed him farther inside. Whenever she left him alone he pined, not trusting that she would come back.

The more adamant Delia's frigidity, the more outrageous became her husband's suggestions. Aghast at the very idea of taking a man's private part into her mouth, of being entered from behind, of simply lying naked together with no specific intent, she at last allowed the normal sexual act, but only if he— unbeknownst to her husband; unidentified, at least— came, too, and so he was entered by her husband and pushed more deeply into Delia, and he received both her passion and her shame.

This baby lived. This one grew, thrived, and for a while he thought, with both trepidation and eagerness, that Delia would have to set him free in order to make room for this child. When the baby was born and Delia fed her, he thought he would starve. But she fed him her shame. Confined in a shrinking space, he grew bigger and bigger between herself and her daughter. He could have brought them together, one long hand stretching to each of them even through the bars, but Delia wouldn't let her daughter so much as glimpse his shadow. For fear he would hurt her. For fear he would frighten her. For fear she would take him away.

He took baths with her. She wouldn't touch herself. Using a very thick washcloth, she treated her body like a sinkful of dirty dishes. He longed for her to touch him; her touch was rough and wonderful. She let him slide with the soapy washcloth between her labia and over the tip of her clitoris, which she had never seen and of whose contours she had no inkling.

After the cancer, her daughter gave her bath oil, but the thought of smoothing and sweetening a body with a tumor in its belly the size, now, of a grapefruit seemed to her obscene and made him swell up like a tumor himself. She dumped a little of the bath oil down the toilet and later told her daughter, "That felt so *good*. That was so *nice* of you," in rather the same sociable tone she'd used with the neighbor who'd brought her an endless stream of ceramic creations that stayed in boxes in the back of her closet.

Her daughter, more a stranger to her than anyone else, did not, all the same, believe her. Dirty and sour-smelling, he made a small noise, and the daughter heard him. But Delia beat him back, beat her daughter back, and was far more stern and determined and practiced than either of them.

When the pain started, and the gold and black clouds from the morphine they gave her from the stopper as if she were a naked baby bird, and still the pain though not for long and not yet very bad—the fear of the pain far worse than the pain itself—he thought then she'd have to let him go. He thought she wouldn't be able to keep up either her guard or her strength. He lay in wait, held himself rigid and absolutely still until he couldn't stand it anymore. Then he paced. Then he rattled the cage, banged his head against the stone wall of her, howled.

Without warning, Delia cried out to her daughter, "It's like I've always had the devil in me!" He was not the devil, but he knew she was talking about him, and proudly he drew himself up, waiting to be introduced.

Taken aback, her daughter asked, "What do you mean?"

But Delia wouldn't say any more. She closed her eyes, rolled onto her side, and moaned.

He was there when her husband shuffled in to lie down beside her. The old man didn't remember from one minute to the next that Delia was sick, Delia had cancer, Delia was dying. But he loved her. "I love you, Delia, you are so beautiful, you made me the man I am, we've had a good life, haven't we? Let me hold you. My sweetheart. I love you."

He longed for her to kiss him. His lips stuck to the cold metal bars. She shrank away from them both. He wrapped his arms around himself.

When the tumor exploded, he thought it would burst his chains. He called out when she did. He begged, like her. The roof collapsed. The walls imploded. His cell blazed. He became so full of fire that he could not bear to touch himself from the inside out. But Delia still would not let him out.

After one long searing morning, the pain melted. Delia pushed herself up on one elbow, fixed her daughter with a look and a smile, flashed the OK sign with circled thumb and forefinger, and fell into a coma. Stunned, her daughter said good-bye. Delia didn't.

He crept out then, through the rubble of her, and didn't know what to do without Delia. He lowered himself onto her on the bed, slid his penis up into the poison that burned through her perineum, settled the hollows of his pelvis into the hollows of hers, covered her mouth with his, and took her last breath.

NECROS

Brian Lumley

I

An old woman in a faded blue frock and black head-square paused in the shade of Mario's awning and nodded good day. She smiled a gap-toothed smile. A bulky, slouch-shouldered youth in jeans and a stained yellow T-shirt—a slope-headed idiot, probably her grandson—held her hand, drooling vacantly and fidgeting beside her.

Mario nodded good-naturedly, smiled, wrapped a piece of stale *fucaccia* in greaseproof paper, and came from behind the bar to give it to her. She clasped his hand, thanked him, turned to go.

Her attention was suddenly arrested by something she saw across the road. She started, cursed vividly, harshly, and despite my meagre knowledge of Italian I picked up something of the hatred in her tone. "Devil's spawn!" She said it again. "Dog! Swine!" She pointed a shaking hand and finger, said yet again: "Devil's spawn!" before making the two-fingered, double-handed stabbing sign with which the Italians ward off evil. To do this it was first necessary that she drop her salted bread, which the idiot youth at once snatched up.

Then, still mouthing low, guttural imprecations, dragging the shuffling, *fucaccia*-munching cretin behind her, she hurried off along the street and disappeared into an alley. One word that she had repeated over and over again stayed in my mind: *"Necros! Necros!"* Though the word was new to me, I took it for a curse word. The accent she put on it had been poisonous.

I sipped at my Negroni, remained seated at the small circular table beneath Mario's awning, and stared at the object of the crone's distaste. It was a motorcar, a white convertible Rover and this year's model, inching slowly forward in a stream of holiday traffic. And it was worth looking at it only for the girl behind the wheel. The little man in the floppy white hat beside her—well, he was something else, too. But *she* was—just something else.

I caught just a glimpse, sufficient to feel stunned. That was good. I had thought it was something I could never know again: that feeling a man gets looking at a beautiful girl. Not after Linda. And yet—

She was young, say twenty-four or -five, some three or four years my junior. She sat tall at the wheel, slim, raven haired under a white, wide-brimmed summer hat that just missed matching that of her companion, with a complexion cool and creamy enough to pour over peaches. I stood up—yes, to get a better look— and right then the traffic came to a momentary standstill. At that moment, too, she turned her head and looked at me. And if the profile had stunned me . . . well, the full frontal knocked me dead. The girl was simply, classically, beautiful.

Her eyes were of a dark green but very bright, slightly tilted and perfectly oval under straight, thin brows. Her cheeks were high, her lips a red Cupid's bow, her neck long and white against the glowing yellow of her blouse. And her smile—

—Oh, yes, she smiled.

Her glance, at first cool, became curious in a moment, then a little angry, until finally, seeing my confusion—that smile. And as she turned her attention back to the road and followed the stream of traffic out of sight, I saw a blush of color spreading on the creamy surface of her cheek. Then she was gone.

Then, too, I remembered the little man who sat beside her. Actually, I hadn't seen a great deal of him, but what I had seen had given me the creeps. He too had turned his head to stare at me, leaving in my mind's eye an impression of beady bird eyes, sharp and intelligent in the shade of his hat. He had stared at me for only a moment, and then his head had slowly turned away; but even when he no longer looked at me, when he stared straight ahead, it seemed to me I could feel those raven's eyes upon me, and that a query had been written in them.

I believed I could understand it, that look. He must have seen a good many young men staring at him like that—or rather, at the girl. His look had been a threat in answer to my threat—and because he was practiced in it I had certainly felt the more threatened!

I turned to Mario, whose English was excellent. "She has something against expensive cars and rich people?"

"Who?" He busied himself behind his bar.

"The old lady, the woman with the idiot boy."

"Ah!" He nodded. "Mainly against the little man, I suspect."

"Oh?"

"You want another Negroni?"

"OK—and one for yourself—but tell me about this other thing, won't you?"

"If you like—but you're only interested in the girl, yes?" He grinned.

I shrugged. "She's a good-looker. . . ."

"Yes, I saw her." Now he shrugged. "That other thing—just old myths and legends, that's all. Like your English Dracula, eh?"

"Transylvanian Dracula," I corrected him.

"Whatever you like. And Necros: that's the name of the spook, see?"

"Necros is the name of a vampire?"

"A spook, yes."

"And this is a real legend? I mean, historical?"

He made a fifty-fifty face, his hands palms up. "Local, I guess. Ligurian. I remember it from when I was a kid. If I was bad, old Necros sure to come and get me. Today," again the shrug, "it's forgotten."

"Like the bogeyman." I nodded.

"Eh?"

"Nothing. But why did the old girl go on like that?"

Again he shrugged. "Maybe she think that old man Necros, eh? She crazy, you know? Very backward. The whole family."

I was still interested. "How does the legend go?"

"The spook takes the life out of you. You grow old, spook grows young. It's a bargain you make: he gives you something you want, gets what he wants. What he wants is your youth. Except he uses it up quick and needs more. All the time, more youth."

"What kind of bargain is that?" I asked. "What does the victim get out of it?"

"Gets what he wants," said Mario, his brown face cracking into another grin. "In your case the girl, eh? *If* the little man was Necros. . . ."

He got on with his work and I sat there sipping my Negroni. End of conversation. I thought no more about it—until later.

II

Of course, I should have been in Italy with Linda, but . . . I had kept her "Dear John" for a fortnight before shredding it, getting mindless drunk, and starting in on the process of forgetting. That had been a month ago. The holiday had already been booked and I wasn't about to miss out on my trip to the sun. And so I had come out on my own. It was hot, the swimming was good, life was easy, and the food superb. With just two days left to enjoy it, I told myself it hadn't been bad. But it would have been better with Linda.

Linda . . . She was still on my mind—at the back of it, anyway—later that night as I sat in the bar of my hotel beside an open bougainvillea-decked balcony that looked down on the bay and the seafront lights of the town. And maybe she wasn't all that far back in my mind—maybe she was right there in front—or else I was just plain daydreaming. Whichever, I missed the entry of the lovely lady and her shriveled companion, failing to spot and recognize them until they were taking their seats at a little table just the other side of the balcony's sweep.

This was the closest I'd been to her, and—

Well, first impressions hadn't lied. This girl *was* beautiful. She didn't look quite as young as she'd first seemed—my own age, maybe—but beautiful she certainly was. And the old boy? He must be, could only be, her father. Maybe it sounds like I was a little naïve, but with her looks this lady really didn't need an old man. And if she did need one it didn't have to be *this* one.

By now she'd seen me and my fascination with her must have been obvious. Seeing it she smiled and blushed at one and the same time, and for a moment turned her eyes away—but only for a moment. Fortunately her companion had his back to me or he must have known my feelings at once; for as she looked at me again—fully upon me this time—I could have sworn I read an invitation in her eyes, and in that same moment any bitter vows I may have made melted away completely and were forgotten. God, *please* let him be her father!

For an hour I sat there, drinking a few too many cocktails, eating olives and potato crisps from little bowls on the bar, keeping my eyes off the girl as best I could, if only for common decency's sake. But . . . all the time I worried frantically at the problem of how to introduce myself, and as the minutes ticked by it seemed to me that the most obvious way must also be the best.

But how obvious would it be to the old boy?

And the damnable thing was that the girl hadn't given me another glance since her original—invitation? Had I mistaken that look of hers?—or was she simply waiting for me to make the first move? *God, let him be her father!*

She was sipping martinis, slowly; he drank a rich red wine, in some quantity. I asked a waiter to replenish their glasses and charge it to me. I had already spoken to the bar steward, a swarthy, friendly little chap from the South called Francesco, but he hadn't been able to enlighten me. The pair were not resident, he assured me; but being resident myself I was already pretty sure of that.

Anyway, my drinks were delivered to their table; they looked surprised; the girl put on a perfectly innocent expression, questioned the waiter, nodded in my direction, and gave me a cautious smile, and the old boy turned his head to stare at me. I found myself smiling in return but avoiding his eyes, which were like coals now, sunken deep in his brown-wrinkled face. Time seemed suspended—if only for a second—then the girl spoke again to the waiter and he came across to me.

"Mr. Collins, sir, the gentleman and the young lady thank you and request that you join them." Which was everything I had dared hope for—for the moment.

Standing up I suddenly realized how much I'd had to drink. I willed sobriety on myself and walked across to their table. They didn't stand up but the little chap said, "Please sit." His voice was a rustle of dried grass. The waiter was behind me with a chair. I sat.

"Peter Collins," I said. "How do you do, Mr.—er?—"

"Karpethes," he answered. "Nichos Karpethes. And this is my wife, Adrienne." Neither one of them had made the effort to extend their hands, but that didn't dismay me. Only the fact that they were married dismayed me. He must be very, very rich, this Nichos Karpethes.

"I'm delighted you invited me over," I said, forcing a smile, "but I see that I was mistaken. You see, I thought I heard you speaking English, and I—"

"Thought we were English?" she finished it for me. "A natural error. Originally I am Armenian, Nichos is Greek, of course. We do not speak each other's tongue, but we do both speak English. Are you staying here, Mr. Collins?"

"Er, yes—for one more day and night. Then—" I shrugged and put on a sad look. "—Back to England, I'm afraid."

"Afraid?" the old boy whispered. "There is something to fear in a return to your homeland?"

"Just an expression," I answered. "I meant I'm afraid that my holiday is coming to an end."

He smiled. It was a strange, wistful sort of smile,

wrinkling his face up like a little walnut. "But your friends will be glad to see you again. Your loved ones—?"

I shook my head. "Only a handful of friends—none of them really close—and no loved ones. I'm a loner, Mr. Karpethes."

"A loner?" His eyes glowed deep in their sockets and his hands began to tremble where they gripped the table's rim. "Mr. Collins, you don't—"

"We understand," she cut him off. "For although we are together, we, too, in our way, are loners. Money has made Nichos lonely, you see? Also, he is not a well man, and time is short. He will not waste what time he has on frivolous friendships. As for myself—people do not understand our being together, Nichos and I. They pry, and I withdraw. And so I, too, am a loner."

There was no accusation in her voice, but still I felt obliged to say: "I certainly didn't intend to pry, Mis.—"

"Adrienne." She smiled. "Please. No, of course you didn't. I would not want you to think we thought that of you. Anyway I will *tell* you why we are together, and then it will be put aside."

Her husband coughed, seemed to choke, struggled to his feet. I stood up and took his arm. He at once shook me off—with some distaste, I thought—but Adrienne had already signaled to a waiter. "Assist Mr. Karpethes to the gentleman's room," she quickly instructed in very good Italian. "And please help him back to the table when he has recovered."

As he went Karpethes gesticulated, probably tried to say something to me by way of an apology, choked again, and reeled as he allowed the waiter to help him from the room.

"I'm . . . sorry," I said, not knowing what else to say.

"He has attacks." She was cool. "Do not concern yourself. I am used to it."

We sat in silence for a moment. Finally I began: "You were going to tell me—"

"Ah, yes! I had forgotten. It is a symbiosis."

"Oh?"

"Yes. I need the good life he can give me, and he needs . . . my youth? We supply each other's needs."

And so, in a way, the old woman with the idiot boy hadn't been wrong after all. A sort of bargain had indeed been struck. Between Karpethes and his wife. As that thought crossed my mind I felt the short hairs at the back of my neck stiffen for a moment. Goose-flesh crawled on my arms. After all, "Nichos" was pretty close to "Necros," and now this youth thing again. Coincidence, of course. And after all, aren't all relationships bargains of sorts? Bargains struck for better or for worse.

"But for how long?" I asked. "I mean, how long will it work for you?"

She shrugged. "I have been provided for. And he will have me all the days of his life."

I coughed, cleared my throat, gave a strained, self-conscious laugh. "And here's me, the nonpryer!"

"No, not at all, I wanted you to know."

"Well," I shrugged, "—but it's been a pretty deep first conversation."

"First? Did you believe that buying me a drink would entitle you to more than one conversation?"

I almost winced. "Actually, I—"

But then she smiled and my world lit up. "You did not need to buy the drinks," she said. "There would have been some other way."

I looked at her inquiringly. "Some other way to—?"

"To find out if we were English or not."

"Oh!"

"Here comes Nichos now." She smiled across the room. "And we must be leaving. He's not well. Tell me, will you be on the beach tomorrow?"

"Oh—yes!" I answered after a moment's hesitation. "I like to swim."

"So do I. Perhaps we can swim out to the raft?"

"I'd like that very much."

Her husband arrived back at the table under his own steam. He looked a little stronger now, not quite so shriveled somehow. He did not sit but gripped the back of his chair with parchment fingers, knuckles white where the skin stretched over old bones. "Mr. Collins," he rustled, "—Adrienne, I'm sorry. . . ."

"There's really no need," I said, rising.

"We really must be going." She also stood. "No, you stay here, er, Peter? It's kind of you, but we can manage. Perhaps we'll see you on the beach." And she helped him to the door of the bar and through it without once looking back.

III

They weren't staying at my hotel, had simply dropped in for a drink. That was understandable (though I would have preferred to think that she had been looking for me) for *my* hotel was middling tourist class while theirs was something else. They were up on a hill, high on the crest of a Ligurian spur where a smaller, much more exclusive place nestled in Mediterranean pines. A place whose lights spelled money when they shone up there at night, whose music came floating down from a tiny open-air disco like the laughter of high-living elementals of the air. If I was poetic it was because of her. I mean, that beautiful girl and that weary, wrinkled dried-up walnut of an old man. If anything I was sorry for him. And yet in another way I wasn't.

And let's make no pretense about it—if I haven't said it already, let me say it right now—I wanted her. Moreover, there had been that about our conversation, her beach invitation, which told me that she was available.

The thought of it kept me awake half the night. . . .

I was on the beach at 9:00 A.M.—they didn't show until 11:00. When they did, and when she came out of her tiny changing cubicle—

There wasn't a male head on the beach that didn't turn at least twice. Who could blame them? That girl, in *that* costume, would have turned the head of a sphinx. But—there was something, some little nagging thing, different about her. A maturity beyond her years? She held herself like a model, a princess. But who was it for? Karpethes or me?

As for the old man: he was in a crumpled lightweight summer suit and sunshade hat as usual, but he seemed a bit more perky this morning. Unlike myself he'd doubtless had a good night's sleep. While his wife had been changing he had made his way unsteadily across the pebbly beach to my table and sun umbrella, taking the seat directly opposite me; and before his wife could appear he had opened with:

"Good morning, Mr. Collins."

"Good morning," I answered. "Please call me Peter."

"Peter, then." He nodded. He seemed out of breath, either from his stumbling walk over the beach or a certain urgency that I could detect in his movements, his hurried, almost rude "let's get down to it" manner.

"Peter, you said you would be here for one more day?"

"That's right," I answered, for the first time studying him closely where he sat like some strange garden gnome half in the shade of the beach umbrella. "This is my last day."

He was a bundle of dry wood, a pallid prune, a small, umber scarecrow. And his voice, too, was of straw, or autumn leaves blown across a shady path. Only his eyes were alive. "And you said you have no family, few friends, no one to miss you back in England?"

Warning bells rang in my head. Maybe it wasn't so much urgency in him—which usually implies a goal or ambition still to be realized—but eagerness in that the goal was in sight. "That's correct. I am, was, a student doctor. When I get home I shall seek a position. Other than that there's nothing, no one, no ties."

He leaned forward, bird eyes very bright, claw hand reaching across the table, trembling, and—

Her shadow suddenly fell across us as she stood there in that costume. Karpethes jerked back in his chair. His face was working, strange emotions twisting the folds and wrinkles of his flesh into stranger contours. I could feel my heart thumping against my ribs . . . why I couldn't say. I calmed myself, looked up at her, and smiled.

She stood with her back to the sun, which made a dark silhouette of her head and face. But in that blot of darkness her oval eyes were green jewels. "Shall we swim, Peter?"

She turned and ran down the beach, and of course I ran after her. She had a head start and beat me to the water, beat me to the raft, too. It wasn't until I hauled myself up beside her that I thought of Karpethes: how I hadn't even excused myself before plunging after her. But at least the water had cleared my head, bringing me completely awake and aware.

Aware of her incredible body where it stretched, almost touching mine, on the fiber deck of the gently bobbing raft.

I mentioned her husband's line of inquiry, gasping a little for breath as I recovered from the frantic exercise of our race. She, on the other hand, already seemed completely recovered. She carefully arranged her hair about her shoulders like a fan, to dry in the sunlight, before answering.

"Nichos is not really my husband," she finally said, not looking at me. "I am his companion, that's all. I could have told you last night, but . . . there was the chance that you really were curious only about our nationality. As for any 'veiled threats' he might have issued: that is not unusual. He might not have the vitality of younger men, but jealousy is ageless."

"No," I answered, "he didn't threaten—not that I noticed. But jealousy? Knowing I have only one more day to spend here, what has he to fear from me?"

Her shoulders twitched a little, a shrug. She turned her face to me, her lips inches away. Her eyelashes were like silken shutters over green pools, hiding whatever swam in the deeps. "I am young, Peter, and so are you. And you are very attractive, very . . . eager? Holiday romances are not uncommon."

My blood was on fire. "I have very little money," I said. "We are staying at different hotels. He already suspects me. It is impossible."

"What is?" she innocently asked, leaving me at a complete loss.

But then she laughed, tossed back her hair, already dry, dangled her hands and arms in the water. "Where there's a will . . ." she said.

"You know that I want you—" The words spilled out before I could control or change them.

"Oh, yes. And I want you." She said it so simply,

and yet suddenly I felt seared. A moth brushing the magnet candle's flame.

I lifted my head, looked toward the beach. Across seventy-five yards of sparkling water the beach umbrellas looked very large and close. Karpethes sat in the shade just as I had last seen him, his face hidden in shadow. But I knew that he watched.

"You can do nothing here," she said, her voice languid—but I noticed now that she, too, seemed short of breath.

"This," I told her with a groan, "is going to kill me!"

She laughed, laughter that sparkled more than the sun on the sea. "I'm sorry," she sobered. "It's unfair of me to laugh. But—your case is not hopeless."

"Oh?"

"Tomorrow morning, early, Nichos has an appointment with a specialist in Genova. I am to drive him into the city tonight. We'll stay at a hotel overnight."

I groaned my misery. "Then my case *is* quite hopeless. I fly tomorrow."

"But if I sprained my wrist," she said, "and so could not drive . . . and if he went into Genova by taxi while I stayed behind with a headache—because of the pain from my wrist—" Like a flash she was on her feet, the raft tilting, her body diving, striking the water into a spray of diamonds.

Seconds for it all to sink in—and then I was following her, laboring through the water in her churning wake. And as she splashed from the sea, seeing her stumble, go to her hands and knees in Ligurian shingle—and the pained look on her face, the way she held her wrist as she came to her feet. As easy as that!

Karpethes, struggling to rise from his seat, stared at her with his mouth agape. Her face screwed up now as

I followed her up the beach. And Adrienne holding her "sprained" wrist and shaking it, her mouth forming an elongated "O." The sinuous motion of her body and limbs, mobile marble with dew of ocean clinging saltily . . .

If the tiny man had said to me: "I am Necros. I want ten years of your life for one night with her," at that moment I might have sealed the bargain. Gladly. But legends are legends and he wasn't Necros, and he didn't, and I didn't. After all, there was no need. . . .

IV

I suppose my greatest fear was that she might be "having me on," amusing herself at my expense. She was, of course, "safe" with me—insofar as I would be gone tomorrow and the "romance" forgotten, for her, anyway—and I could also see how she was starved for young companionship, a fact she had brought right out in the open from the word go.

But why me? Why should I be so lucky?

Attractive? Was I? I had never thought so. Perhaps it was because I *was* so safe: here today and gone tomorrow, with little or no chance of complications. Yes, that must be it. *If* she wasn't simply making a fool of me. She might be just a tease–

—But she wasn't.

At 8:30 that evening I was in the bar of my hotel— had been there for an hour, careful not to drink too much, unable to eat—when the waiter came to me and said there was a call for me on the reception telephone. I hurried out to reception where the clerk discreetly excused himself and left me alone.

"Peter?" Her voice was a deep well of promise. "He's gone. I've booked us a table, to dine at 9:00. Is that all right for you?"

"A table? Where?" my own voice was breathless.

"Why, up here, of course! Oh, don't worry, it's perfectly safe. And anyway, Nichos knows."

"Knows?" I was taken aback, a little panicked. "What does he know?"

"That we're dining together. In fact he suggested it. He didn't want me to eat alone—and since this is your last night . . ."

"I'll get a taxi right away," I told her.

"Good. I look forward to . . . seeing you. I shall be in the bar."

I replaced the telephone in its cradle, wondering if she always took an apéritif before the main course. . . .

I had smartened myself up. That is to say, I was immaculate. Black bow tie, white evening jacket (courtesy of C & A), black trousers, and a lightly frilled white shirt, the only one I had ever owned. But I might have known that my appearance would never match up to hers. It seemed that everything she did was just perfectly right. I could only hope that that meant literally everything.

But in her black lace evening gown with its plunging neckline, short wide sleeves, and delicate silver embroidery, she was stunning. Sitting with her in the bar, sipping our drinks—for me a large whisky and for her a tall Cinzano—I couldn't take my eyes off her. Twice I reached out for her hand and twice she drew back from me.

"Discreet they may well be," she said, letting her oval green eyes flicker toward the bar, where guests stood and chatted, and back to me, "but there's really no need to give them occasion to gossip."

"I'm sorry, Adrienne," I told her, my voice husky and close to trembling, "but—"

"How is it," she demurely cut me off, "that a good-looking man like you is—how do you say it?—'going short'?"

I sat back, chuckled. "That's a rather unladylike expression," I told her.

"Oh? And what I've planned for tonight is ladylike?"

My voice went huskier still. "Just what is your plan?"

"While we eat," she answered, her voice low, "I shall tell you." At which point a waiter loomed, towel over his arm, inviting us to accompany him to the dining room.

Adrienne's portions were tiny, mine huge. She sipped a slender, light white wine, I gulped blocky rich red from a glass the waiter couldn't seem to leave alone. Mercifully I was hungry—I hadn't eaten all day—else that meal must surely have bloated me out. And all of it ordered in advance, the very best in quality cuisine.

"This," she eventually said, handing me her key, "fits the door of our suite." We were sitting back, enjoying liqueurs and cigarettes. "The rooms are on the ground floor. Tonight you enter through the door, tomorrow morning you leave via the window. A slow walk down to the seafront will refresh you. How is that for a plan?"

"Unbelievable!"

"You don't believe it?"

"Not my good fortune, no."

"Shall we say that we both have our needs?"

"I think," I said, "that I may be falling in love with you. What if I don't wish to leave in the morning?"

She shrugged, smiled, said: "Who knows what tomorrow may bring?"

* * *

How could I ever have thought of her simply as another girl? Or even an ordinary young woman? Girl she certainly was, woman, too, but so . . . *knowing!* Beautiful as a princess and knowing as a whore.

If Mario's old myths and legends were reality, and if Nichos Karpethes were really Necros, then he'd surely picked the right companion. No man born could ever have resisted Adrienne, of that I was quite certain. These thoughts were in my mind—but dimly, at the back of my mind—as I left her smoking in the dining room and followed her directions to the suite of rooms at the rear of the hotel. In the front of my mind were other thoughts, much more vivid and completely erotic.

I found the suite, entered, left the door slightly ajar behind me.

The thing about an Italian room is its size. An entire suite of rooms is vast. As it happened I was only interested in one room, and Adrienne had obligingly left the door to that one open.

I was sweating. And yet . . . I shivered.

Adrienne had said fifteen minutes, time enough for her to smoke another cigarette and finish her drink. Then she would come to me. By now the entire staff of the hotel probably knew I was in here, but this was Italy.

V

I shivered again. Excitement? Probably.

I threw off my clothes, found my way to the bathroom, took the quickest shower of my life. Drying myself off, I padded back to the bedroom.

Between the main bedroom and the bathroom a smaller door stood ajar. I froze as I reached it, my senses suddenly alert, my ears seeming to stretch themselves into vast receivers to pick up any slightest sound. For there had been a sound, I was sure of it, from that room. . . .

A scratching? A rustle? A whisper? I couldn't say. But a sound, anyway.

Adrienne would be coming soon. Standing outside that door I slowly recommenced toweling myself dry. My naked feet were still firmly rooted, but my hands automatically worked with the towel. It was nerves, only nerves. There had been no sound, or at worst only the night breeze off the sea, whispering in through an open window.

I stopped toweling, took another step toward the main bedroom, heard the sound again. A small, choking rasp. A tiny gasping for air.

Karpethes? What the hell was going on?

I shivered violently, my suddenly chill flesh shuddering in an uncontrollable spasm. But . . . I forced myself to action, returned to the main bedroom, quickly dressed (with the exceptions of my tie and jacket), and crept back to the small room.

Adrienne must be on her way to me even now. She mustn't find me poking my nose into things, like a suspicious kid. I must kill off this silly feeling that had my skin crawling. Not that an attack of nerves was unnatural in the circumstances, on the contrary, but I wasn't about to let it spoil the night. I pushed open the door of the room, entered into darkness, found the light switch. Then—

—I held my breath, flipped the switch.

The room was only half as big as the others. It contained a small single bed, a bedside table, a wardrobe. Nothing more, or at least nothing immediately apparent to my wildly darting eyes. My heart, which was racing, slowed and began to settle toward a steadier beat. The window was open, external shutters closed—but small night sounds were finding their way in through the louvres. The distant sounds of traffic, the toot of horns—holiday sounds from below.

I breathed deeply and gratefully, and saw something projecting from beneath the pillow on the bed. A corner of card or of dark leather, like a wallet or—

—Or a passport!

A Greek passport, Karpethes's, when I opened it. But how could it be? The man in the photograph was young, no older than me. His birth date proved it. And there was his name: Nichos Karpethes. Printed in Greek, of course, but still plain enough. His son?

Puzzling over the passport had served to distract me. My nerves had steadied up. I tossed the passport down, frowned at it where it lay upon the bed, breathed deeply once more . . . and froze solid!

A scratching, a hissing, a dry grunting—from the wardrobe.

Mice? Or did I in fact smell a rat?

Even as the short hairs bristled on the back of my neck I knew anger. There were too many unexplained things here. Too much I didn't understand. And what was it I feared? Old Mario's myths and legends? No, for in my experience the Italians are notorious for getting things wrong. Oh, yes, notorious . . .

I reached out, turned the wardrobe's doorknob, yanked the doors open.

At first I saw nothing of any importance or significance. My eyes didn't know what they sought. Shoes, patent leather, two pairs, stood side by side below. Tiny suits, no bigger than boys' sizes, hung above on steel hangers. And—my God, my God—a waistcoat!

I backed out of that little room on rubber legs, with the silence of the suite shrieking all about me, my eyes bugging, my jaw hanging slack—

"Peter?"

She came in through the suite's main door, came

floating toward me, eager, smiling, her green eyes blazing. Then blazing their suspicion, their anger as they saw my condition. "Peter!"

I lurched away as her hands reached for me, those hands I had never yet touched, which had never touched me. Then I was into the main bedroom, snatching my tie and jacket from the bed (don't ask me why!), and out of the window, yelling some inarticulate, choking thing at her and lashing out frenziedly with my foot as she reached after me. Her eyes were bubbling green hells. *"Peter!"*

Her fingers closed on my forearm, bands of steel containing a fierce, hungry heat. And strong as two men she began to lift me back into her lair!

I put my feet against the wall, kicked, came free, and crashed backward into shrubbery. Then up on my feet, gasping for air, running, tumbling, crashing into the night. Down madly tilting slopes, through black chasms of mountain pine with the Mediterranean stars winking overhead, and the beckoning, friendly lights of the village seen occasionally below. . . .

In the morning, looking up at the way I had descended and remembering the nightmare of my panic flight, I counted myself lucky to have survived it. The place was precipitous. In the end I *had* fallen, but only for a short distance. All in utter darkness, and my head striking something hard. But . . .

I did survive. Survived both Adrienne and my flight from her.

And waking with the dawn, and gently fingering my bruises and the massive bump on my forehead, I made my staggering way back to my still slumbering hotel, let myself in, and *locked* myself in my room— then sat there trembling and moaning until it was time for the coach.

Weak? Maybe I was, maybe I am.

But on my way into Genova, with people round me and the sun hot through the coach's windows, I could think again. I could roll up my sleeve and examine that claw mark of four slim fingers and a thumb, branded white into my suntanned flesh, where hair would never more grow on skin sere and wrinkled.

And seeing those marks I could also remember the wardrobe and the waistcoat—and what the waistcoat contained.

That tiny puppet of a man, alive still but barely, his stick arms dangling through the waistcoat's armholes, his baby's head projecting, its chin supported by the tightly buttoned waistcoat's breast. And the large bulldog clip over the hanger's bar, its teeth fastened in the loose, wrinkled skin of his walnut head, holding it up. And his skinny little legs dangling, twig-things twitching there; and his pleading, pleading eyes!

But eyes are something I mustn't dwell upon.

And green is a color I can no longer bear. . . .

Tricks or Treat

Jeff Gelb

*T*here were pussies everywhere.

There were dicks, too, but that didn't matter to me. Or to my partner, Jake. Not only because we weren't gay, but because it wasn't what we were looking for.

No, it was pussy we were after. Not just any pussy, either. Not the pussy over in the corner, on the woman with the tiny titties. Her pussy lips were the size of mudflaps. Nor was it the pussy on the tall, leggy blonde in front of me, who was looking at my private parts while I was ogling hers, which were tattooed with angel's wings. Wincing a bit at the thought of what she'd gone through for that particular piece of body art, I said something to end our meaningless if sexually-charged conversation and walked over to another part of the crowded party room, where I could catch a better view of all the pussies in evidence. And like I said, there were plenty, of all shapes, sizes, and colors.

I mean, I felt like Cheech Marin in *From Dusk Till Dawn,* touting the variety of pussies in the Titty Twister bar he managed in the movie. But what else could I do but stare at each one of them? After all, it was my job. Really. Scout's honor.

I could have stared at their faces, but they were all wearing masks. Monster masks, Nixon masks, gas masks, Mask masks. So you see, I hadda look at their pussies. I mean, their boobs didn't count.

I winked at Jake, who was having a hell of a hard time disguising the fact that he was hard as a rock from looking at all the female fun flesh on display in that sweaty room. He put his hands in front of his privates, but then it just looked like he was playing with himself. I could tell he was terribly uncomfortable with the whole situation. Me, I was surprised to find that being around so much twat had the opposite effect. Jake would have given me some sort of nickname. He always gave me nicknames. Maybe he woulda called me Shriveldick. In any case, my balls had drawn so far up my scrotum I coulda licked 'em. I swear my dick looked as tiny as a cocktail pickle. Pussy overkill—who'da known there was such a thing?

But I'm getting ahead of myself. . . .

Actually, it started three weeks earlier when my homicide partner Jake and I were called to an apartment building in West L.A., one of those Wilshire Boulevard high-rises, where hundreds of people spend hundreds of thousands of dollars to live right on top of one another, with a view of dozens of other high-rises. Not my idea of home sweet home, but what do I know? I'm just a dumb cop. Dan Chesterfield by name, but Jake often called me "Smokey," even though I don't. Smoke, that is. Jake's idea of a joke, I guess, except I'm not laughing. Which is kinda funny, considering how it was us who found the million-dollar TV sitcom king.

The panicked building manager had called the

police after he'd smelled something not-so-funny coming from under the door to one of the building's more famous tenants, Jerry Kramer, the TV show comedian. The manager feared something had died in the room, because one time he'd smelled the same aroma coming from one of the other condos that made up the twenty-story building. And sure enough, it had turned out that old Mrs. Mavis Maple had succumbed to heart failure in the middle of her precious daytime soaps and afternoon snack of gorgonzola cheese and crackers. By the time we'd got there, I don't know what had smelled worse, Mrs. Maple or her snack. Being dead for a few days in a closed room with no air-conditioning in the middle of the summer will do that to a body.

But that's neither here nor there. Jake and I had the manager open the door to Jerry Kramer's condo, and sure enough, it smelled just like Mrs. Maple's place, maybe even worse, if that's possible, and that's with no gorgonzola in sight. Jake's nose twitched like Samantha's on the old *Bewitched* show. I loved that Elizabeth Montgomery—she was one sexy little witch. Anyway, I just put the smell out of my mind as I looked around the condo. It was the kinda place that they'd put in the dictionary, with a photo next to the words "richly appointed." On one of three fireplace mantels, I saw the Emmys and other awards for Jerry's hit TV show, and then I saw Jerry, with one of the awards stuck in his crushed skull, and another stuck in his backside. Hadda hurt—if he was still alive when the award was given.

"Jesus," Jake said. Not a man of many words. But I hadda agree; I crossed my heart and said a quick prayer for Jerry, even if he was Jewish. I figured, what the hell, couldn't hurt.

"Is he . . . is he dead?" whispered the manager, who was virtually hiding behind Jake's bulky back.

The big man nodded, asked the manager to leave the room. The little man was only too happy to oblige. I couldn't blame him.

Once we were alone, I looked at Jerry more closely. Without makeup he looked a few years older than he did on his TV show, which I never actually found funny. In fact, the few times I had tuned it in, it was only in hopes of seeing Gloria, the girl who played his ex-girlfriend. She had great hair, the kind I'd love to have running all up and down my body while she was teasing me in bed. So I've got an active imagination— it ain't no crime. Yet.

"Jealous actor?" Jake jarred me loose from my sexy thoughts as he gazed at the award that stuck, half in and half out of Jerry's cranium. "Deranged fan?"

I shrugged. "All I know is that the shit is gonna hit the fuckin' fan big time when the media hears that its favorite nighttime sitcom star has gone to that big comedy club in the sky."

Which it did. Hit the fan, that is. By the next week there were cover articles in *People, TV Guide, Entertainment Weekly,* and the *Enquirer,* all of whom speculated about the killer. The *Enquirer* said they had proof it was O.J. All Jake and I knew was that our asses were on the line like never before. We hadda find the killer, and fast, before our ratings went down the toilet—for good.

But we just couldn't catch a break, no matter what crackpot we interviewed who claimed to have done the dirty deed—some whackos will say anything to bask in the limelight. But none of them knew how Jerry'd died, which left us exactly nowhere. In fact, we might never have caught the killer if it weren't for Batman.

We were back at Jerry's apartment for yet another look around, our fourth or fifth in the two weeks since

Jeff Gelb

his death. The chief was losing patience with us; hell, *we* were losing patience with us. So we had returned to the apartment hoping something would seem out of place, when suddenly Jake yelped. A strange sound, that yelp. Like a dog who's just had his balls crushed by his master stepping on him. Or so I imagined.

Anyway, I looked over and saw Jake smiling like a kid in a candy shop, holding up a copy of a Batman comic book. Well, any fan of the show knows that Jerry was a real fan of Batman. As it happens, so was Jake. In fact, he once told me over coffee and doughnuts that reading Batman comics as a kid made Jake want to go into law enforcement in the first place. Can you imagine that? What a gullible guy! I always figured Bats for a fag, myself. I mean, if I coulda picked a teenage ward to live with me, it would've been a blond high school cheerleader, not a boy from a circus.

So Jake was looking through a stack of Jerry's Batman comics, saying shit like "Hey, I remember this story!" Or "I used to have this one till my dog Andy puked on it!" He fell silent for a while till he found a bound volume of older issues. The front of the book claimed it held issues numbered one through ten. Jake whistled as he motioned me over. "This has gotta be worth a hunnert grand easy," he whispered as he opened the front cover, only to find the insides were nothing but newsprint, hollowed out at the center. And in the middle of the fake book was a diary, which fell into Jake's lap. "Huh," was all the enthusiasm he could muster. Nothing phased Jake.

The thing had no lock—I guess Jerry thought no one would ever find it. So me and Jake started looking through it. I tell ya, we learned some things about his co-stars in there that would curl your toes. Like how that cute girl, Gloria what's-her-name, who plays his old girlfriend, had been sleeping with him *and* his co-stars, Hyman Schwartz and Mitchell Foster. I tell ya, it was hot stuff. In fact, reading it made my dick pulse a bit, I gotta admit. I mean, I don't know anybody who wouldn't wanta make it with Gloria, what with all those cute curls and everything.

Anyway, the diary said that Jerry'd also been sleeping with some young female fan he'd met at a taping of his show. And get this: It turns out the bimbo was a weekend member of one of those nudist colonies somewhere east of Malibu, up in the hills. Jerry had apparently taken to going there with her, but with sunglasses and a phony beard, so no one would recognize him. Imagine that: One of the biggest stars in the world could let his cock hang out in public with no fear of the paparazzi, with just a simple disguise. What a pisser!

The bitch of it was, the diary never mentioned the girl's name—maybe Jerry was paranoid about someone finding the book after all. But according to what he wrote, she was a wanna-be actress, like every pretty piece of pussy west of Las Vegas and east of the Pacific Ocean. Jerry had promised her a bit part on his show, but according to the diary, it was just a ruse to get in her bell-bottomed pants. Which he had, repeatedly. And he wrote about it in great detail, which made both me and Jake adjust our dicks in our pants repeatedly, because the guy was not only funny, he was actually a pretty good writer. And lemme tell ya, some of what those two did together was—well, it was certainly beyond my admittedly limited sexual experiences. The lucky dog.

The last diary entry said that Jerry was planning to see the girl at a big Halloween bash the colony was going to have, where his identity would still be safe because everyone wore masks—and nothing else. He wrote that the party was just an excuse to swap partners for the night, something Jerry was apparently looking forward to. Raise a little hell on Halloween, and all that.

We knew we hadda find the girl; according to the diary, she was the last person to see him alive, and that made her a prime witness and maybe even our prime suspect. So we hadda go to that party, even if it meant taking off our clothes in the line of duty. Not that I ever wanted to be naked in the same room as Jake. But a job's a job, and we hadda find Jerry's little actress friend.

So here we were, our dicks hanging out like it was business as usual, searching the party for Jerry's girl. The diary gave us the only solid clues to her identity: She had a heart-shaped birthmark just to the left of one of her eyes. And her clit was pierced. They do that kinda shit out here. Go figure. Jerry's diary said she wore a diamond stud right through her clit hood. Jesus. So we hadda eyeball all the pussy that walked in and hope she would run true to form and wear her little piece of pussy jewelry. It was virtually her only visible unique trait, because like I said, everyone at the party was masked.

Suddenly one more woman walked in, and I gotta admit, she made my dick twitch like one of those divining rods that finds water in the desert. She was, in two words, fuckin' gorgeous. So far as what I could see was concerned anyway. Long blond hair, pert upturned breasts with perfect circular aureoles and gumdrop pink nipples. But she had so much pubic hair, finding her pussy would have taken a rake. Problem was, she was the only girl at the party whose privates I hadn't eyeballed.

Jake sized up the problem immediately, leaned in to me and whispered, "You know what this means, don't you?" I shook my head. "You're gonna have to fuck her."

That Jake sure had a way with words. I'll sure miss that about him. Anyway, I knew that Jake might be right: I just might have to fuck her to find out if she was our girl. All strictly in the line of duty, of course.

Just then, one last, late partygoer entered the room, and damned if she didn't match Jerry's girl's description equally well as the one I'd claimed as mine for the night. He looked the newcomer over, trying in vain to hide his erection, which, I couldn't help but notice was throbbing away like a geiger counter. Jeez, it was disgusting. And small, the poor slob. On the other hand, the dame was gorgeous, so it just proved the guy was still breathing. She leaned in to him and said loud enough so I could hear too, "See anything you like?"

He winced in embarrassment. "How about everything?" he asked, jockeying in vain for a better view of her privates.

"I'm Carrie," she said, the voice behind her New Orleans–style ornamental face mask as breathy as a warm breeze from the Mississippi. "Are you taken?" she asked. Jeez, this girl had bigger balls than Jake!

He shook his head and allowed her to lead him by the hand to the exit. He turned back, winked twice at me, which was our signal to meet back here in an hour, and left the room.

I walked over to my sexy suspect and introduced myself. "I'm Dan Chesterfield," I said.

She formed a perfect O with her perfect lips and then said, "Got one?"

"Excuse me?"

"A Chesterfield. You know, a smoke."

"Oh. That. Yeah, well, believe it or not, I don't smoke. With a name like that, I figured I was destined to be an addict or abstain totally."

She leaned in to me so I could feel the electric touch of her nipples against my bare chest. It felt wonderful, let me tell you. She whispered, "I hope that's the only sin you abstain from."

"Why don't we find out," I suggested, grabbing for her hand. She did one better, grabbing for my dick. I gasped in surprise and, I gotta admit, delight, as she guided me and my dick out of the room and in the direction of one of the many little cottages behind the party room. She introduced herself as Peggy.

"You—uh—come here often?" I asked, gasping for breath as she tugged at me while she unlocked the door and we entered the studio. It wasn't much of a room; a throw rug, small writing table, and chair. It was dominated by a queen-size bed that looked like it had seen its share of pickup parties like the one I was attending tonight. The room looked artificial, like a bad movie set, smelled dank, and made me feel a bit depressed.

But I remembered why I was there and turned to Peggy. She was still wearing her mask. I gestured to mine, which was a kid's Dick Tracy mask. That was Jake's choice, another example of his corny sense of humor. I made him wear a Porky Pig mask in revenge, though it's been a few years since anyone's called us pigs—at least to our faces. "Shall we undress? . . ."

She shook her head and smiled. It was a pretty smile, under her half-mask. "I have a better idea," she breathed in my ear, while she massaged my member with her very accomplished hands. Although it felt like I'd died and gone to heaven, the circumstances were so bizarre I wasn't getting particularly hard. After all, Peggy could have the clap, or worse. She could be an insane killer.

She noticed the trouble I was having getting it up and looked at me questioningly with her gorgeous baby blues. I tried to see around them, to spot the birthmark, but the damned mask got in the way. "Trouble, sailor?" she asked.

"Uh . . . I guess I'm not used to this."

She stopped for a moment, patted the bed, and sat down. I stared at her crotch and hoped she didn't notice, but I still couldn't see beyond that dark patch. I sat down.

"You're new around here, aren't you?" she asked with a voice that could melt butter. "I haven't seen you here before, or have I? Sometimes it's hard to tell with these masks."

"So let's take 'em off already. Maybe that'll help me get in the mood."

She laughed. "Is that the problem?"

"Well, it's just that, you know, with all our clothes off, there's not much mystery left, is there?" I felt tremendously uncomfortable and aware of my body, like a gawky teenage boy on his first make-out date. Briefly, I wondered whether Jake was having better luck.

She laughed. "Maybe we should put our clothes back on for a while and get acquainted . . . is that what you really want?" she purred, pulling at her nipples, making them even bigger than they already were. "I think I know how to get you in the mood," she said as she stood up. I hoped she was about to do a naked lap dance for me or something, so I could see her privates better, but instead, she went over to the room's light switch and plunged the room into darkness! Now how was I supposed to see the diamond, or at least the piercing?

I quickly rose to my feet. "Uh, no, actually I'd prefer the lights on," I said as I flicked the switch. "It's a guy thing." I shrugged. "We're very visually-oriented, you know."

"But not very romantic," she complained as she clasped her hand over mine and flicked the lights back off, and then pushed me back to the bed, where we both fell in a heap of flesh. Her breasts were pressed against my chest and it felt good, I gotta admit. They were firm in a way I hadn't experienced in a woman in years. Shit, I hadn't experienced a woman in years, let alone one as young and gorgeous as she was. Her nipples were so hard they almost felt like bullets against my body. Only softer. Warmer. Less dangerous. Nicer to suck on, too. I finally felt myself starting to rise to the occasion.

She noticed. Pulling on my johnson, she murmured, "I'll be your witch if you be my broomstick," and started to guide me toward her privates. I felt the head of my dick kiss the moist pussy lips that I could feel but not see in the dark. I pushed her away.

"What's wrong?"

"I need to warm up a bit. How about I go down on you?"

"Thanks, but I'm already wet. Or couldn't you tell?" she asked as she put a finger inside her wet pussy and then stuck the dripping digit between my lips. She tasted like cinnamon, and I was having a hard time concentrating on the job at hand, as it were.

"Humor me," I said as I pushed her hand away and moved into position so that my face was inches from her pussy. Trouble was, my own head was blocking the scant moonlight entering the room. I couldn't see anything down there, let alone a diamond or any sign of a piercing. Added to that, she smelled so damned good that I all but decided to forget why I was there and just go for it. I could imagine Jake was probably already finishing up—he's told me he's not much of a foreplay kinda guy. If he was, he might still be my partner.

Well, I figured, maybe if I play with her with my fingers, or even my tongue, I can feel it. I started to go down on her, but she yanked me by my hair back up to her breasts. "Lick me here," she whispered throatily, pushing my head down on one of her firm but somehow also pliant breasts. I could hardly complain since my mouth was full of a salty-tasting nipple. But darn, I just wasn't getting anywhere—well, I wasn't getting where I needed to go, anyway.

I licked and bit and chewed for a while, till she started breathing harder, and then I pulled away. "Let me catch my breath," I said. She sighed. "You older men are all alike," she complained. "Just can't keep it up very long, can you?"

I had an idea. "Hey, you like TV?"

"Huh? You want the TV on?"

"No, I mean, I was just wondering—what's your favorite TV show?" I propped my head on one elbow so she wouldn't yank it back to her boob. If only I could get her talking about Jerry. . . .

"Shit, Chesterfield, you are one funny guy."

"Hey, speaking of funny guys, you like Jerry Kramer?"

She was silent for a moment, and I swear I felt her whole body stiffen.

"Why do you ask?" Her voice was noticeably less friendly.

"Well, he was my kinda comedian. I loved his show. Ain't it a bitch what happened to him?"

She laughed, but it was a cold smirk with no trace of humor. "Some people get what they deserve," she hissed.

"Sounds like you knew the guy," I prompted.

"You don't know the half of it. Now are we gonna fuck or talk about dead TV stars all night?"

With that she jumped back on top of me and grabbed my dick, and before I could complain, she slid it right into her pussy, burying me to the hilt. "By the way," she said, "I've been tested this month, how about you?"

I grunted something, barely hearing her words. I was too busy noticing how good it felt to be sliding in and out of this luscious blonde's body, her privates massaging mine with their own secret oils and muscles. What a romantic rubdown!

"Shit, this feels good," she said as she arched her back and took me for a ride, playing urban cowgirl, bucking on my dick like she was trying to win a rodeo prize. She'd won mine already.

I got my mind back on business by thinking of taxes and my dead grandmother, and reached in the darkness for her clit. "Let me make you feel even better," I said as I searched for her little nasty nub. But something hard blocked my way—something multifacted. A diamond!

She grabbed for my hand, pulling it away. "I don't like men touching me down there." She put my hand back on one of her perfect boobs, but I moved it to her mask. "Let me see your face," I said. "You know us guys—we're really visual." Before she could complain, I pulled it off and just enough moonlight hit her face to show a heart-shaped birthmark next to her left eye. Holy shit—it was her!

Peggy gasped and put the mask back on. "That's against the rules, you know," she complained. "You could get thrown out of the club for doing that." She regarded me more closely, as if seeing me for a human being, not just a sex object, for the first time that night. "Say, who are you anyway? How'd you get in here?"

I noticed that I was becoming my alter ego, Shriveldick, again. This situation had become decidedly unsexy, and my gun was back in the unmarked car. After all, I couldn't exactly hide it up my butt. I pulled out of her and tried to move, but she grabbed my arms with surprising strength and held them to my side, pinning them between her legs, which straddled my sides. Her gams were amazingly strong, but then, I don't work out much, and this honeypot probably did two hours daily at her favorite gym. All pretty California girls do—I think it's the law. Anyway, she squeezed against my arms till my fingers were nearly numb.

I was suddenly not in the mood to squeeze, fuck, or anything else as I saw her pull a knife out from under the pillow and point it at my privates. I swear I felt the hair on my balls stick straight up as a wave of fear swept through me, from my guts to my gonads.

She was talking. I tuned back in. "You're a friend of Jerry's, aren't you? Did he tell you about me?" She poked at my dick with the dangerous-looking knife, and I wriggled around like a worm on a hook, but I remained trapped by her astonishing legs. "Did he tell you that he promised to marry me and then went off and fucked that slut Gloria?" She poked me again with the knife, and I felt blood ooze from the tip of my dick. It was decidedly unpleasant, which gave me the strength I needed to push her off me.

I rolled off the bed and hit the floor hard, smashing my elbow against the hard wood grain. I saw stars for a moment, and then felt a terrible stab of pain in my leg as I felt the knife slice through calf muscle and out the other side. My stomach flipped like a pancake on a griddle as I struggled to hold on to the nachos and margarita I'd had at the party. I prided myself on the fact that I hadn't thrown up since 1988, and I didn't plan on starting now.

"What's she got that I haven't got?" Peggy was asking me, like I had a clue. I swear I could see spittle surrounding those pretty lips. "Maybe her hair?" She tossed her own wild mane. "Well, catch this news flash: Jerry told me that Gloria's hair is just a fucking wig. Can you believe that? A wig!" She accentuated the announcement with more pokes and prods of the knife, and I was losing focus and strength by the second as I flipflopped across the floor, trying in vain to get away from her, but slipping in my own blood and banging my chin against the floor. I think I even bit my tongue. Geez, every damn part of my body was screaming out in pain!

My brain was reeling. Peggy was off her rocker, and I had seen the results the last time she'd lost her marbles. This time there were no awards around, but that knife had become equally dangerous. I mumbled, "Peggy, I'm a cop. Stop now and it'll go a lot easier on you."

She screamed then, as bloodcurdling a sound as I have ever heard come out of a human being. I wondered whether Jake could hear it, wherever he was. I sure as shit hoped so; in fact, my life depended on it. Just as suddenly the screaming stopped, and in an eerily emotionless voice she said, "Sorry. It's too late for you."

She aimed for my heart this time. But with the moon now behind some clouds, she scraped my collarbone instead. It still felt like I'd been sliced wide open. I gasped in blinding pain. "Hey, I lied: I don't even think Jerry's funny," I offered in hopes she might take pity on me. But I hadda admit, right then it looked like I was about to go to that big Rerun Channel in the sky. I had a clear vision of the inevitable tabloid headlines: COP SCREWED TO DEATH BY CRAZED KRAMER KILLER. It was no way to go.

And I would have, if not for Jake. Just then, he barged in the door, running into the darkened room, gasping, "Smokey, where are you?"

I yelled, "She's fucking psycho! Get her off me!"

The next thing I heard was the sound of the earth exploding. Actually it was the sound of his .357 going off in the tiny room, deafening me and hitting Peggy. She screamed and rolled off me, but I had lost too much blood to do anything but lay there like a beached whale, which was pretty much how I felt. In the far distance I heard Jake explain, "I've been looking all over for you. My blonde wasn't the one, so I knew you were with our suspect."

I wanted to warn him, I really did. Through fuzzy eyes I saw her creeping in the darkness toward him with the knife, but I just couldn't concentrate on what he was saying or the situation. In fact, I was blacking out.

When my eyes opened again, it was obvious I was in a hospital room. In my experience, they all look pretty much the same: depressing as hell. I mean, if I built a hospital, I'd sure try and liven up the rooms a little, so people would want to live through their stays, you know? Anyway, a nurse came in. At first, I thought she was naked, but I blinked and realized it was just my little panicked imagination on overdrive. Actually, she was a sweet-faced, big black woman of forty or so, who tidied my bed and refilled my water glass.

"Hello, Mr. Chesterfield. Nice to finally see the color of your eyes. How do you feel today?"

"Today?" I croaked. She handed me a plastic container of orange juice, and I sipped at it greedily. My throat felt as parched as concrete in the noonday sun. How long had I been here?

She must've read the confusion on my face. I have that kinda face: easy to read. Not good for a cop. In fact, it's probably what gave me away to Peggy. "You've been here for three days now."

Three days? I tried to raise myself up on one elbow, and fell backward immediately, weak as a puppy and aching from places in my body I'd forgotten existed. "What—what happened to Jake?" I thought I knew but prayed I was wrong.

The sweet-faced nurse smiled sadly and shook her head. "I'm sorry, Mr. Chesterfield. Your friend didn't make it."

"Peggy . . ."

"That girl was just plain crazy, Mr. Chesterfield. Even after being wounded by your friend, she was able to find the strength to put her knife in his heart before she died." She wiped away a tear. "Still, if it weren't for him, you wouldn't be here right now."

I felt numb. "I know, I know." *Jake. God.* I'd sure miss the big damn lug.

"What'd she have to go and do that for, Mr. Chesterfield?"

I thought of Jerry Kramer, world-famous TV comedian with a sexual appetite for his young female fans, and what it had cost him. And Jake. And me. I shook my head. "It's a long story, ma'am."

The nurse nodded, regarding me with soft, liquid brown eyes. I musta looked like I was about to break into a flood of tears, which to be honest, is about how I felt. She touched my face with her warm hand. "You need some cheering up, Mr. Chesterfield." She looked at her watch. "Say, it's nine o'clock. How about I put on some TV? Jerry Kramer's on. That should cheer you up."

That made me sit up for a moment. "Jerry Kramer?" Was it all some sort of dream, then? Was I coming off some incredible bender or something? "I thought . . ." I couldn't complete the sentence.

She clucked her tongue. "Oh, well, since that terrible murder, they've been showing reruns. The show's more popular than ever. Figures, doesn't it?" She shook her head.

Yeah, it figures. She turned on the TV, placed the remote control mechanism next to my orange juice, and quietly left the room. Onscreen, Jerry was saying something stupid to that sexy Gloria, only she didn't look so sexy to me anymore. And in fact, the hair *did* look kinda fake. Funny I'd never noticed it before.

Absently, I wondered whether Jake had at least gotten laid before he died. I sure hoped so.

I aimed the remote controller for the middle of the TV set and threw it with all my remaining strength, which was modest. Nevertheless, I was rewarded with the sound of breaking glass. It was cold comfort, but by the time that sweet nurse ran back into the room, I found myself chuckling anyway. Couldn't stop myself, in fact.

You know, that was the first and only time Jerry Kramer had ever made me laugh.

CURS

Tom Piccirilli

Heavy ice crystals had formed on Achilles's nose, clinging to whiskers, sleek husky fur, and the edges of ears, his breath hot on Collins's cheek as they climbed over the three-foot-high snowbanks. The killing blizzard had struck two days ahead of schedule, and within an hour the roads were too hazardous to traverse, the pass leading back down the mountain completely cut off. Four miles from the cabin, Collins had left his truck nearly buried off among a stand of Doug fir and thrown everything he could carry into his backpack, cursing himself for not being prepared. He'd forgotten the snowshoes.

Misjudging the weather badly, he once again realized how far out of touch he'd become during his two-year marriage to Lynn. The streets of Manhattan had eaten away his north woods instincts and replaced them with certain gutter knowledge he'd always fought against, and so never truly learned. It made the ending that much more a shearing of manhood; there was something awful in the fact that he'd seen clues of her infidelity the entire time, yet had let it sneak up on him anyway.

The orange fur of Achilles's wolfish face was so frosted with rime that he looked like a half-eaten Creamsicle. "She got almost all of it, Killy," Collins said. The dog's intense sapphire eyes stared at him warmly, explosive hot breaths heating the back of Collins's neck as they trudged on, hip-deep in snow. "But not everything that mattered."

At twenty-two, with a degree in architecture he'd never bothered framing, Collins started building the cabin, taking the better part of a year just to complete the landscaping and foundation; it took another eight months before the two-story, three-bedroom main-frame, masonry, and nominal wiring was completed. He'd had greater notions then, before he'd met her, so that the cabin stood now composed half of logs he'd cut himself, the other half a modern backdrop ranch reminiscent of his grandmother's home in Colorado.

It took almost two hours to cover the distance to the cabin. Nearing midnight the full moon on the snow made it seem like daylight. He came up out of the last rolling bank hardly feeling his legs anymore, shivering uncontrollably and gasping for breath, throat raw from the freezing air, and could barely make out tendrils of black smoke trailing from the chimneys.

"No, damn it . . ." he breathed.

She'd beaten him back home.

Christ, not only had she abandoned him, but now she'd try to take his only possession left, the house he'd built with his own hands. Enraged, a nice adrena-line surge kicking back his fatigue, Collins threw himself against the roiling blizzard. He spotted the hint of her crimson Firebird in the driveway and thought, *Good, that thing will slide right off the mountains in this weather,* and realized as his nausea rose that she wouldn't be going anywhere—he was stuck here with her—the snow having already reached the windshield. There was another car beside it he didn't recognize.

Flopping against the front door, Collins took off his right glove and stuck his fingers into his mouth, sucking them back to life. Finally able to grasp his key, he jammed it into the lock and shoved open the door, not expecting to see anyone in the living room.

A startling figure in white lurched from the couch, illuminated in the weak firelight. Wind and ice tore at Collins's back as Achilles crawled inside past him, sniffing madly, sneezing with the sudden blast of heat and burning pine, only to be beset by a yapping toy poodle.

Disgusted, Collins said, "Shut up, Juliet."

The poodle fell back with a puzzled grimace and yeeped a few more times into Achilles's face, pirouetting on her hind legs.

Lynn's sister, Amanda, came toward him then, a specter free in the darkness. She wore a bulky cotton sweater over an ankle-length silken nightgown, apparently caught unaware by the blizzard, too. "Collie?" she said. "My God, how did you get through this snow? What are you doing here? Killy!" Achilles ran forward two bounding steps, shaking and whining, ecstatic to see her again. Even as a puppy he'd shown her more loyalty than Lynn.

Not quite as voluptuous as her sister, Amanda was infinitely more attractive to Collins now; he'd always known she would have been better for him, without her sister's vampish demeanor; bobbed blond hair framed her face perfectly, pouty lips gleamed, those lightly etched lines around her eyes full of concern.

Oddly enough, his first question was "What are you doing on the couch?" Three bedrooms were on the second floor, each with fireplaces, making it much more comfortable, cozier, and warmer up there. Then, frowning, his voice dropped nearly an octave. "Where's Lynn?"

Taking him by the shoulders, a gesture of sympathy, Amanda's mouth worked silently before she pulled her hands away as if burned by the ice covering him. "Uhm, Collie, you'd better let me explain. Listen, she told me that this was all okay with you, that the two of you had . . ." No good, she should have understood her sister had lied. Searching his face, she shrank from him, eyes flitting as she finally acknowledged the noises upstairs.

So, they were in his bedroom.

With a hideously happy voice, Lynn called, "Yeah, come on, uh-huh!" Without thinking, red fury pressed Collins forward, cold sweat exploding across his forehead as he limped up the steps still mostly frozen and opened the door. He grunted as if physically struck by the sight.

Lynn and Zack, her latest lover, rolling and smacking the ornate oak headboard that had been in the Collins family for three generations, cracking out rhythmic *ka-thunks*. The sheets twisted and *scritched* along the mattress, and that blanket Collins's grandmother had crocheted lay kicked down in a knotted bundle. Zack's wet lips left silvery tracks down Lynn's large breasts, her nipples bleeding slightly, drops welling, his spit pooling with her sweat between them. His kisses were loud, obscene, and inhuman—Collins knew Lynn didn't kiss so much as she gnawed and nipped, sank her teeth in the painfully sensitive areas of flesh. She moaned, their rhythm speeding, groaning louder now, once, twice, and again, and then painfully so, the sheets shifting along the contours of their bodies.

The television burned in the darkness, so at least somebody had been smart enough to refill the generator. For a moment Collins thought he was in the movie, too, and that he was the man being ground beneath her bucking, controlling nature. Collins swallowed a sound of anguish and arousal—"Huhn"— and turned, only to find himself seeing the television again; and yes, he really was there on the screen, watching himself watching the television with them screwing behind him. He couldn't get away, spun and saw the video camera on the tripod, its cyclopean red light blinking only slightly slower than Zack's hairy thrusts, like a two-hundred-pound bear rug on top of her, his bloated, pale flesh only occasionally seen in spots beneath all that black fuzz—*cripes, he ought to be in a freak show.* Collins had only allowed his wife to film them making love once, and had never been able to watch the tape for more than a minute.

Lynn started to shriek, her voice growing louder as the pitch rose, mostly in her penultimate orgasm and riding the rapids of her own fluidity, both of them as wet as if bathing on his bed, Zack laughing like some maniacal child—as she opened her eyes in such all-encompassing ecstasy, both of them coming and now nearly howling, and finally noticed her ex-husband standing above her now.

And at the foot of the bed, as usual, lay Muggins licking his balls.

Muggins—always there—vicious mongrel rottweiler-retriever, a hefty hundred pounds of prime and angry muscle, with scarred black hindquarters where Achilles had taken out a couple of nice chunks during one of their bloody throw-downs, bleak brown eyes like a pair of Times Square toilets, his ever-present tumescent lipstick erection and handball-sized testicles hanging like deformed hornets' nests, ready to rip and rage and screw your leg, your arm, hip, sneaker, VCR, your G.I. Joe dolls, anything in his path. Muggins turned slowly away from the scene on the bed, looked at Collins, and came as close to smiling as a dog could.

Retreating, the fury going from red to black, clawing within him, Collins moved out the door, down the stairs to the den. Amanda wavered, unsure of where to go. His drafting table lay broken and leaning against the wall, and with sudden clarity Collins knew they'd tried to fuck on top of it, too, smashing his desk to pieces. Amanda made a halfhearted attempt to soothe him. "Uhm, hey listen, Collie, we . . ." He held up a hand to stave further explanation. Juliet yeeped urgently. He turned in time to see Zack rushing into the room, naked except for all that black wiry fur like he was wearing a mohair suit, holding Collins's father's shotgun, with Lynn in a ratty kimono standing close behind him.

Amanda shouted, "Zack, no!"

Collins kept the guns perfectly oiled and clean, but he could see that Zack must have gone hunting sometime in the last couple of days; dried earth clogged the barrel. He fantasized contentedly about letting the jackass pull the trigger, the gun exploding and shredding his face: instant electrolysis. He sighed as Zack stepped closer, the shotgun swinging up to point directly between Collins's eyes.

Zack said, "You son of a bitch. You get your rocks off watchin' other people? That what you're into?" He shoved the gun another inch closer, until it pressed against Collins's eyebrows. "Why are you here? Why are you hounding us?"

Achilles was already *en garde,* turning his muzzle from Zack to Muggins in the background, a low and solid growl in his throat proving he was primed for war. If Collins said the word *rip,* the husky would jump and tear out Zack's throat or die trying. So many ways to kill the chubby little bastard just standing there, his gnarled pecker making an almost ninety degree bend—*Christ, how'd she guide that thing into herself?*—acting tough, thinking he had the upper hand. Collins closed his eyes and fought down the temptation, tried not to think of the fluid leaking down Lynn's leg to *dap dap dap* on his den rug.

He didn't know how it happened that he should ever have fallen in love with her; it made no sense, there was no reason. The hidden masochistic streak in him had come on too strong and shoved him straight at her, like a self-flagellating puritan searching out his pain. "Damn you, Collie," she said. "What are you doing here?"

"This is my home," he said. Sometimes the simplest and most honest statements sounded the dumbest.

"Like hell it is."

"It's in our final settlement. What, you thought you were going to get everything I owned, Lynn, and leave me with nothing?"

She countered with "The papers only went out a week ago."

Collins actually smiled, the shotgun still pressed at his skull. "So that makes the truth any less legal? Less right? You can't even let me have one thing, a single haven not infected with you? Poisoned by you?"

"Who the hell do you think you're talking to!" Lynn screeched, the *dap dap* crashing like thunder.

Over four miles in the snow, every muscle aching, and now to find her here in his home, damning him, the photographs of his family on the bureau having been forced to watch this perverse path his life had taken . . . Collins's hands tightened into fists, no way to back down now if he had to keep looking at her. He was fairly certain he could take the shotgun away from Zack and shove it up his fat, hairy ass without much trouble. Achilles sensed his mood and began whimpering, ready to rip. Muggins rolled over onto his side and went back to licking himself.

Squelching the lit fuse with her calming voice, Amanda moved in front of Collins, staring at Zack and her sister as she slowly pushed aside the shotgun. "Why don't you two go on upstairs, get yourselves cleaned up and dressed, and then we'll all have some coffee and figure this situation out, all right?" She waited, immovable. "Go on."

Collins wondered if the heat at the back of his brain had been hiding beneath his head ever since those first jealousies forced him into battle over girls he didn't even like. He got up and watched Lynn and Zack receding from the den, tasted his own blood, and wanted more.

At the kitchen table, wearing a sweatsuit he'd bought her last Christmas, Lynn said, "We were planning to leave in the morning, anyway."

Collins nearly burst out laughing and sat there shaking his head. "Too late. The pass down the mountain is impenetrable by now."

"What do you mean?"

He stood and pointed at the frosted window being battered by wind-driven snow. "Jesus, when was the last time you looked out a window? A major blizzard hit this afternoon. It'll snow off and on for the next week, probably longer. Your car is buried. It'll take at least another week before they clear out any of the access roads up here."

Lips set together, a know-it-all grimace crumbling his brow, Zack shifted in his seat calmly and murmured, "So? We'll hike down."

"Sure, like a nice spring walk in Central Park, take you no time at all, right. It's eighteen miles down off the mountain and into the nearest town. You're talking about drifts that reach twelve feet in some spots. I parked only a few miles off and nearly froze just making it this far. With windchill and temperatures at minus ten or twenty out there, we can't leave until the system's moved on."

Her face in her hands, gazing through slatted fingers as if looking through the bars of a jail cell, his prisoner rather than vice versa, Lynn said in a pained whisper, "Why are you here, Collie? Why did you do this?"

The absurdity of truth left him with a stunned smile sagging on his face. "To get away from you."

"Enough of this, all right?" Amanda made a severing motion between them. "We're in this together, so let's see where we really stand, just how bad it actually is, or if we're just living out paranoid fantasies of the Donner party. How long are we talking?"

"A week at least, possibly as long as two."

"I can't take off for that long!" Zack said. "My boss'll kill me. I'll get pink-slipped if I'm not back by Tuesday at the latest."

"Food, Collie?" Amanda asked. "Heat?"

"There are enough supplies packed away in the cellar storage to last one person a couple of weeks. It'll hold the four of us over, and the dogs, too, I suppose, if we ration it. We'll turn the generator off during the day and save on gas, but that's the least of our problems. Firewood's going to be worse. How long have you three been here?"

After another heavy silence, Amanda said, "I met them a couple days ago. They've been here since last Monday."

"Making bonfires? You've used a month's worth of wood."

He'd forgotten how life-and-death all the small things became out in the country; he had to recover his instincts fast. "There's not much left, but the cabin is well-insulated." Of course it was, he'd built it, but it took no time to spot chew marks at the floorbase where Muggins had cleaned his teeth. "If push came to shove we could chop some more, try to dry it out, but I don't think it'll come to that. Dress warmly and we'll hold out fine."

"Will we now?" Zack said.

No. Collins eyed him for a moment, letting his gaze move over the three of them, the three dogs, and then staring out the window, knowing in his heart they wouldn't be able to make it. Too much subterfuge: all these undercurrents of anger and agony, his own lust and hatred for his wife, and her indifference like salt in each of his emotional scrapes. Too many guns in the house, too many teeth.

Achilles got up and sauntered to him, a short whine in the back of his throat, and rested at his master's feet. Collins petted the dog's beautifully innocent yet dangerous face; he didn't want to make his dog kill anyone, and wondered if he'd have the strength to resist trying for the next two weeks.

Three days later, after the rationing had left them irate and hungry, Lynn told Zack, "Okay, I'll give you head for what's left of your Chunky Soup."

"You'll give me head anyway."

"You think so?"

"I know it."

Wrong play, Collins thought, as pangs of jealousy neatly sliced into and dug him up; his knowledge of her came so adroitly to the surface. Couldn't the idiot see it? Just check out the coy glint in the corner of her eyes, that survivor's stance in each move she made.

With her luscious voice, slowly licking her lips, she said, "Not like I would be willing to do for you now, dearie."

Finally getting the point, Zack shoved his plate forward. "Okay, sold."

Turning to her sister, the light of triumph reflected heavily off those lips. "Believe it or not, this was how I got my new coffeemaker." She hiked a thumb at Zack. "Can you believe he wouldn't buy it for me unless I gave him ten blow jobs?"

Amanda screwed up her face and shot a worried glance at Collins. The sensible sister trying not to step on too many toes. "Listen, Lynn, this is bad enough, y'know, why don't you try to control yourself a little. The way you phrase things, your tacky openness, for God's sake. In front of your ex? Knock it off."

Lynn shrugged and lifted her hand in a poo-poo gesture. Collins understood her so well—the grin lifting the corner of his mouth even though his gaze grew more dead, every nuance of Lynn's so transparent to him now as he watched her eating the soup. She'd survive no matter what; she continued playing only a game at the moment, but she had the sex to sell and at least one willing buyer. She'd leave the hairy idiot starving to death in their bed if need be, as she drew herself on top of him once again, strong and healthy and always well-fed, and drained the rest of the life out of him—out of anybody, out of everybody, if it really came to that.

Hatred grew palpable as the nights passed. Collins could barely sleep with all the nightmares and memories pounding through his subconscious, one after the other. His wife's loud and delighted squeals in the other bedroom, directed at him, each thrust a knife cutting him open, every sob of ecstasy a white-hot poker sizzling in his brain. Muggins and Achilles glared at each other the same way Zack and Collins locked gazes, dares of death always in the air, one just waiting for the other to jump. Achilles's sapphire gaze kept catching Collins's eyes, as if the dog were asking, *Now? Can I do it now?*

Muggins's pecker prodded everyone in the cabin, the dog constantly on the prowl. In two days he banged the armchair, a fishing pole in the corner, an empty Styrofoam coffee cup, a stack of Vogue magazines.

Leaning down, and warming himself against the weak fire, Zack commented on Muggins's prowess with inanimate objects. Collins mentally echoed the word *rip,* imagining torn cartilage, exposed bleeding windpipe, Achilles's foaming muzzle working into flesh. A couple hours later he cleaned out the shotgun and put it under his bed.

Amanda came to him in the middle of the night; she slid under the blankets, different from her sister and yet so alike. "Hi," she whispered, kissing him softly, like this was the most natural meeting in the world. Perhaps, in its own way, that was actually the case. Juliet followed her in, hopped up on the bed, and yeeped twice. One of them kicked her onto the floor as they tumbled gently against each other.

Initially, her touch was painful, his skin electrically ticklish as she pressed him—her breasts were slightly smaller and more upturned than Lynn's, nipples larger. She fed them to him and he suckled her, a mockery of mothering, perhaps, perhaps not, feeling good anyway. Slow going for a time, but eventually her tongue brought him to erection—her mouth took him in and she licked him for hours, the length of his legs, thighs, spending an inordinate amount of time on his shaft. Although he knew he was robbing her of pleasure—of consummation and his thanks—and realized she truly didn't mind if the favor was returned tonight, what she did was too fulfilling in its sincerity for him to slow or stop. Sometime near dawn she slept. Achilles, outside the door sniffing at the jamb, whimpered in his own loneliness.

The next night, seconds after he entered Amanda, in the other room Lynn screamed twice in a terrifying fashion, enough to make him leap out of bed. He waited, curious to know if it was another sex game, just her hitting the multiorgasmic peak or if something had finally snapped in Zack and he'd actually hurt her this time. The third shriek made Collins move against his better intentions. He rushed into the hallway and to their door—his own bedroom door— and found it ajar, the reeking, sweet smell of marijuana slinking free. Inside, cocaine lay scattered on the throw rug, a cracked hand mirror overturned. Muggins's studded collar fit snugly around Lynn's throat, her heaving breasts swaying as she moved on all fours, leash tight against her neck while Zack pulled roughly on it, yanking her around the room even while he slunk behind her doggie-style. Bored, Muggins stared without interest at the television screen.

Smiling lusciously, Lynn looked up and said his name as he'd never heard it spoken before. *"Collie."*

He returned to Amanda, knowing for certain that somebody had to die before this was all over.

Too soon, he found the animosity was there within each of them—she, so much her sister at certain moments, the same throb throughout her body as he entered her, the same out-of-control thrashing as she orgasmed—but he had to readjust to the tenderness in-between. Amanda's caresses and kisses felt strange after the years of *abandoning* sex, turning his back on passion and attachment, not much biting. Having

Amanda so *near* him during their lovemaking—all this touching, so much skin to cover—gave him an odd sensation. Every time he drew away, to turn to another position, she lunged up against him to hold him close. "I've dreamed about loving you since you first came home with her," she told him. Juliet yeeped, Achilles whined. Murmuring words into her mouth that might actually mean something, at some point if not now, he was almost able to forget how low he'd allowed himself to be beaten by his wife. Maybe sex could bring him back, or love, or simply blood. Collins wondered if the same sadomasochistic romanticism that had shifted into pure mean-spirited lovemaking with her sister would also happen now with Amanda. He looked into her eyes, searching for his own destruction.

Hours later he said, "It can't really be this good, can it?"

"Trust me," she told him, nuzzling his neck, jugular pulsing heavily against the side of her nose.

"You're asking for more than you think."

"No, I'm not," she said. "I realize what it's all about. Believe me. I know." Their stomachs grumbled from hunger. "And you will learn. You have to. You'd better."

Their intensity moved up a gear each time they made love over the following three nights. Something began, changed, and ended then, as well; he heard it crack as loudly as a spine breaking. An exciting phoniness entered their act, and he couldn't be certain if it came from him or Amanda. He couldn't always see where Lynn ended and she began. He had more teeth than he wanted but not quite as many as he needed now. Their hunger was twofold as thoughts of death crossed and recrossed their minds, so obvious in her eyes. She said, "Trust me" again but sounded frightened by the notion, acknowledging the fact that the one responsibility in the world she didn't want was his wholehearted faith.

She nibbled at his throat, snapping harder now, sipping, and he bit down on her left shoulder. Yelping, she glanced at the dotted half circle of bloody beads rising and slapped him lightly, then backhanded him harder, and again until his ears rang. "Is this the way it has to be?" she asked. "Can't you have it any other way?"

He'd been right in not trusting the extent of their purity, something always fouled the work. She grunted loudly, the first truly ferocious sound from her, that savage look sudden in her eyes, Amanda almost entirely gone now, swirling backward in a sea of violent Lynn sex. He turned her over so as not to see it anymore. ". . . no . . . what are you doing?" Under the bed beside the shotgun, Juliet began to whine. Not touching Amanda much, he smiled sadly at the realization of just how corrupted he'd become, how much he'd learned from his wife that he never wanted to believe existed in him.

Collins moved off as she lay sobbing, "You've ruined it all. Your fault! . . . It's your fault!" and he knew that in effect, as his lust and rage consumed the chance for love, that it was most definitely his own fault.

When he awoke in the frigid darkness, snow bashing down hard against the windows, with her lips on him, smooth mouth moving up and down his neck, biting instead of kissing, drawing his blood out of the little jagged incisor rips along his largest veins, he violently pulled her away and said, "Amanda?"

In the glow of the few remaining embers, he saw the side of Lynn's face, that same self-absorbed intensity seeking out his soul, still wanting a piece. He realized, oh, Christ, it really was Lynn.

"Where?"

"Relax, Collie," she told him, the sugary sweetness in her voice spilling out like every false promise she'd ever made him. "Be with me tonight, one last time. It'll be better than ever before."

"You're crazy."

"No, baby, don't you get it yet?"

He leaped off and stepped on Juliet's head, hearing the firm snap of the dog's neck, one final yeep crushed from her lungs. He ran out and kicked open the door to the other bedroom, expecting Zack to be with Amanda, both of them on the floor bundled in dog leashes. Muggins and Zack both glanced up from the bed, looking equally stoned with rheumy eyes, wet noses, penises about the same size and ugly shape, where they lay watching television.

Collins ran downstairs calling, "Amanda? Amanda!" wanting to make up the difference, erase these last hours, change it all back to the tenderness and kill off and cut the umbilical cord still holding him tied to Lynn's sexual sadism, his own attraction for such beatings. Certain that she was dead, or waiting for him with a meat cleaver, he felt the shifting current of night turning once again.

She'd added the last of the wood to the fire, until it blazed and lit the living room in crimson and yellow. She sat with Achilles on the couch, his head in her lap, tail thumping hard, throwing one shadow against him. "What?" she said when she saw him, fear in her voice. "What's the matter?"

"Why are you down here?"

"What do you mean? I wanted to think over some things. What we're all about, you and me, where we're going. Why? What happened?" She looked back up the stairs as Lynn came out of the bedroom, no longer sneaking in the shadows, shameless as she glanced down at them and smiled and returned to Zack and Muggins, always in charge no matter what the madness of the situation.

Amanda's eyes narrowed for a moment, the jagged wrinkle between her brows deep and dark before smoothing away completely. "She came to you again, didn't she." No question. She knew her sister. And now, yes, herself. "I turned my back for ten minutes and she tried to take you away from me, even when she doesn't want you." She swallowed thickly, an utterly defunct smile creasing the corners of her mouth. "Even though she never wanted you." A single, genuine sob broke inside her and she whispered, "Did you even fight her, Collie? Did you struggle?" She peered at him in the firelight and saw all his lost and losing battles, the weakness of his cur's soul, his damnation and possible redemption. "Maybe you did, for a while, but you can't for much longer, huh? Not in this place. Not under these conditions." She sobbed again and patted Achilles's neck, burying her hand deeply in his thick fur. The dog whined as if understanding and looked at her, then turned his own burrowing sapphire gaze on his master; Collins had as difficult a time meeting his dog's eyes as he did his lover's.

She rose and said, "Come on, Killy." Achilles jumped from the couch and followed her, his new mistress, trudging, step by step back up to the second floor. Collins stared into the fire, knowing what was about to be accomplished and where his failures and revenge would lead the only two loyal friends he had left in the world.

A minute later he heard her say the word, clearly pronounced so as not to make a mistake in inflection or meaning—*"Rip!"*—and he wasn't surprised that she knew his secret lethal word or that the shotgun lay hidden under the bed. He talked in his sleep. He did not keep secrets well. But would the dog respond to someone else's fury, even if the agony was shared? He waited, and instantly heard the noises. Achilles sounded like every hatred felt now unleashed against his tormentors; Zack shrieked and almost made it out of the bedroom before Achilles pulled him back inside, leaping, twisting him by the throat, and digging ever inward. Muggins crept out and crawled whimpering to nuzzle the cooling meat of Juliet. The shotgun went off impossibly slow, as if the sisters had stared long and hard at each other up there, a lifetime of regret and pitiful misdemeanors passing between them, until Lynn, even at this moment, laughed her bitter unalterable giggle, and Amanda pulled the trigger.

Again.

And again.

QUICK

Robert J. Randisi &
Marthayn Pelegrimas

*H*e had to be quick.

He tore the flimsy T-shirt from her body, baring her breasts. They were small and perfectly formed, with pink nipples and wide aureola. Next he tore the panties from her. He pinned her to the wall with his body while he exposed himself. His erection sprang forth anxiously. He slid his hands beneath her arms, lifted her and brought her down on his penis. She was dry, but he persisted, and finally she sank down on him, the length of him sliding inside of her.

He began to hump her then, slamming her against the wall. His hand slid once on the blood, but it wasn't really a problem.

He had to be quick, though.

His mouth found her breasts, sucking them, biting them hard. She was moaning now, whether from pleasure or pain, he wasn't sure. It really didn't matter, though. His pleasure was what he was concerned with, not hers.

Quick, quick . . .

Her eyes were open. That always helped. When the

eyes were open sometimes he could use them to gauge how much time he had left.

She bit her lower lip hard enough to pierce it, and he leaned forward and licked away the blood. The blood from the other place was dropping down his side now, and hers, pooling on the floor. Once his foot slipped in it, but he moved it and found purchase again.

She made a sound then, from deep in her throat, and that helped. It spurred him on, made him more excited.

Quickly!

His hips began to move faster and he began to grunt. In his mind a voice was saying, "Oh, yes, oh, yes . . ." and it was her voice, not his. He was imagining that she was urging him on, that she was enjoying it as much as he was.

He slid his hands beneath her buttocks, grabbing them and holding them tightly as he drove into her with more fury. The blood was all over then, but her eyes were open, he could see that he still had time, though not much.

He started to grunt with the effort now, faster and faster, a grunt for each thrust. Her arms were flailing about wildly, as if she had no control over them.

But control seemed to be something she always had.

Quicker!

Talking was forbidden but she tried telling him with her eyes, her mouth that the boy would soon be cold.

It was exciting—all of it. Harvesting the loud ones, turning their noises into calm. Or the lonely ones who huddled in their doorway each night to get a few hours of sleep.

His perspiration glistened, made their bodies even

more slippery. She scraped her plastic nails across his back, hoping she had made him bleed.

The kid on the table had been sweet. His gratitude had been heartwarming when they took him inside, fed him. He talked between gulps, thinking his adolescent stories of woe unusual. They had smiled, though, and nodded, patient while he relaxed and got warm.

The emotional change their actions brought about was always beautiful to watch. Before they were finished, their visitor passed through their own personal seasons.

Gratitude changed to pleasure as they bathed him, gave him clean pajamas. How quickly the calm changed to panic as they forced him downstairs. And terror, like autumn, all in reds.

They had it down to a system, now. The metal table was installed after the second one stained the wooden bench beyond hope. The leather straps, the IV tube, had all been stolen from her workplace.

But the actual gathering of the warmth had taken five tries before they got it right.

Quick.

She was almost there. It was all in the timing. First the taking, then the sustaining.

QUICK.

Pinpricks in the plastic bag attached to the tube brought on the rain. A scarlet shower, she called it. The boy was unconscious, pale, as his life drained into a tube, collected in a bag and sprinkled over them. Small payment for the kindness they had bestowed on the lonely one.

Quick . . . quick . . .

She could see the red clotting in his hair and it excited her. He was biting as he thrust and she could feel his warmth inside her, the boy's warmth all over her, running down her face, into her mouth. She was slick with excitement. It coated their kisses, caked their fingers.

The bag was almost empty.

If they didn't hurry the air would soon cool his blood and the moment would be lost . . .

Until they found another one.

But she couldn't wait. She wanted it now.

The boy was dead, she was sure of it.

Quicker . . . er . . . quick . . . er . . . quick . . . er . . .

Her lover drained himself inside her.

The boy drained himself outside her.

She came loudly. Completely.

Quickly.

THE TROUBLE WITH HITCHHIKERS

Michael Garrett

The smiling face of an attractive waitress was refreshing for a change. Max Jennings had realized years earlier that most sexy young women looked right through a man of his age, as if he didn't exist. The "invisible man syndrome" is what he'd laughingly called it when he'd first noticed the phenomenon, but it wasn't funny anymore. At least here was a female who wasn't repulsed by gray hair.

Regrettably Max had reached a point in life when younger women simply didn't notice him anymore. He'd exceeded the upper threshold at which women in their twenties, and even thirties, seriously evaluated him as a potential social companion. Most were unwilling to engage in even simple conversation unless they happened to be waitresses employing their charms to encourage higher tips. After a while, even that angered Max. It wasn't that he hoped to get laid every time he met an attractive younger woman, either. He still loved his wife despite her changes over the years, but he simply wanted to be *noticed* by the opposite sex, to feel recognized as a *man,* as subtle reinforcement that he wasn't quite yet ready for the grave. A nice roll in the hay would be great, but at this stage of his life Max would settle for a gentle hug or a sweet smile every now and then.

Getting old *sucks,* he often complained to his friends back home. Although the sentiment was as true now as ever, he'd reluctantly accepted it as a sad fact of life.

When she returned to freshen his coffee, Max continued the friendly banter he'd initiated with the shapely brunette when she'd first taken his order. "Can I ask a simple question?" he inquired, admiring the smooth complexion of her youthful face.

"Sure."

She looked like a cover girl, and Max couldn't understand why she was working in a dump like this for substandard wages and tips. She had to be in her late teens or early twenties, with a magnetic personality and not a hint of conceit. In this girl Max saw a successful woman of the future.

He took a sip of steamy coffee and tried not to appear too pushy. "I'm not making a pass at you, I promise," he said tactfully. "But when you think about guys you'll date, how much older can they be before you consider them off-limits?"

She scanned her other customers and was apparently satisfied they didn't need her immediate services. "Well, I've never really thought about it much," she began. Max's eyes darted from the "Becky" name tag on her blouse pocket to the cleavage exposed by the unfastened top button of her white blouse. "I've dated guys ten years older than me and that didn't bother me much," she continued. Then, as she picked up his soiled plate to continue her duties, she laughingly drawled, "But I guess when they start looking too much like my daddy they're out of my range." She smiled as she pivoted toward the kitchen with the coffeepot and soiled plates. Max feigned a weak laugh. She hadn't intended to rub salt in his wound, he knew, but her closing comment certainly wasn't what he'd hoped to hear. Couldn't she have said something like *I judge men by what they are on the* inside, *rather than how they look on the* outside, or *too bad you aren't trying to pick me up; I could go for a man like you.* He tried to convince himself he really hadn't intended to pick her up, rationalizing that his encounter with Becky wasn't about sex; it was only about *age.* Max was becoming more sensitive about his advancing years with every day that passed. He left Becky a generous tip and trudged back into the hot sun of the parking lot.

Traveling alone was nothing unusual for Max Jennings. He'd done it all his working life. With the convertible top of his Mazda Miata down and the tires spitting gravel from the diner's parking lot, he steered back onto the rural eastern Tennessee highway, the humid southern air of August whipping what little remained of his thinning gray hair. He preferred scenic routes these days, off the beaten path, to escape the speed and congestion of I-75. Let everyone else take the fast lane, he thought.

Life wasn't what it used to be for the middle-aged pharmaceutical salesman. His most generous clients had retired and been replaced with young snot-nosed kids barely out of college with whom he couldn't relate. His numbers were sagging, and his boss was no dummy; George Felix knew all too well that Max had become a liability to the company. Max sensed his lifelong career spiraling down the toilet.

At least both of his kids were grown, with new families of their own, so he no longer faced the financial responsibilities of parenthood. But Max's wife was a poor money manager and seemed more concerned about her social circle than about him.

Worse, even Max's libido had waned as of late. On the rare occasions when Margaret was actually willing to have sex, it was often difficult for him to get it up. This was particularly frustrating when he recalled the stiffening of his dick at the sight of young Becky's skirt tightening around her ass as she'd leaned over to wipe off an adjacent table. Where were those erections when he had an opportunity to use them?

Max shook his head. Perhaps it was his age, or stress, or maybe it had to do with the sameness of a twenty-five-plus-year marriage and a spouse who wanted sex only on her own terms. Whatever the hell it was, Max knew one thing for sure—even though he still felt young at heart, it was difficult to compete in a world oriented toward the younger generation.

And that was another reason he preferred traveling the countryside—fewer billboards hawking products to a younger audience by perfectly shaped youthful male and female models. Instead, the quiet environment here—grazing cattle, silos, and cornfields swaying in the warm breeze—created a sense of serenity. The purple ridge of the Great Smoky Mountains in the distance reconnected him with days long past, when he had been a mere boy himself with few cares in the world and had vacationed here with his dad. Max fondly recalled the innocent days of his sexual awakening, when he was so horny in school that he could hardly concentrate. Such instances of sexual excitement had long since passed him by.

Now, so many years later, even his fantasies had begun to fade. After all, Max was realistic enough to know that with a deeply receding hairline and a pear-shaped physique, he offered little to excite the opposite sex. His fantasies of secret liaisons with women half his age had died when he'd awakened from a steamy dream and practically laughed at himself from the implausibility of it all. He didn't care for women of his own age; hell, they only reminded him of his own advancing years. And despite his age and the condition of his body, he still felt young and alive inside. Paying a young hooker could perhaps revive the doused flame he so desperately needed in life, but that would do little to satisfy his ego. Younger women would never be attracted to him again. It was a plain and simple fact. He was out of their range, a mere father figure now. Only in the movies would a young, attractive female go for a man like him, he thought.

Yeah. *Only in the movies.*

Max's interaction with beautiful young women was now limited to the occasional waitress like Becky who might give him the time of day. Exhaling a sigh of boredom, he punched the search button on the radio dial for a stronger country music station as the Chattanooga signal weakened with distance. It seemed hard to believe that he, a heavy-metal child of the sixties, had become a hard-core country music fan, but it was true. Certainly not what he'd expected. Hell, so little in his life had turned out as planned.

His goal of early retirement had all but fizzled. Like so many of his generation, he'd prepared for his senior years too late in life. And Margaret hadn't helped at all. She'd managed to spend what little was left from each paycheck, and now it seemed he'd be forced to work to age sixty-five or beyond.

"Shit!" he cursed. He rarely talked to himself, but on this hot August day Max Jennings was angry at the world, at youth, and himself in particular. The summer sun scorched the bald spot at the top of his head as he steered the convertible forward. He felt the tingle of sunburn at his scalp, having lost his Atlanta Braves baseball cap to an unusually strong gust of wind a few miles back. But with a new country station blasting the airwaves he headed closer to Knoxville, maneuvering the twists and turns of the rural highway with precision in the little red sports car he'd bought when the "middle-age crazies" first struck.

And so it was that when Max Jennings rounded a curve and caught first sight of a female hitchhiker in the distance, her long hair trailing in the breeze, latent fantasies of the past reawakened. She appeared almost like a mirage, and he couldn't help smiling. How many times had he, and every other heterosexual male, dreamed of picking up a sexy hitchhiker and having himself fucked till his dick was sore? Sure, there had been times in the past when it might have been within reason. But not now. Not when he looked more like a college girl's grandfather than a potential lover. And besides, even as the distance between himself and the girl narrowed, he knew that she probably wasn't nearly as pretty as Becky, despite her long willowy hair. Hell, hitchhikers were usually trouble anyway. You couldn't trust them in this day and age, and he rarely picked one up. But the closer he approached this particular lady, the more interesting she became.

She stood at the side of the road, her legs long and lean, darkly tanned, and her hip projecting seductively. Her streaked blond hair hung almost to her waist when the wind died down. She sported thick, bushy eyebrows reminiscent of Kathy Ireland and wore incredibly short cutoffs. Her tight undersized T-shirt restrained full rounded breasts that bulged against the thin white fabric and outlined erect nipples. She appeared to be in her early-to-mid-twenties.

Even as his foot hit the brakes, though, Max knew this was too good to be true. It was similar to the opening scene of a *Twilight Zone* episode, his favorite childhood television series. A gorgeous young woman dressed like this would never hitchhike alone in the backwoods without an ulterior motive. But perhaps she'd only had car trouble and was walking to the next town for help. He didn't recall having passed a stalled car, though. Obviously something was missing from this picture, and Max envisioned Rod Serling stepping from behind a black-and-white spotted cow to introduce the setup. Max had learned long ago to be cautious. Travelers were too often victims of crime, and as he slowed the car to a stop he couldn't help thinking of the "spider and the fly" scenario. But glancing at the gently sloping field behind the hitchhiker he saw no accomplice, and couldn't resist the urge to learn the secret of the sexy young lady in the Tennessee hills. Perhaps she was only a naive and innocent young lady too trusting of a violent world. Perhaps she only needed a helping hand.

"Where are you headed?" he asked as he braked to a stop. Her rating on the proverbial ten-point scale jumped a notch higher. Max knew sex was out of the question, but it had been years since an attractive woman had accompanied him in a car. They could attempt to bridge the generation gap and continue the discussion begun earlier with Becky. Perhaps luck would strike twice on this otherwise average day.

"Maryville," the girl answered in a voice even sweeter than Becky's. "To school."

Max smiled, too smitten by her beauty to consider the credibility of her statement. She was hitchhiking to school, yet she carried no books—only an oversized handbag that couldn't hold nearly enough supplies for a legitimate traveler. She dropped the bag into the cramped space between the driver's seat and the rear deck as she settled into the passenger's seat. She didn't seem the collegiate type, either, especially when Max noticed the body piercings. She raked her fingers through her tangled hair, then laid her hands to rest on her knees. Small golden rings adorned the loose skin between the weblike base of the fingers of her left hand, glistening in the sunlight. He'd never seen piercings in that particular location before, and he had his own preconceived notions about people who deface their bodies in such a way, but as long as she wasn't accompanied by a boyfriend, Max didn't care. Instead he imagined where else on her body she might be pierced.

He surveyed the terrain again and saw no one ready to jump him, but he still felt a bit nervous. It could be a setup after all, and he'd have to stay on his toes. The girl seemed a bit uneasy, too, but why shouldn't she if she were, indeed, innocent and in need of help? She was placing her safety in the trust of a complete stranger, and Max noticed she didn't buckle her seat belt, perhaps to make a quick escape should he pose a threat. He revved the engine and guided the Miata back onto the molten asphalt, glancing at her golden legs stretching down to the adjacent floorboard. Embarrassed to have been caught staring, he looked up at her face, but she avoided eye contact, her long hair fanning in the wind.

"I'm surprised to see someone like you hitchhiking," he commented in an attempt to start a conversation. "It's awfully dangerous, you know."

She didn't respond; not nearly as friendly as Becky.

"You never know who might pick you up," Max continued. He tried to be nonthreatening, but felt self-conscious in the presence of such a beautiful young woman. "I rarely pick up hitchhikers," he continued awkwardly, "but I guess you're special."

She flashed a smirk of disgust as if she'd heard that one a thousand times before. Max decided to keep quiet for a while.

But less than a mile down the desolate county

highway a long-haired unshaven man in an unbuttoned blue work shirt and tattered jeans sauntered from a drainage ditch to block the narrow highway ahead. Max was surprised that the man's appearance registered with him at all. It was the revolver the man pointed directly at Max's face that most attracted his attention.

"You'd better pull over," the girl said. "He means business."

Max slowly shook his head and exhaled. He'd been set up after all. But then a rush of adrenaline surged through his body. He'd been pissed off before he picked the girl up, and he was even more pissed off now. This confrontation was about old versus young. His mind shifted into high gear as he downshifted the Miata to stop. The gunman's smug level of confidence obviously grew as the sports car slowed. When the vehicle was no more than ten feet from the threatening stranger Max stomped the accelerator and swung past in a sharp turn, clipping the con man in the process and sending him spiraling backward toward the drainage ditch. A larger automobile couldn't have maneuvered such a sharp cut, though the Miata failed to escape unscathed; an errant gunshot put a hole in its windshield inches from the young girl's head.

Beads of sweat blurred Max's vision as he mashed the accelerator to the floor, checking the rearview mirror for any sign of movement from the gunman. The girl twisted in her seat. "Skip!" she screamed. "Oh, my God!"

Max exhaled and tried to regain control. He hoped he hadn't killed the guy, though the gunman had intended robbery as a minimum motive, and probably worse. And seated beside Max was a woman who had participated in the whole scheme, who was likely capable of watching her punk boyfriend put a bullet through his balding head. His nerves shattered, Max slowed the car.

The girl covered her face with her hands and shook her head. "I knew he'd fuck up," she groaned.

Max studied her unsympathetic reaction with a mixture of anger and pity. "Why did you ever get mixed up with a guy like that?" he asked. "He probably has a criminal record as long as his arm."

She stared blankly ahead. "He's an idiot," she said calmly. "I told him to concentrate, to expect anything. He didn't pay attention. He deserved what he got."

Max was stunned that she could be so heartless. And then he gazed at her magnificent legs and her T-shirt flapping in the wind, accentuating her breasts. Months of sexual neglect were strong enough to overcome even the tension of the moment, and he eased off the accelerator a bit more. His dick felt like Rip Van Winkle, or in his case, Rip Van *Wrinkle,* awakening from a twenty-year sleep. How the hell could he become sexually excited over someone who'd just attempted to set him up? It was as if the threat intensified his sexual energy. He took in every square inch of what he could see of her body and recognized that without a doubt she was every bit as ravishing as anyone he'd ever imagined.

"It's not too late for you to turn your life around, you know," he advised her, but she completely ignored him. "What's your name?" he finally asked, but she still averted his sight. Visibly shaken, she reached behind the seat for her bag, and before he knew it Max faced the menacing barrel of still another revolver.

"Pull over," she demanded.

Max sat motionless, maintaining a steady speed and mentally reviewing options.

She pulled back the hammer. "I mean it," she hissed. "I'll blow your fuckin' brains out."

Max's face turned to stone. He watched the highway curve like a ribbon over distant hills and pressed the accelerator harder.

"What the fuck are you doing?" she screamed. "I said to pull over *right now!*"

Max pushed the Miata past eighty. "What? And take the chance of getting my head blown off?" he answered. "No way."

She held the weapon with both hands, her arms shaking from the pressure of the situation and the jerking motion of the automobile. Max prayed she wouldn't accidentally pull the trigger, but he had to maintain control.

"Don't make me do it," she threatened. "I'll do it. I swear I will."

Max sensed that she was weakening. "Shoot me and we both die," he said with growing confidence. "Throw the gun out or I'll crash this car into the next tree, so help me, I will."

Her face blossomed with beads of sweat. "You're bluffing."

Max tried to remain calm. "I've got nothing to lose," he said. "Nothing's going right in my life anymore. If I die in an automobile accident, my wife will get plenty of life insurance, enough to compensate her for the embarrassment of her husband dying in the company of another woman. So if I die, *you die,* and my wife becomes a wealthy widow."

He watched the muscles in her neck constrict as she swallowed nervously. "We've got to go back for Skip," she gasped as if she hadn't heard a word he'd said. "Turn around. *Now.*"

Max slammed on the brakes, not to turn around but to avoid crashing into the embankment of a sharp curve in the highway. The resulting jolt jarred the girl off balance and jammed her against the dashboard and the windshield. The gun misfired high into the air, and Max had an opportunity to grab it but was afraid he'd lose control of the car at this excessive speed. By the time she straightened to a safe position he had pushed the car closer to ninety. "Next time I won't be able to make a curve like that," he warned her. "Throw the gun out. Get rid of it or we'll both look like ground beef at the next curve."

She looked ahead. Another sharp curve loomed in the distance. Max noted the mounting fear in her eyes and tried to hide his own. Her arms shook harder, and he jerked the steering wheel again, squealing the tires to frighten her more, and in one swift motion, without even looking, she tossed the revolver backward out of the car and collapsed into a pile of frazzled nerves in the passenger's seat beside him. Thank God, he thought, finally slowing to a more respectable speed.

"You're a fucking idiot!" she exclaimed. "You're crazy!" She dropped her head to her knees and Max saw the crack of her ass as she bent over and her shorts and the thin elastic band of her panties bulged slightly at her backside.

Max shook his head. How could he feel any attraction toward her at all after he'd almost been killed? Hell, he'd just survived two threats on his life and was thankful to be alive. But Max suddenly discovered an inner strength he hadn't previously known. Having always been the first to buckle under pressure, he was proud of himself. He'd faced death and won. He'd outwitted two criminals who were half his age and lived to tell about it. For once youth hadn't mattered; the elder had prevailed. For several miles neither of them spoke, and Max finally felt his adrenaline return to normal.

When the girl raised her head, her face was red from a fit of crying. Stunned that he still pitied her at all, Max tried to calm his anger. "My name is Max. What's yours—Lizzie Borden?"

She seemed to stare off into blank space. "T.J.," she finally answered. "Just T.J."

It didn't make sense. In one moment he wanted to put his arm around her and console her. In another he wanted to slap the shit out of her. It would be far easier to maintain realistic emotions if she wasn't such a sexpot. Max shook his head slightly as he glanced at her out the corner of an eye. He couldn't help wondering what could have driven such a lovely young woman into the arms of a man who had obviously ruined her life. She'd be lucky if the asshole hadn't survived the hit-and-run.

T.J.'s trancelike manner continued as a Tennessee highway patrol car approached in the opposite lane. "What will you do with me?" she asked when Max made no attempt to get the officer's attention. "Are you gonna turn me over to the cops?"

Max took a deep breath and noted how vulnerable she now appeared compared to the wild-eyed threat she posed moments earlier. "I haven't thought about that yet," he answered. "It's about forty minutes before we hit the next town. I'll have to think it over." His attention was riveted to the roundness of her breasts.

T.J. laughed half-heartedly. "Sure," she answered, rolling her eyes. "I know exactly what you're thinking." She shook her head and leered at him in disgust. "Men are all alike, no matter how old they are. It all comes down to a blow job, right?"

Her comment caught Max off-guard because that hadn't been a consideration at all. But since she'd brought it up and addressed him as "old" he couldn't get the possibility off his mind. What would be wrong with exchanging her freedom for sex? Hell, she'd pushed him to the brink of death. She'd forced him into behavior he'd never thought possible. She owed him *something*.

He watched her expression change to revulsion. "I've fucked my way out of jams before," she groaned. "Once more won't make any difference."

Max was so overcome by visions of her nude body spread out before him that he could still say nothing. He imagined squeezing her breasts, burying his nose in her pubic hair, and feeling himself sink into her vagina. His dick was harder than he could remember in years.

"Well?" she asked, exhaling in obvious boredom. "I would imagine that, unless you're gay, we've got ourselves a deal, right? After all, it'll only be your word against mine. I could tell the cops you tried to rape me if you took me to them."

Max's sweaty palms slipped on the steering wheel. Could she set him up even yet? He didn't think so. Her boyfriend would be found, dead or alive, and probably had a criminal record. The police were likely looking for him already, and she could easily be connected to him. Max seriously doubted she could turn the tables on him if he handed her over to the cops. But of course if he did that he'd miss out on the opportunity of a lifetime, to have sex with a woman who looked like she'd just stepped out of the pages of *Playboy*. Not even in his younger days had he made it with someone so stunning. It had been months since he'd even had sex with his wife. How could he possibly turn this down?

Max looked her over, wondering if she could detect his embarrassment. "A blow job in the car won't do. It'd have to be an all-nighter before I'd even consider it." He felt ashamed as he voiced his thoughts.

T.J. reached into her bag again and Max flinched, but she only pulled out a cigarette this time. Before she could even light it, he snatched it from her mouth and tossed it out of the car. "No smoking in the car," he said. "You might not be concerned about your own health, but I am about mine."

She laughed hysterically and doubled over to her knees until he could see her ass again. "You're such a fucking idiot," she finally said with a sneer. "You think one measly cigarette is unhealthy, but fucking someone you don't even know who's been with more men than she can count isn't? Shit, man, I don't claim to have AIDS. I've never been checked. But it wouldn't surprise me if I've got that and anything else you can catch by fucking strangers. I've been had by everything with two legs."

She made him feel like a fool. He'd stop for condoms; he was glad she reminded him, and he'd worry about the logistics of getting them later. But he resented her now more than ever. He wanted to fuck her hard, fuck her so savagely she'd never forget it. He wanted to fuck her for what she'd tried to do to him, for representing what he could no longer have at this stage of his life, for being so much sexier than his wife, for *knowing* how irresistible she was, and for using it to control the opposite sex. The egotistical cunt. He wanted to tie her down, something he'd never done with any other woman, and take out the rage of growing old in every orifice of her perfect smart-ass body.

"Lift your shirt," he said. "Show me what you've got."

She complied without batting an eye and displayed two of the shapeliest, most perfect breasts he'd ever seen. And they were real, too. No implants like the ones that bounced around in titty bars. Both nipples were pierced, just as he'd expected. An eighteen-wheeler suddenly approached from the distance. "Cover up," he said, not wanting to attract attention.

She refused, and in fact began to tug the T-shirt off

and over her head. *"Cover up!"* he demanded as he reached over to jerk the white cotton fabric down himself. The truck driver blasted his air horn as Max momentarily lost control of the car and it wandered slightly across the solid yellow line into the opposite lane. The tires screamed again as he righted his course, and T.J. did nothing but laugh.

"Not an all-nighter," she finally said in a serious tone. "I'd be too tempted to split your skull open after you fall asleep." Max wondered if she was all talk, if it had been pure bullshit when she'd threatened him before with the gun. But it probably wouldn't be wise to take any chances. He'd been lucky so far. The next time could prove fatal.

T.J. tried to unravel her windblown hair, but it was hopeless. Max wondered how the pierced rings between her fingers kept from snagging her hair. "Stop at the next motel, though, and let's get it over with. I want to get out of here."

They were about fifteen minutes from the next town, Max knew. And he also knew he wouldn't take her to the police regardless of whether she fucked him. He just didn't want to get involved. It would be far too embarrassing that he'd allowed himself to be duped not once, but twice. No, it was either pull over and let her out and say good-bye to the best piece of ass of a lifetime or stop at a motel and allow her to repay him for the torment she'd caused.

Before he could give his decision, T.J. made a wrinkled face and said, "I've got to pee real bad."

"We're not far from the next town," he said.

She shook her head. "I can't make it that long. I've got to pee *now.*"

Maybe she'd run if he stopped. Maybe that would be the end of it. He could make her leave her bag with him for security, but what would it matter if she ran? Hell, he was too old for this kind of shit. He needed rest. He wanted to forget this had ever happened. Maybe it wasn't worth the risk after all. Max exhaled, shook his head slightly, and pulled over to the side of the road near a cluster of pines. *"Pee,"* he said.

She was out like a flash, running toward the trees, and she hadn't taken her bag. Maybe it wasn't an escape attempt after all. He kept a steady eye on her until she disappeared behind tall brush, and then a speeding pickup truck slammed a wake of hot steamy air from the asphalt-melting highway into his face, rocking the small sports car as it passed.

Minutes crept by. Maybe she thought he'd come looking for her. She was probably hiding behind a tree with a rock or a heavy branch from a tree to brain him when he passed by. T.J. might be gullible, but she sure as hell wasn't stupid. This adventure was apparently over.

Max reached for her bag to toss it out for her as he drove away when she came trotting back from behind the trees. "Hey! You weren't gonna just *leave* me here, were you?" she asked incredulously. The touch of her smooth skin returned in an instant to his vivid imagination.

T.J. slumped back into the car and was actually giggling. "I peed on my leg," she said, laughing. "Man, I had to go *bad.*"

She must've had drugs in the pocket of her shorts, he mused. All of a sudden she was way too happy, like she was high on something. T.J. grinned at him and he noticed the only flaw in her appearance, nicotine-stained and slightly crooked teeth. But that wouldn't matter. Everything else looked so damn good, he could overlook that. She twisted in her seat to face him and placed her hand over his on the gearshift knob as he shoved into first to get back onto the highway. "Wait," she teased. "I brought you something."

Crumpled in her left hand were her soiled panties. "I thought you might like a sniff of things to come." She giggled as she dangled the bikini briefs in his face. When he raised his hand to snatch them, Max felt a sharp pain at his side.

The blade was short, probably no longer than a kid's pocket knife, but she'd buried it to its hilt in his side and the pain was excruciating. He reached back to grab her arm, but the confined space of the small sports car kept him at bay. "We don't need a motel," she said. "We can do it here, right up behind those trees." She pulled the blade out and jammed it in a second time.

Max shrieked in agony. The knife must have been concealed in her tight shorts, too difficult to remove while seated in the car without giving herself away. "Come on, let's go, big guy," she said, "before you bleed all over my new car."

"Please . . ." Max begged. "Just leave me and take the car. I won't—"

"Shut up, old fart," she interrupted.

Before he knew it, she was helping him out of the car, holding the knife at his side, and guiding him along the path to the pines before another car passed. Every step intensified the pain, and Max thought he'd pass out before reaching her destination. Maybe it was all for the best, he thought. Maybe he actually deserved this.

She prodded him farther until they were out of sight of the highway, then she stared him eye-to-eye in silence. Max held the wound at his side to slow the bleeding when, without warning, she kicked him hard in the groin. He crumpled to the ground, unable to determine which pain was worse. Max held the bleeding wounds with one hand and his groin with the other as she fished through his pockets for his wallet and anything else she could find.

Looking up as he lay flat on his back, Max watched late afternoon clouds drift slowly by. Pine needles on a nearby tree rustled from hot gusts of wind. A jetliner droned high overhead, its passengers likely enjoying snacks and a movie, oblivious to the carnage unfolding on the ground below. Sweat pooled across Max's forehead and dripped into his eyes, stinging and blurring his vision. And then she came into view again, standing at the foot of his crumpled form. There was a wickedness on her face like none he'd ever seen as she stripped the T-shirt up and over her head to free her breasts. "Men always think with their dicks," she gloated. *"I'm* the one with a criminal record as long as my arm. That jerk you ran over back there never committed a crime in his life. He was just pussy-whipped, that's all."

In his crippled condition and facing certain death, Max couldn't enjoy the display of raw nudity before him. He had no idea how much blood he'd lost; he just prayed he might live if she didn't inflict any further wounds.

"I thought you might like to see what you missed out on," T.J. hissed, "before you shrivel up and *die."* Sunlight glistened from the golden rings of her pierced nipples and between her fingers. She unbuckled and unzipped her shorts and dropped them to the ground, then danced and swayed around him as if to an imaginary beat only she could hear. Tossing back her hair, she swiveled her hips and bent her knees, bumping and grinding to the music inside her mind. Another ring glowed from her labia. Max knew in an instant she had danced in strip joints before. She had all the right moves, all the right curves—everything a man could ask for. Everything a *living* man could ask for. To a dying man the show meant nothing.

Max gasped for air. She stood with her feet planted at each side of his head to reveal a clear view of her bush and vagina. Then she swiveled her hips again, bending lower and lower, gyrating endlessly as her sex moved closer to his face. He reached up to push her away, but she slashed the top of his wrist, leaving a fresh thin trail of blood. God, if he'd only left her on the highway. If he had only been satisfied with the boring existence he'd shunned before, instead of opening the passenger door for this mindless killer to enter his life . . .

Her pubic bush tickled his nose as she continued the tease, the lips of her hot vagina brushing lightly against his own lips and chin. The ring at her labia teased his cheeks. As she gyrated to a standing position again, Max was partially blinded by the piercing rays of sunlight reflected from the golden rings all over her body. She reversed the dance and pivoted away from him, then repeated the bump and grind, lowering her perfectly rounded ass to his face. The cheeks of her butt pressed his nostrils closed, and it became difficult to breathe. And just as he passed out he felt the knife jab repeatedly at his left arm and shoulders.

When Max awakened the sky was dark, a dim half-moon barely illuminating his surroundings, but thank God he was still alive. He struggled to raise an arm to assess the damage to his body. Blood soaked his clothing in several places but at least the pain had diminished. Fortunately it seemed she had missed a major artery or vital organ with the short blade of the pocket knife. Max rolled to his side and tested his strength. There was no way he could stand or walk, but perhaps he could crawl back to the highway for help.

The journey took seemingly forever. Night creatures skittered through the nearby brush, probably rats, opossums, or snakes. More than once Max blacked out momentarily, then continued the trek. Struggling for air, he dragged his dead weight across the dusty ground, dead and dried pine needles jabbing his exposed skin. As he neared the rocky edge of the highway he found a small patch of fabric—her panties. Just as he'd expected, the Miata was gone, but a couple of his country music cassettes had been tossed to the ground nearby. Occasionally the headlights of passing cars illuminated the surroundings but no one could see him as he lay against the ground.

Got to stand up, he thought. *Got to get where someone will see me.*

Struggling to his knees, he saw approaching headlights top a nearby hill. He filled his lungs with air, then wobbled to his knees, watching the dual lights grow brighter and brighter until blinding his vision. He waved the panties like a white flag, to desperately signal an appeal for help, then felt the desolation inside his stomach multiply as the car sped past.

According to the emergency room nurse, the rural hospital was busier tonight than usual. He occupied a gurney and lay semiconscious but groggy as he was wheeled down the hallway toward the recovery room. A nurse, overweight and seemingly close to his own age, smiled down at him and patted his shoulder. "You're awfully lucky, sir," she said in a soothing voice. "You only needed minor surgery since the wounds weren't deep, but you would have almost certainly bled to death if a passing motorist hadn't called 911."

He tried to remember how he had come to be in the hospital, but for the moment couldn't even recall his own name, his memory impaired from the physical trauma and anesthesia. The nurse tenderly massaged his shoulders and there was something about her expression of compassion that seemed to contrast with whatever he'd experienced only a few hours earlier. When the anesthetic wore off and he'd rested sufficiently, he knew he'd remember, but he feared the memories would likely be unpleasant. "Thank you . . . for your help," he grunted in a rasping voice, but the nurse motioned for silence.

"You need to rest," she said as she pushed the gurney down the corridor leading to a bank of elevators. "Someone from the hospital staff will talk to you soon. You weren't carrying any identification, and the police have already asked how soon you'll be able to talk. In the meantime, just try to get some rest." It seemed strange that he might have been a crime victim. He'd assumed until now that he'd been involved in a traffic accident, but his head was so groggy that nothing made much sense just yet.

A body covered from head to toe with a blood-soaked sheet rounded a nearby corner too sharply on its gurney and shifted from the motion. A bloody female arm slipped from beneath the soiled sheet and there was something vaguely familiar about the brightly painted fingernails and the golden rings piercing the loose skin between the base of the hand's fingers. He nodded toward the crimson gurney as it passed in the opposite direction. "What happened?" he asked the nurse.

She slowly shook her head. "I'm not sure about the details," she finally commented. "She came in a couple of hours before you. I heard she lost control of her car at a pretty high rate of speed. Poor girl crashed into an embankment without wearing a seat belt. One of the orderlies told me she was driving one of those fancy topless sports cars and was thrown from the car against some rocks. I believe she was D.O.A."

Perplexing thoughts raced through the male patient's mind. Was there some sort of connection here?

Within moments he lay safely inside his own private room, becoming more cognizant moment by moment. He recalled his name, the kind of car he'd been driving, the gyrating motion of a young woman's genitals in his face, her hands planted firmly on her hips, one of which displayed an array of pierced rings between its fingers . . .

The police would be here soon.

He didn't know exactly where to begin.

STARR BRIGHT WILL BE WITH YOU SOON!

Joyce Carol Oates

At the Golden Sands, Las Vegas, Nevada

She was here, somewhere. He'd know when he saw her and maybe, even, she'd know him.

He carried himself through the crowds with the cocky air of a man bearing a secret too good to keep for long. Sucking a cigarette, licking his upper lip with his tongue as if savoring it, eyes roving, searching. He wore $150 cowhide boots with a substantial heel, designer jeans, a sporty wide-shouldered Italian-style gunmetal-gray silk-cotton-and-polyester jacket, and a black silk shirt open at the throat. He was, with the heels, almost five foot ten; muscular through the chest and shoulders (a former athlete, maybe? high school football?); his flesh just slightly soft, going flaccid at the waist (but the stylish jacket hid that); his hair, receding sharply at the temples, was brush-colored and wiry and had been combed at artful angles to minimize hair loss. With his close-set watchful eyes and sharp-boned western-looking face he resembled a hawk ever vigilant for prey. Here in Vegas for the weekend he was thinking he deserved a good time, deserved some goddamned happiness like anybody else and he meant to get it.

In the Barbary Coast casino into which he'd stepped out of a sun-glaring temperature of 97°F, a blast of refrigerated air caressed his forehead like a woman's soothing fingers. *Mmmmm,* he liked the sensation; he believed it was his due.

Back home in Sumner County, Nebraska, he had a life known to many; a "career"; an identity linked primarily to the career. He was proud enough of this without being blind to the fact that probably he'd never be promoted much beyond his present rank. When thinking along these familiar lines he was in the habit, when alone, of shrugging and muttering aloud, "So? What the hell." Smiling a quick pained smile as if some asshole had told a joke meant to be hilarious and, sure, Ernie Fenke was a good sport, he'd laugh.

It wasn't the first time he'd flown to Vegas for a weekend. And this time a three-day weekend, end of October. Leaving the Omaha airport late on Thursday, taking a single suitcase containing his Vegas clothes, which were not clothes he wore in Sumner County, Nebraska. They were not clothes his wife knew about, nor anyone in his family; he kept them in a locker at headquarters. Going to Vegas once or twice a year was his own business, nobody else's. None of his colleagues knew, either. In dreams he saw himself illuminated and virile as on a video screen. In dreams he had the power to gamble away all the cash in his pocket, reaching deep into his pockets and drawing out more, more, more, no end to the cash he had, he'd live forever. At craps, at blackjack, at poker betting ever higher stakes and winning as strangers watched in awe; beautiful women watched in awe. He worried he might be a binge gambler, maybe a binge drinker, he knew from professional experience what a deadly combination this was, what it did to even intelligent, decent people; but he was too smart to allow any such weakness to overcome him. *It's just I deserve a good time, shit, a man deserves some happiness doesn't he!*

His wife Lynette, poor sweet dumb girl he'd married, already pregnant, out of high school, the best-looking of the varsity cheerleaders, but he'd always known how to keep her in line. Not scared of him exactly but never fully at ease, not her or the kids, never taking Ernie Fenke for granted the way the wives of most of his friends took them for granted. Why couldn't I come with you just once, Lynette would ask, and he'd tell her bluntly no, these were professional trips, not vacations; these were "conferences" and "seminars" he had to attend, not in Vegas but, for instance, Salt Lake City, another time Albuquerque, this time Des Moines—hardly places a man would choose to spend a three-day weekend. And maybe Lynette believed him, and maybe she didn't; looking sometimes as if she had more to say but hesitated to say it.

Though never once in eighteen years of marriage had he hit her, and vowed he never would, Ernie Fenke wasn't that kind of man. Not in Sumner County, Nebraska.

In Vegas he rented a car and checked in, not at one of the big hotels, but at the Golden Sands Motor Lodge on the strip, a motel of no distinction, moderate-priced with a pool he wouldn't use and where each room opened out directly onto the parking lot. Which was what you required when you required privacy. Not like the high-rise hotel, the Sahara, he'd made the mistake of staying in on his first Vegas visit six or seven years ago, bringing a girl back to his room and when things got too rough the girl had lost it and started screaming and within minutes a house dick had pounded on the door and he'd had no choice but to open it, disheveled and sweating and wearing only trousers he'd hastily yanked on, but managing to say in an offended voice, "Officer, there's nothing wrong here, just my girlfriend and me," and the detective said pleasantly, "I'll need to look around, it's just routine." And so the man had come in and looked around, sniffing like he smelled a bad odor, and the girl was in the bathroom hurriedly fixing herself up, and Ernie said, "My girlfriend is a screamer, that's all it is. Somebody called down to the desk?" and the detective said, pausing outside the bathroom door upon which, too, he knocked, "Oh, yeah? Is your girlfriend a screamer?" and Ernie said, managing to laugh, laughter like clearing his throat of clotted mucus, "Yeah, but I don't hold it against her." The girl then emerged from the bathroom, in a kimono wrapped tight about her short-legged, chesty body; she'd slapped on makeup to disguise the welts on the underside of her jaw, and she was wearing bright lipstick, and she was smiling; stiff-bleached hair falling over half her face, and her eyes glassy as marbles. "Tell this officer there's no problem, Sonya," Ernie said, and Sonya said, "Officer, no problem," with a twitchy smirk. Ernie was wondering if he should offer the detective a bill or two, fifty dollars maybe; or would that be a mistake of offering him money which was a goddamned insult— as if he, Ernie Fenke, was looking for bribes; as if he, Ernie Fenke, was in fact bribable!—which maybe in another set of circumstances he might be, but these days sting operations were so common, in the papers and on TV, so anyone who imagined Ernie Fenke was stupid enough or desperate enough to be tempted to take a bribe had insulted him doubly. So he decided no; and the girl was convincing enough; and the detective seemed to want to believe them, backing off and saying in a bored voice, "Okay, kids, but take it easy from now on." So it was okay, but Christ he'd resented having to deal with it. He resented his privacy invaded and scrutinized by some S.O.B. private cop near enough to him in age, size, disposition, and possibly income to be his twin brother. So he'd never returned to any big hotel again, much preferring the small two-story motels along the strip like the Golden Sands, which was about two miles from the center of Vegas.

At Caesar's Palace, at Pleasure Island and the Mirage and the Hilton and the Sahara. At craps, at poker, at blackjack and at craps again. He'd won a few bucks, and lost; lost, and won; drew on his American Express card taking a chance he'd win enough to keep going, and so he did; for five hours of strain coming out a lousy $238 ahead. And he hadn't yet hooked up with a girl, he'd been so anxious waiting to get hot, really hot; but it wasn't happening.

I need one, I need a woman. For luck.

He had a habit, not nervous exactly but half-conscious, of slipping his hand inside his jacket and rubbing his chest; touching the .32-caliber pistol he carried close beneath his heart everywhere he went as if to check yes it's there, he's okay.

At last at a crowded roulette table he sighted a good-looking redhead in an eye-catching costume: sexy gold lamé minidress and high-heeled cork shoes, she appeared to be alone, though plenty of guys were noticing her; numerous rings on her fingers so he couldn't tell if she wore a wedding band, but in the case of a woman like this, what would a wedding band signify if the husband wasn't within a hundred feet of her? A divorcée Ernie supposed; maybe spending a few days in Vegas to clear out her head; looking for a pickup, too—maybe. It was Saturday night, after all. (In Vegas it was always Saturday night except for a few depressing hours on Sunday morning.) He saw her pushing chips out, and not getting chips back; pushing chips out, and not getting chips back. He saw a hurt, stung, scared look in her face that was the look of a woman losing a bet; he couldn't see how much she'd lost, but he was glad she'd lost; when a woman wins, she isn't likely to need a man. He followed her when she left the table abruptly, walking quickly in her high-heeled shoes, her pale face slightly flushed, a breathless look to her, hoped to hell she wasn't meeting up with some guy. Red-haired and sexy and not too old for him, in her late twenties possibly; reminded him of Sharon Stone, that tough-sexy look. Like her legs would wrap around you and practically break your back and you'd love it. He didn't like it that she was tall, preferred shorter women, of course the heels added inches to her height and when she kicked them off she'd be more to his taste. A creamy-pale face smooth as a mask, not much expression, a bright red mouth like something gouged into flesh. He followed her through the casino, in and out of crowds, possibly she was aware of him by now and not minding it that he, a good-looking guy, was following her; you don't dress like that, wear your hair tousled like that unless you want men to look seriously at you, and think serious thoughts about you. Jesus!—that gold lamé dress that fitted her slender but voluptuous body as if she'd been poured into it! The sight turned him on, shiny gold fabric tight as a tourniquet especially at her belly, pelvis. Her legs were long as a dancer's legs, maybe she was a showgirl, or had been; long, bare, smooth legs; a thin gold chain around her left ankle. *Honey look at me: Ernie Fenke's your man.* He was disappointed, though, she'd gone to the slot machines; losing at roulette and back to playing slots, both of them sheer blind chance and slots the lowest form of casino gambling. And she wasn't having luck here, either. Slots was a sucker's game, took no brains at all, still there's always the flutter of hope you *might* win; rigged to favor the house ninety-nine times out of one hundred, but you *might* win; there were wins timed regularly in a row of machines to keep the credulous hopeful; to keep the suckers going, going, and gone. Until the last quarter is gone. And the good-looking redhead was losing; playing with an air of expectation tinged with hurt; a childlike look to her glamour-face; she was playing and losing, playing and losing so Ernie felt sorry for her; it was an emotion he enjoyed, feeling sorry for women. As long as it wasn't expected of him. This woman was looking anxious now, and she was looking more and more like someone in need of company. She paused in her playing to open a blue-sequined purse to look for, Ernie guessed, a pack of cigarettes she couldn't seem to find. "Here y'are," Ernie said, his own pack in his hand, there he was smiling and available and ready to assist; the woman lifted her eyes to him in mild surprise, pleasantly, as if she hadn't been aware of him watching her intensely for the past ten minutes or more. She smiled in return, and accepted the cigarette, and said in a throaty, husky voice so soft Ernie Fenke had to lean close, inhaling her perfume, to hear, "Why, thank *you.*"

So they met in the Century, in the midst of numerous strangers avidly playing slots, and became acquainted; very quickly acquainted, for in Vegas there isn't time to spare. "What's your name?" he asked, and in her soft-sweet-sexy voice she said, "Sherrill," and he said, "'Sherrill'—I like that name. Sherrill what?" and she said, "Sherrill Dwyer," so easily and looking him full in the face so he believed absolutely she was telling the truth. He grabbed her hand and shook it, squeezing the soft, rather cold fingers hard, "I'm Earl Tunley," which was the name of a right-wing state congressman from Sumner County, Nebraska, and she said, " 'Earl'—I like it, I've never known any 'Earl' close up," and he said, "There's always a first time, Sherrill, right?" and they laughed together as if this was quite a joke. And he saw that Sherrill Dwyer's eyes were a cool bluish-gray, like pebbles washed by rain; he saw without exactly noting that he saw, in the excitement of the moment, white near-invisible lines radiating outward from the corners of her eyes. He smelled something metallic and ashy beneath the ripe-peaches scent of her perfume. He liked what he saw, and what he smelled, and the effect she was having on him, a sexual stirring he understood to be the stirring of his luck, returning to him. He asked would she like a drink, and she said yes; and later he asked would she like something to eat, and she said yes; it was clear they got along, Earl and Sherrill, they liked each other a lot, understood each other it seemed; maybe even, as Sherrill speculated, they'd somehow met before, in another lifetime. Wasn't that possible? So Earl Tunley laughed indulgently and said, "Sweetheart, in Vegas anything's possible."

It was 2 A.M., a giddy crazy hour in Vegas and not really a time for serious eating. So they left most of their food on their plates and retired to the Golden Sands, to room nineteen, to become better acquainted. Ernie who was Earl bought a bottle of Jim Beam en route and two packs of Camels and they were feeling good, keyed up and amorous and grateful to have found each other. Their first time in bed, to be specific on top of the king-size bed, was so great so terrific so fantastic it truly did seem, as Sherry insisted, they'd known each other in another lifetime.

And Earl sighed yes, could be. Lying then naked and luxuriant smoking cigarettes, sipping whiskey out of tumblers, still too excited to sleep. In Vegas, who wants to sleep? Earl Tunley was saying he was from Council Bluffs, Iowa; owned a TV-video store; Sherrill who'd become Sherry in his arms, blowing in his ear and moaning in sexual heat, described herself as a P.R. girl from Fresno, California, between jobs. She was staying in a motel farther out on the strip, not liking the congestion of the big hotels—"And all these crude guys hitting on you." Earl wasn't a married man any longer, he'd been married for almost ten years and lucky he and his wife hadn't had any children so he was spared child support and his ex-wife was remarried so she was out of his hair permanently; and what about her, Sherry?—and glamorous red-haired Sherry said, sighing, for a fleeting moment sad, that she'd been married, too, at the age of eighteen; but it had ended a few years later, and she tried never to think about it. She said, "I was just a child, back in—this small town in Pennsylvania no one's ever heard of. I thought it was true, deep love Michael and I felt for each other but it was a delusion, oh, I was flattered this rich man's son, who'd been a football hero at our high school a few years ahead of me, was crazy about *me.*" And she wiped carefully at her eyes, not wanting the silvery-blue eye shadow and the inky black mascara to run; perhaps the makeup was waterproof, since it didn't run.

In a playful growling voice Earl who was Ernie, unless he was Ernie who was Earl, said, "Sweetheart, anybody'd be crazy about *you.*" And it was time to make love again. Jesus, he was feeling good!—feeling his old luck return, coursing through his veins, into his cock, like molten gold. Whoever he was, Earl, Ernie, Tunley, Fenke, or somebody not yet known, he was grateful to this terrific woman, and he was the kind of good-sport good-hearted basically generous guy to show it. Only watch.

Am I afraid?—I am not.
Am I despairing?—I am not.
For You have given me a sign, & Your blessing. & I am patient, I have learned to bide my time.

The next man, maybe. Always there was the promise of the next man. When she danced, always there was the promise of being singled out, raised above the others, a photo-feature in a newspaper, or in *Nevada By Night:* "Starr Bright." Always the promise of a really serious male admirer who would love her for herself alone and wish to marry her.

Now, no longer dancing, lacking that arena for display, "Starr Bright" was temporarily disadvantaged. And her money was rapidly running out.

Not just money for food, for necessities, and a decent place to stay, but money sufficient to maintain "Starr Bright's" cultured-classy appearance; the crucial "Starr Bright" appearance that made all the difference. For you can't attract the attention of a worthwhile man unless you look good; and looking good, even if you're a beautiful woman, doesn't come cheaply.

Where had the money gone?—*her* money she'd earned. She'd counted $692 from the man's wallet before tossing the wallet away in a developer's landfill off route 80 where no one would ever find it; $692 which should have been enough to stake her for a while, staying at the cheapest motel in Vegas she could tolerate, and mainly playing the slots which was minimal risk with the possibility of a big jackpot; in fact she'd won a $444 jackpot at Vegas World on her second night but hadn't been able to repeat the win; believing that her luck was building up, gradually building up like steam pressure that had to explode eventually. When the slot machines disappointed, she'd tried blackjack, roulette, keno, and the Nevada State Lottery, praying *Just this once, O Lord, and I will never ask another favor of you.* And perhaps she believed this, and meant it. As years ago, when they were little girls, she'd cajoled her sister Lily into praying with her, reasoning that double prayers had double power.

One of "Starr Bright's" problems was that if she'd been drinking she was susceptible to wild mood swings. She was susceptible to behaving impulsively. Bursting into tears—tears of happiness?—when she'd won the $444 in silver coins. And later that night meeting up with a sobbing fat woman who'd lost all her money in the casinos and said she had nowhere to go and the woman's name was Lilia (which could not have been a coincidence, could it?) and "Starr Bright" had peeled off three crisp $50 bills to press into the woman's hand. And the woman had stared at her in disbelief, and stammered thanks, and blessed "Starr Bright" as an angel of mercy sent direct from God.

Just this once, O Lord. And I will never sin again.

Though knowing that God disapproved of gambling. Disapproved of these sinful cities of the plain Sodom and Gomorrah. As in her innermost heart she disapproved. For hadn't she been brought up in a devout Christian household to love God and her savior Jesus Christ above all earthly vanities; brought up to know that the wages of sin are death. But: There are times of upheaval when you have no choice except to gamble, gamble your very life, you're desperate and run to earth and this was one of those times, He would understand, surely He would understand. A God of wrath but also a God of mercy and forgiveness.

For this was the one true fact: He was always guiding her hand.

"Starr Bright's" trembling hand gripping the razor-sharp carving knife that was her secret protection.

For if He had not guided her hand, how could she have acted? How could she have defended herself against her violator?

As, that morning in October, she'd driven in the rental Infiniti from Sparks to Reno, from Reno to Vegas, how many solitary hours in the desert singing hymns at the top of her lungs she hadn't sung in more than twenty years, singing a tune of her childhood:

> Starr Bright will be with you soon!
> Starr Bright will be with you soon!
> Starr Bright, Starr Bright!
> Starr Bright will be with you soon!

And laughing, and talking to herself, and already she'd begun to forget; what had happened in the Paradise Motel she'd begun to forget; for forgetting is part of healing, and God's grace is to heal. At dawn, as the fiery eye emerged from the dark side of the earth, she'd known that she would be guided, she would not come to harm. A wind rose out of the desert blowing dust and tumbleweed across the highway and she'd arrived in a gritty cloud obscuring the sun. Calmly locking the Infiniti with a gloved hand and tossing the keys beneath the car and walking away unobserved carrying her Gucci bag and other items, traveler's items, through the sea of vehicles parked at the Mirage. *And I saw a sea of glass mingled with fire and knew I had come to the right place.* In this Sodom and Gomorrah of the desert "Starr Bright" stepped into a dream, but it was not a dream of her own, it was not a dream that depended upon her to sustain it, it was a dream already existing, in which she could hide, as a hunted creature can hide in the wilderness; she'd been in such cities before, and knew the solace of such anonymity. And in a women's rest room at the Mirage she'd changed certain of her outer garments and fitted her beautiful red wig exactingly to her head, it was a finely woven #300 human-hair wig she'd purchased for professional reasons in Miami that had the power to change her appearance, and her personality, utterly. And so if pigs' eyes moved onto her snagging onto her they were not eyes to capture *her*.

Thank you O God for this safe passage.

Strange then the next morning to read in the tabloid *Las Vegas Post* the banner headline

BLOODY RITUAL EXECUTION
"PIG DEATH" IN SPARKS MOTEL ROOM

because already she'd forgotten so much. Because already she'd begun to heal. Like the ugly welts on her breasts and her belly and between her legs that were beginning to heal, with God's grace. Like the bruises at the nape of her neck and at the small of her back where he'd straddled her. It was an ugly, lurid but fascinating story the *Post* had featured on its cover and inside front pages. How many times such had happened, and would happen. In the desert, beneath the vast empty sky into which you might fall, fall forever. A DO NOT DISTURB sign had hung outside the door of a motel room for a full day, the blinds of the room had been closed tight and the customer's car was gone from the lot and there appeared to be no activity and at last a maid unlocked the door to discover to her horror what waited inside to be discovered. *A forty-seven-year-old California man lying in a pool of congealed blood. A corpse bloodied, mutilated, naked. His throat slashed so he'd bled to death and there were multiple stab wounds in the*

*genital area and there was blood splattered everywhere,
even on the ceiling. And on the wall beside the bed in
eight-inch bloody letters:*

DIE PIG FILTH
DIE SATAN

Trying not to be scared, living as she was from day
to day, hour to hour. The slots, blackjack, roulette and
keno and the lottery and again the slots. Waiting for
her luck to change. Waiting for a man, the right man.
Waiting for a sign. And there was Earl Tunley so
powerfully attracted to her, she saw desire shining in
the man's eyes suffusing her like flame. Hadn't she
reason to believe her life might be changed for the
better? Hadn't she reason to believe her bad-luck
streak had ended?

Wanting to believe that Earl Tunley in his cowhide
boots, black silk shirt, and Armani-style jacket, Earl
Tunley with his hot, quick hands and mouth was truly
from Council Bluffs, Iowa; for she had the idea that a
man who sold TV and video equipment in Council
Bluffs, Iowa, was a man you could trust. And he'd
promised to stake her "as much as required" and this,
too, she wanted to believe.

Except hadn't there been, from the start, something
swaggering and authoritarian in his manner. As if,
somehow, she'd met this man before?

After their fantastic lovemaking, there she lay naked and content in Earl Tunley's king-size bed in the
Golden Sands Motor Lodge lazily stroking Earl
Tunley's chest, running her long polished fingernails
through his steely-gray chest hairs and stroking the
glittering gold chain he wore around his neck which

looked like the real thing, 24-carat, and she'd thought with girlish naiveté *This one, this one maybe I could love, maybe* seeing in her mind's eye dimmed and confused by alcohol and by the late hour something looming chalky white, a dreamy image of Council Bluffs, Iowa. And her new lover was smiling saying, "You want it, sweetheart? Take it." And for an instant she ran her hands rapidly over his muscular body, stroking his clammy-cool penis reverently until he groaned, forgetting any sarcasm, any doubt of her motives, and it was all right between them again. Or seemed so.

"Oh, lover. Oh, my God—"

Later, in the bathroom, readying herself for another stint of casino gambling (though in fact she'd rather have soaked in a hot tub and gone to bed to sleep, alone) she realized that the ugly moment between "Sherry" and her new lover had been her own damned fault. She'd made the guy anxious alluding to a former husband—a "boyfriend"—God knows, men are worried about their sexual performances, this one had tensed up at even the hint she might have been comparing him to some teenage "football hero" stud. That was it!

An error "Starr Bright" vowed never to make again with Earl Tunley, or another.

JACKPOT!
$1000 SILVER DOLLARS JACKPOT!

"Oh, Earl! Look!"—as the slot machine released a cascade of silver dollars like madness.

Laughing, incredulous, cigarettes clenched between their lips, they held CASINO AMERICANA buckets to the machine's opening, to catch the miraculous coins. "Baby, you've got the touch. Congratulations!" Earl said, kissing her as a small crowd of onlookers cheered and applauded. Envy shining in their eyes, "Starr Bright" could see even in the midst of her exhilaration. Envy not just that "Starr Bright" had won a $1000 SILVER DOLLARS JACKPOT—the machine lighted up red, white, and blue like a berserk American flag, hurdy-gurdy music playing loudly—but that she was a beautiful glamorous sexy redhead in a gold lamé dress tight as a tourniquet across her breasts and pelvis and she had a lover, good-looking, manly, a gold chain glinting around his neck, clearly crazy for her. *Thank you God thank you God thank you God.*

"Now, let's play craps. Slots is small-time."

"Oh, but Earl, honey—"

"Baby, don't worry, I'll stake you—$500. The $1000 is all yours."

"But, Earl, craps scares me; you can lose too much too fast. I trust the slots."

"Baby, I told you: Slots is small-time. Craps is the real thing."

Earl had staked "Sherrill Bright" for the slots; she'd played as many machines simultaneously as she could manage, while he looked on indulgently, supplying them both with drinks, cigarettes. Now it was 3:43 A.M. in the casino at the Americana amid lavish neon-flashing red-white-and-blue American flags, eagles, replicas of Uncle Sam and Abraham Lincoln, George Washington, John F. Kennedy gazing out over the swarming sea of gamblers. "Starr Bright" had been playing the slots only twenty minutes when she'd won the jackpot and she owed her good luck to Earl Tunley, leaning now against the man, twining herself around him, inhaling his rich ripe manly odor, liking that people were watching them, sad-faced fattish women with too much makeup who hadn't ever won a jackpot and hadn't any man to love them like Earl Tunley. "All right, lover," she said, sighing, hugging the bucket of gleaming new-minted silver coins, "you know best."

So they left the slots, and went to play craps; "Starr

Bright" dazed with excitement, exhaustion; smiling upon everyone she saw; in a state of bliss. Her lover Earl was excited, too; edgy, positioning himself at the craps table with "Starr Bright" beside him, at his left elbow—"Now don't budge. You're my good luck, baby." Calling her "baby" so frequently now she guessed he'd maybe forgotten her name.

Earl pushed out $300 worth of chips and got into the game immediately. And when "Starr Bright" opened her eyes again he'd won: Chips were being pushed in his direction. "Starr Bright" kissed him, crying, "Terrific, lover!" But Earl scarcely paid attention, gathering in his new chips and mingling them with the old. He counted out $500 worth of chips for "Starr Bright" and told her to do what he said; they'd both be betting, and he intended to win, big. "Starr Bright" pretended enthusiasm; she'd been drinking whisky sours, on a near-empty stomach; she smiled, smiled and looked gorgeous which was what a gambling man required, a great-looking redhead beside him at the craps table. "Okay, baby," Earl said, drawing in a deep, exhilarated breath, like a man on a high diving board, "bet *pass.*" When "Starr Bright" hesitated, Earl closed his hand over hers and pushed out a pile of chips. The principal player at the table was a fattish flush-faced man with startling blue eyes; he was the one who wielded the dice, and all eyes avidly fastened upon him as he shook, and rolled— and whatever it was, half the players at the table seemed to have won, along with him; and half the players seemed to have lost. Earl grunted with satisfaction, squeezing "Starr Bright's" hand so hard he nearly crushed the bones, so she figured they'd won. How much? It looked like a lot.

At 4:10 A.M. it was Earl Tunley's turn to shake the dice. "Starr Bright" had been drifting off, woozy and blissful in her private space thinking *My jackpot! My one thousand silver dollars!* She hated craps, a fast, cruel, confusing game involving numerous players, side bets on bets, "points" that were made, or lost; the rapid motion of dice, chips, dice, chips was too much for her eye to follow; the pattern of numerals and figures on the tabletop, the calm expressionless manner with which the uniformed casino girl (beautiful, years younger than "Starr Bright") raked in piles of chips with a little Plexiglass rake, taking hundreds or even thousands of dollars from losing players without a blink of an eye—God, what a cruel game! "Starr Bright" followed Earl's directions betting he'd make his point, she wasn't aware of how much she was betting, only that he'd staked her and she couldn't lose, could she?—the bucket of silver dollars was at her feet. She wanted him to love her, she'd experienced, almost, a glimmer of emotion, and of sexual excitement, in his arms, in his king-size bed at the Golden Sands Motor Lodge. There was something consoling about Council Bluffs, Iowa—wasn't there? *A pig like any of them, a mask of Satan. You know.* Earl was nudging her impatiently to place a bet, "Everything you have, baby," and "Starr Bright" said in a pleading little-girl voice, "Oh, Earl honey— *everything?* I'm scared to go all the way." Earl's face shone with an oily perspiration and the gold chain glittered around his neck like a living thing. His eyes were red-veined, but sharp. He was saying, boasting, "Redheads are my good luck," loud enough for other players, men, to hear. "Starr Bright" saw both her hands, trembling just visibly, push out a messy pile of chips onto the pass line. How much? How much was she risking? Grandly, Earl shook the dice, shook and rolled and all stared as the dice turned up four and three.

"Seven! Won!"

Earl was grinning, excited as a kid. The casino girl scarcely gave him a glance as she pushed a large pile of chips in his direction. Cool as swabbing down an emergency room splattered with blood, "Starr Bright" thought. That was the kind of professional hauteur you needed to be an exotic dancer, too.

Thank God, they'd won. Five thousand? Or more? Earl gulped down the remainder of his drink, sex-moaned in "Starr Bright's" ear, "Oh baby, baby—" but didn't otherwise pause. No time to rest, no time to catch his breath, Earl wanted to stay in the game now he was hot. "Starr Bright" was beginning to feel faint. Not long ago she'd been a terrified passenger in a Porsche being driven at one hundred miles an hour along a rain-slick highway and it was the identical sensation—exciting, exhilarating, but crazy and dangerous. Too much too fast.

By 4:35 A.M. they'd won—what? Thirteen thousand, Earl was saying. He was counting his chips, muttering to himself, grinning and wiping his damp face; his eyes were glassy and bright and his lips slack, loose. There was something about him "Starr Bright" could almost identify, some characteristic, trait—but what? As if she'd met him before this night, or someone very like him. He was looking flushed with success. He hadn't wanted to take time to shower or even wash himself after they'd made love, eager to get back to the casinos, and now a powerful odor wafted from him, "Starr Bright" hoped no one else at the table could smell it—male sex, male heat, male passion. *A filthy pig like any other. You know.* She had to admit, winning made a man sexy; winning made a man desirable; this was a man she could love, maybe. Except he'd developed a habit of nudging her in the breast saying, irritated, "Stand still, right here, don't be moving around, I told you. You're my good-luck piece of ass." And he laughed loudly, and "Starr Bright" tried to smile. He was shaking dice again, he'd pushed out half his enormous pile of chips and wanted "Starr Bright" to bet he'd make his point so vaguely, blindly she pushed out half her pile of chips, too.

Thinking *God, don't let us lose. Let him love me.* A dazed-groggy prayer that was the same prayer mouthed everywhere in Vegas by hundreds, thousands of anxious gamblers every second of every hour of every day.

Another time, Earl Tunley rolled and won.

Following this things became even more confused. A roller coaster going faster, faster, faster. They'd won twelve thousand dollars? Fifteen, twenty? Her lover from Council Bluffs, Iowa, and glamorous sexy red-haired "Sherrill Dwyer" from—somewhere in California. Earl was saying, gloating, "Jesus, I'm hot. Back home they can kiss my ass. A man needs respect and this is *it.*" He'd been squeezing "Starr Bright's" upper arm, there were red welts in the flesh. Now that she had money again, she could repay the loan from her sister—what had it been? $500, not much—she'd had the feeling that her sister's husband, whose name she couldn't remember, resented the loan, or loans; well, fuck him! Lily's sister Sharon always repaid her loans and with interest, too.

"Starr Bright" must have been easing away, her feet aching in the ridiculous high-heeled shoes that pinched her toes, forcing the weight of her body into a tiny pointed space, for Earl Tunley gripped her arm again and smiled hard at her and repositioned her at his side. "Now stay still, baby. We're going for broke." "Starr Bright" winced. "Please, Eddy—that hurts," and Earl said, his voice slurred, "'Ernie' you mean— no: 'Earl.' You mean 'Earl,'" and "Starr Bright" said quickly, "'Earl'—that's what I said, honey. 'Earl' is your name," and Earl laughed harshly saying, "Fucking 'Earl' is my fucking name, not fucking 'Eddy,'" his laughter explosive as a sneeze. He took up the dice again exuberantly and "Starr Bright" murmured, "Here we gooo! Sky's the limit!" and planted a kiss on his burning cheek; but instead of rolling the dice as everyone expected, Earl turned to her, his lips drawn back from his teeth in a savage grin, and said, "Watch it, cunt. I'm warning you." So "Starr Bright" went very still, and contrite. And Earl rolled the dice, and came up with a number that wasn't good, muttered, "Shit," so "Starr Bright" thought in a panic they'd lost, but, as it turned out, he had another roll and another chance, and this time he rolled—two sixes. And this wasn't good, either. "Starr Bright" said in a giggly-drunken little-girl voice, a voice meant to dispel the sickening sensation in the pit of her belly, "Oh, damn! You'd think a twelve would be better than an eleven, wouldn't you?"

But no one laughed. Glazed-eyed Earl didn't hear.

No pause in the game. Not a heartbeat. A few of the players avoided Earl's eyes out of brotherly sympathy perhaps. "Starr Bright" stared as the casino girl coolly raked in Earl's big pile of chips—and "Starr Bright's"—without an eyeblink. How much had they lost? "Starr Bright" was whispering, "Oh, lover. Ohhhh." She meant to console him slipping her arm through his, but he shook her off, muttered something she didn't catch, stooped to take up the bucket of silver dollars from the floor and as "Starr Bright" stared uncomprehending after him he went to a nearby cashier's counter to cash the silver dollars into chips. And came back, grim, determined, sweat gleaming on his face like congealed grease, and the look in his eyes warning her not to fuck with him. "Starr Bright" tried to protest faintly, "Earl, honey, those silver dollars were mine, you said—you promised," and Earl repositioned her at his side and said, "Just stand still, baby. And shut the mouth."

So Earl bet one thousand dollars worth of chips on

a single roll and "Starr Bright" hid her eyes behind her trembling fingers praying *God oh God!* though seeming to know the prayer was helpless to intervene. And even as Earl threw the dice, sent them flying and bouncing across the table, "Starr Bright" must have suffered a moment's weakness, a mini-blackout— falling against him, so that, even as he lost the roll, he'd turned to her and slapped her across the mouth, the movement of his hand so swift that no one at the table saw, or seemed to see; and "Starr Bright" herself could not comprehend what had happened, except her lower lip throbbed with pain and began to bleed. Earl's face had gone the color of bread dough and his bloodshot eyes glared. "Cunt, I told you not to fuck me up," he said, advancing upon her as others at the table scrambled to get out of the way, leaving "Starr Bright" to her boyfriend's mercy, "didn't I tell you *not to fuck me up.*"

"Earl, I'm sorry—"

"Y'know what you cost me, cunt?—*twenty-seven thousand dollars!*"

Abruptly, as if he'd emerged from out of a trapdoor, a casino security guard appeared, a hefty black man of few words, "That's enough, mister, come this way please," and before they knew what was happening they were being escorted politely but unerringly out of the casino. "Starr Bright" supposed that the girl at the craps table had summoned the guard with a secret buzzer. Earl was sullen, blustering, and intimidated, his words slurred, "Butt out, asshole, this is a private discourse, this cunt cost me a bundle," and "Starr Bright" was trying earnestly to explain, "Sir, he doesn't mean it, he's my friend, he didn't hurt me, he's excited 'cause he just took a big loss," and Earl said angrily, "Shut it!" and "Starr Bright" said, "Really, sir, he's the sweetest man, he never meant—" But the robotlike guard who was six-foot-five, two hundred fifty pounds, and dark-skinned as a polished hickory nut seemed scarcely to hear as if this, his task, was too familiar and too boring to require from him more than a few clipped words mechanical as a recitation, "Thank you for patronizing the Casino Americana and perhaps another time you will revisit us under more favorable circumstances." When Earl hesitated at the exit, the guard hoisted him into the revolving door and gave the door a fierce spin and a moment later Earl and "Starr Bright" were out in the warm, faintly sulphurous night.

Earl said, aggrieved as a lost child, wiping his face on the sleeve of his Italian-style jacket, "Craps is my *game*. I was *w-winning*."

"Starr Bright" slipped her arm around his waist (which was warm and rumpled as damp laundry) and said, soothingly, "That's right, Earl, you *were* winning. You *were*. You can win again. You can draw on your American Express card, can't you, lover? Sure you can."

Because I had hope, still, that he would love me. I would love him.
Because I was afraid to be alone that terrible night.
Because I wanted the $1000 he owed me.
Because I knew that my heavenly father would watch over me in time of peril.

And at first it had not seemed an unwise decision. She had not seemed in immediate danger.

Taking a cab back to the Golden Sands Motor Lodge because the man who'd introduced himself to her as Earl Tunley wasn't in any condition to drive. Stumbling into the dim-lit room that smelled still of their bodies, and stained bedclothes; fecund odors of sweat, semen, damp wadded towels, and insecticide.

Always the odor of insecticide. And Earl was amorous in his misery, wishing not to think of the many thousands of dollars he'd lost which seemed to him in his confusion to have been his money from the start, stolen from him by the cruelty of chance and a woman's blundering. Kissing "Starr Bright" roughly with his tongue, burying his hot face in her neck and between her breasts and moving his hands swiftly and hungrily over her. Like a drowning man he groaned, "Oh, baby, baby—"

"Starr Bright" eased her neck and head away from her lover's fumbling caresses, cautious he might dislodge her wig; the human-hair miracle-wig that fitted her head snug as a bathing cap. He'd slapped her pretty hard there in the casino and her lip was swelling but in the urgency of the moment she wasn't thinking of it; anyway, other men had struck her and she'd survived; and maybe deserved being struck now and then for *you're a cunt, you know it* and she guessed she knew and accepted this judgment for hadn't she abandoned her own baby years and years ago, wished even to drown her own baby years and years ago and the very memory by now vague and faded like a Polaroid snapshot too long exposed to light. But, oh, God: if he would let her alone and she could shower and cleanse herself and fall into bed and sleep, sleep. The sweet sleep of dreamless sinless oblivion. The sweet druggy-alcohol sleep like dying. And next day he could withdraw cash with his credit card and they would hit another casino, another craps table, and just maybe win, and win big. Because it did seem plausible to her that Earl Tunley deserved to win back the $27,000 he'd lost; he'd been winning, he'd been on a roll, and it had been taken from him unfairly. For this was gambler's logic and it was "Starr Bright's" logic in her innermost heart. *That which you sow, you shall reap.*

And when her lover got back the $27,000 that was rightfully his, she would share in it, too.

It seemed to be dawn. Hazy tendrils of flame in the eastern sky. The venetian blinds of room nineteen, at the far end of the long graceless concrete-block Golden Sands Motor Lodge, were tightly drawn. On top of the TV was a nearly empty bottle of Jim Beam, and greedy Earl Tunley snatched it up and gulped its contents like a thirsty man. And "Starr Bright" sighed, and was going to make a practical suggestion about a little sleep, and suddenly Earl turned on her, cursed her, "—told you not to fuck me up, didn't I?" and when she protested he grabbed her, and they struggled, and he said, grunting, "—could smash your face, cunt—make you ugly like you deserve! Strangle you—" and she was too terrified to scream for help, knowing that no one would hear, no one would wish to hear, and she was too weak suddenly to defend herself as the man pushed her backward, threw her onto the rumpled bed, and reached with grasping fingers up inside the tight lamé skirt to take possession.

God help me.

Waking with difficulty, her head aching, pounding where he'd struck it repeatedly against a wall. Slowly she disentangled herself from the snoring man, cautious of waking him. His hairy sweaty limbs had been flung over her, pressing her to the bed; his heavy torso, slack belly. And how heavy his head, his eyes shut upon a thin crescent of white-like mucus. Eddy? Earl? Though knowing he had surely lied to her she saw again a fleeting vision of chalk-white cliffs— Council Bluffs, Iowa? Her mouth throbbed with pain, the lower lip was grotesquely swollen. Like a bee sting she'd had as a child, and her sister Lily had said *Oh, I wish the nasty bee would sting me, too!* Her left eye, too, was swollen—he must have punched her there. And the nipples of both breasts had been pinched, hard. He hadn't removed her dress but had pushed it up to nearly her armpits. He'd threatened to kill her if she screamed and perhaps he had killed her, it was not "Starr Bright" but her child-spirit Rose of Sharon who awakened in her now. *Because the spirit cannot be extinguished, the spirit liveth and abideth forever.*

The man stirred, groaned as if in pain—but didn't wake. A wet whistling snore issued from his slack mouth. Except for black silk socks on his feet, the lower half of his body was stark naked; his shirt was unbuttoned and open upon a fattish-muscular chest covered in isolated wirelike hairs. The skin was creased, the color of rancid lard. No beauty here. Only the glittering gold chain around his neck.

Recalling in shame how he'd jeeringly offered her that gold chain. As if he'd thought her a prostitute. Why hadn't she fled him, then!

Pig, fornicator, and despiser of women.

Emissary of Satan.

"Starr Bright" extricated herself from the man who'd raped her, beaten her, threatened death. It was just 7 A.M. She'd been unconscious for more than an hour. A fierce fiery light penetrated the slats of the window blind and the crack beneath the door. "Starr Bright' tried to smooth down her dress, which was badly stained, torn at the shoulder. In the bureau mirror she saw her wavering, cringing reflection. Yet the .ed wig was still in place. Her makeup had been rubbed virtually off, her face was white, pinched-looking, sickly; her left eye blackened, her lower lip swollen to twice its normal size. *Is that me? Is that who I've become? God, have mercy . . .*

"Starr Bright" would have slipped from the room and left behind the snoring man except: headed for the door, she stumbled upon the man's jacket on the floor, and stubbed her toe against something heavy in an inside pocket.

She investigated, and discovered—a pistol.

A pistol! It shone like blue steel, with a short barrel of about four inches; compact, and deadly. "Starr Bright" stared at it in astonishment. She knew little about guns, she'd held a gun in her hand upon occasion but had never fired one and could not have identified this except to know that it was a revolver, each bullet in its chamber in the revolving cylinder. What a good clean metallic venal about it.

Its make was Ruger. Of this, she'd never heard.

As soon as the pistol was in her hand, "Starr Bright" felt a deep suffusion of relief. Though her hand visibly trembled, and her head and body were encased in pain. She understood that the child Rose of Sharon would be protected now, inviolate. "Starr Bright" knew that the man could not hurt her now. God had gifted her with unexpected power over the man.

"Thank you, God! Praise God!"

In other pockets of the jacket she discovered the man's wallet, and a badge, and a law officer's ID, with a photo: ERNEST D. FENKE DEPUTY SHERIFF SUMNER CO. NEBRASKA.

"Deputy sheriff—!"

And now she began to laugh. "Starr Bright" hooked up with a cop! An off-duty cop, one of the enemy.

You never could predict God's designs. For the God of wrath was also a God of jokes, tricks. You had to have a sense of humor to comprehend Him.

Playful as a mischievous child, "Starr Bright" affixed the shiny brass badge to the gold lamé fabric above her left breast. It snagged in the material, but held. Wild! She stood very tall in her bare feet, tall enough it seemed to brush the ceiling of the room with her head. She was suffused with strength and joy like a sudden fountain of clear, pure water; almost, she could stand on her tiptoes, a graceful ballerina.

"Wake up."

She was standing above the snoring man, gripping the pistol in both hands to steady it. She'd released the trigger guard and cocked the hammer. She'd spoken calmly, with assurance; though very excited; when the snoring man failed to wake, she prodded his shoulder with the gun barrel. His eyes flew open, at first unfocused. Then he saw her. Saw the gun. The badge above her left breast.

She said, smiling, "'Deputy Sheriff Ernest D. Fenke, of Sumner County, Nebraska.' You are under immediate arrest."

Fenke blinked rapidly as if a bright light was being beamed into his bloodshot eyes. A look of incredulity tightened his features, a stab of quick fear. The worst thing that could happen to a cop had happened to him: His gun had been taken from him. He said, "H-Hey! Honey! Don't kid around with that—"

"Deputy Fenke, get up."

"Jesus, look—honey? Give that gun to me, it might go off and—you wouldn't want—"

"So you're a cop? That's your secret? 'Deputy Fenke of Nebraska'? Why'd you lie to me?"

"Please, honey—"

"You get to carry a gun, eh? Deputy Fenke? Persecute people? How many people has this gun killed, Deputy Fenke?"

"N-Nobody."

"You're a liar." "Starr Bright" spoke with a strange sort of authority. Her voice serene, glistening. As if the deep soothing peace coursing through her had brought with it an eloquence not her own; the purity of the child Rose of Sharon, that sweet clear delicate soprano voice.

"Out of bed, and on your knees. Now."

And he obeyed her. Groveling, cowardly like all such craven men—he obeyed her. It was fitting that the man, part-naked, should tremble before the woman, his pig-eyes shining with fear, awe, trepidation; his limp fleshy genitalia like a skinned baby creature prominent between pale trembling thighs. "Starr Bright" saw the logic of it, how God had once again guided her hand in His shrewd wisdom. A man, kneeling before a woman of such power, has become, by mock-miracle, *a woman.*

"Starr Bright" said, "You raped me, and you defiled me, and you stole my money from me, Deputy Fenke—*my* jackpot, *my* one thousand silver dollars. And now you must repay me."

Fenke pleaded, "Honey, I—I didn't mean to hurt you! Ever! I thought we were—just—" He gestured toward the bed as if to say just *fooling around, screwing around—nothing serious.*

It wasn't clear whether "Starr Bright" meant to arouse such fear in the man or whether, barefoot, her gold lamé dress riding up to her thighs, the glinting badge on her left breast, she was being playful, seductive in a new way. In almost an incantatory voice she said, "Rapist. Filthy pig. And thief—common thief, Deputy! Taking my jackpot from me when you'd promised it was mine to keep."

"Honey, I'll pay you back—I was going to pay you back—"

"You were, Deputy?"

"—I was going to draw $5000 on my credit card tomorrow. Get back into action, the two of us—"

"That's the truth? You lied to me once, Deputy Fenke, why should I believe you now?"

"Baby, I didn't lie to you. I was maybe drinking too much—I got carried away. I'm crazy about you."

"Yes? That's why you raped me?"

On his knees, trembling before her, the man tried to

smile. A sick guilty feeble smile. Staring at "Starr Bright" with his bloodshot eyes as if trying not to see the pistol in her hands, aimed at his face; trying not to acknowledge that he saw it. He was saying, "I—didn't r-rape you, honey. That's a terrible thing to say. I would never force a w-woman——"

"No?" "Starr Bright" indicated her swollen lip, her throbbing eye. Lifting her skirt to show bruises, welts. Torn black-lace panties.

And the man gaped at her miserably. Could only shake his head as if in honest befuddlement. *I? I did such a thing? No!*

"Starr Bright" began an interrogation. Asking the man did he love her and he said quickly sure, oh, sure he was crazy about her! She asked was she beautiful in his eyes and he said eagerly oh, yes, yes, she was beautiful—"Baby, you know it! You're terrific." And she said coyly, redheads were his good luck, yes? Was she his good luck? and Fenke was nodding yes, emphatically yes when in a gesture of triumph "Starr Bright" yanked off the red human-hair wig, revealing her ashy-blond hair flattened and matted, pinned in unflattering clumps around her head. And Deputy Fenke's slack pale hung-over face showed yet more astonishment, incredulity.

Slyly "Starr Bright" asked, *"Am* I beautiful, Deputy?"

He'd swallowed hard, and was stammering, "Y-Yes . . ."

"Starr Bright" laughed in delight. Like the cruelly prankish girl she'd been long ago. Rose of Sharon who was the unpredictable Donner sister but of course you forgave little Sharon, she was so vivacious, so beautiful. Taunting the man now, "Crazy about me, eh?"

"Yes . . ."

Laughing heartily at the look on his face. Sick sinking flailing look of a man who's trapped. It was cruel, it was heartless, such taunting, but she could not resist. "Say, Deputy, a law officer is supposed to be observant. How old d'you think I am?"

"I—don't know—"

"When you picked me up last night, put your moves on me, what age were you estimating?"

"I—don't know—"

"Starr Bright" laughed even more loudly, thoroughly enjoying this interrogation. "I'll be thirty-seven, my next birthday."

Fenke laughed nervously. "That's—not old. I'm thirty-nine . . ."

"Would you have picked me up, if you'd known my age, Deputy Fenke?"

"Yes!"

"You *do* think I'm a beautiful woman?—desirable?"

"Baby, I'm crazy about you—I said. Only please—maybe you should give me the gun now? So nobody gets hurt? And we can get dressed, and go out, and I'll get some cash, and—"

Fenke was reaching out toward her, hesitantly; in appeal; but "Starr Bright" stepped away, frowning. She waved the pistol at him.

"No! Stay right where you are, mister. Or I swear I will shoot you right in the face."

"Jesus, Cheryl—"

" 'Sherrill.' "

"—S-Sherrill. I meant to say."

"My name is 'Starr Bright.' "

" 'Starr'—?"

"You never saw 'Starr Bright' dance. You aren't the one—that was another one—did you know him? 'Cobb.' " For a moment she was confused in time; the men were confused, interchangeable; perhaps in fact they were the same man. It seemed to "Starr Bright" that in some mysterious way the men, or the man, knew her; and knew his ineluctable fate. So they might discuss it together calmly, as if reminiscing. "They said in the papers, on TV—'Starr Bright' slashed a man's throat and danced barefoot in his blood. Drew the sign of the star in pig's blood on a wall. I don't know if it's truth or falsehood, it was something that happened in Sparks, Nevada, at a certain hour and it was not a choice." The memory of what had happened in that other motel room in the desert was as blurred as tissue in water; this man's frightened dough-face was a barrier between her and the memory. Or perhaps it was no memory at all, perhaps she'd only read about it in the *Las Vegas Post* and studied the photographs of Cobb and the blood-smeared wall. She said, smiling, "Oh, that one bled like a stuck pig, he *was* a stuck pig. All of you—*pigs.*"

'W-What are you saying, Sherrill?"

"Cobb. You know—'PIG DEATH.' It was written up in all the papers, it was on TV."

Fenke stared at her, his eyes glazing over in horror. In a hoarse voice he said, "You're kidding, aren't you? My God."

"Starr Bright" laughed in girlish delight. How like performing before an audience this was. She'd known, at age thirteen, this would be her life.

She told Fenke how, immediately, she'd liked him; he'd stepped forward to offer her a cigarette in a moment of need, a weak moment of hers and she'd been grateful to him. She had a hopeful heart, she was a professional singer-dancer and yet a woman who craved love; a woman who wanted to be respected, treated right. And she'd thought, at first, for a while last night, that he was the man for her. "But then you spoiled it, Deputy. You raped me, and you defiled me. And you stole my $1000."

"I—I—I'm sorry—oh, God, Sherrill, I'll make it up to you, I promise—"

"You *are* sorry? That's the truth? You won't do it again?—hurt me again?"

"Honey, I promise."

"You apologize? On your knees? To me? And to all the women you've defiled in your life?" As Fenke nodded with pathetic eagerness, "Starr Bright" continued to point the pistol at his head. She said, "Your wife?—do you have a wife? Yes? Back in Sumner County, Nebraska?" Fenke nodded, his eyes snatching at hers guiltily. "You apologize to her, too? You, an adulterer? Fornicator? How many times, Deputy? You apologize on your knees to all the women you've defiled? You beg forgiveness from them, and from God?"

"Y-Yes . . ."

"And you'll pay me back my $1000 jackpot?"

"Yes! I'll withdraw $5000 from my account right now, Sherrill. Let me get dressed, and we can go out and find a bank—"

"Stay on your knees. Why should I trust you, Deputy?"

"Please, you can trust me. . . ."

"Why should I believe you? Any word out of your mouth? You say you're sorry? But men are never sorry."

"Sherrill, baby, I *am* sorry . . ."

"Starr Bright" was speaking more rapidly, in her high sharp soprano voice like flashing shears.

"Men are masks of Satan, never sorry. They can't get it up unless they hurt women."

"No, no! I'm not like that," Fenke said desperately. "Jesus, I got a daughter—I'm the father of a daughter. I'm not like that."

"Father of a daughter?—*you?*"

"Please, honey, let me make it up to you? Give me the gun, and nobody will get hurt. . . ."

"Starr Bright" stood staring at the man. This part-naked man on his knees. But his shoulders were straighter now, his head higher. He seemed less afraid. *Father of a daughter—him?* A terrible clarity was opening in her brain, a tiny pinprick of light like a distant star rushing closer. Almost softly she said, "You won't be angry with me, if I give you back your gun?"

"No! I promise, Sherrill."

Fenke reached out hesitantly to accept the gun from "Starr Bright" and for a moment it almost seemed that she would surrender it to him. But there was a tawny light in her eyes, her smile slipped sideways like grease. Nimbly she sidestepped him, and raised the pistol higher to take aim between his eyes. She laughed. "And if I do? You won't change your mind and be cruel again? And hurt me again? And say you'll kill me?"

"Jesus, no. Honey, I was drunk. I didn't mean it."

"Because it's in your power, Deputy. You're a man, and a man's got the power. And 'Starr Bright' has no power. Only just this." She indicated the gun, smiling. "And if I surrender my power, what will stop you from hurting me again?"

"Sherrill, honey—no. I promise."

"Starr Bright" backed away to the air-conditioning unit near the window and turned the fan to high. She switched on the TV, loud. A morning talk show dissolved in peals of laughter switching abruptly to a jingly cartoon-bright advertisement for Sani-Flush.

Fenke blinked as if she'd slapped him. "W-what are you doing?"

"Deputy, tell me: Are you in a state of sin?"

"S-Sin?"

"Have you been washed in the blood of the lamb?"

"I—I was baptized—"

"Baptized what?"

"Catholic."

"Catholic! You! So—you believe?"

"I . . . I believe."

"In God, and in Jesus Christ?"

"Yes . . ."

"In Satan, and in sin?"

"Y-Yes . . ."

"You believe God is watching over you? At this moment?"

"Yes . . ."

"God would not allow harm to come to you, then. Unless it was his wish."

"Sherrill, please, honey. I said I was sorry. . . ."

"Starr Bright" spoke rapidly, and clearly, to be heard over the noises of the fan and the TV. "A man is a mask of Satan, Deputy, and maybe can't help himself. Like a scorpion. Born in sin and travail and lust and wickedness and a love of inflicting hurt on weaker creatures. Jesus saw, and didn't judge. He said, 'Forgive, and love they enemies as thyself.' But God says, 'I am a God of wrath, and none shall hide from my vengeance.'"

Now she was wrapping a towel carefully around the pistol, and around her hand that held the pistol. Until the tip of the barrel was only just visible.

Fenke said, in a quavering voice, "Why are you doing that, Sherrill? Baby, please—"

"'This is the Father's will which hath sent me.'"

"Sherrill—"

"One thing about Vegas, people mind their own business. You might hear women screaming—you might hear firecrackers—might even hear guns sometimes. But people respect each other's privacy." She was advancing upon the kneeling man dancerlike, knowing how, in his terror, she grew ever taller, more radiant. The light from her face alone was enough to blind him! He tried to shield the naked part of himself with his arms, and by cringing, hunching over; bringing his thighs closer together. As if ashamed of the fleshy thing between his legs, shrunken now, of the hue and texture of a slug. "My first boyfriend, the first boy I loved, I told you his name was Michael, but that was not his name. He raped me, took my love for him and defiled it. And shared me with his buddies. I was fifteen; never told a soul. Too ashamed. You count on us being shamed." She paused, breathing quickly. "A cop raped me once—more than once. In Miami, and in Houston. Cops prey on the weak because they have the power. All this fallen world *is,* Deputy, is those with power preying on those without. You made a mistake, Deputy. You stole 'Starr Bright's' $1000 jackpot."

A sickly jaundice-light shone in the man's eyes. He was begging, shivering. "Please, don't. Don't shoot me. . . ."

"Look, I'm a sinner, too. I am 'Starr Bright' and I am a fallen angel. My daddy warned me as a headstrong child and I failed to heed. My daddy was a man of God, a shining man of God and he spoke to his flock who adored him of the dark heart of mankind. He spoke of Jesus as his brother, and of Satan the fallen angel as his brother. The one walking at his right hand and the other walking at his left hand. I broke his heart, I betrayed my daddy's love. All the days of my life I am accursed. I have not seen that man in fifteen years. Wishing to drown my own baby girl in sickness and despair and lashing out at those who would forgive me, and love me." She wiped her tearful stinging eyes on her forearm. Her vision wavered as if about to be extinguished; then came into sharp, painful focus again. She saw the kneeling man cringe before her, yet saw his eyes ratlike and alert, waiting for an advantage. She said, slyly, "Well, Deputy—all I need is your credit card."

"Sherrill, no. I'm begging you . . ."

"For what?"

"My life . . ."

"Then down. *Down.*" She was moving, dancerlike, closer to him. The high-humming air-conditioner and the noise of the TV made the air jangle. If she stumbled, if she weakened—he would know. By instinct he would know. He was cringing, craven and terrified yet ratlike he would know. The fact excited her, like sex. Like sex as it had once been. In her ecstasy, in her exultation, she was drawing dangerously near to him. Whispering, "Pray for forgiveness from the Lord, and 'Starr Bright' will forgive you, too."

Fenke clasped his hands together clumsily, in an eager display of piety. His chest gleamed with sweat and his face was a mask of sweat, the creases in his forehead shining like metal.

In a stammering voice, a tremulously sincere-sounding voice, he began to pray, "Our F-Father who art in heaven—" then seemed to lose his breath, and needed encouragement, so "Starr Bright" said, "—hallowed be thy name—" and quickly he continued, "—h-hallowed be thy name—Thy k-kingdom—" and again he paused as if his throat had closed, and "Starr Bright" was obliged to lead him, as small children, years ago in Shaheen, New York, she and her sister Lily had been led tenderly and firmly in prayer by their parents, "—thy kingdom come, thy will—" and the man eagerly repeated, "—thy w-will be done—on earth as it is in—in—"

Suddenly then making his move. Lunging at her, trying to grab the gun. (But "Starr Bright" was prepared for this. Oh, yes: "Starr Bright" was prepared for this. As if she'd been watching the kneeling man from a far corner of the room, or from a distant prospect of time. Noting how, his head bowed, chin creased against his chest, he'd been watching her covertly, desperately, in an attempt to deceive.) "Starr Bright" gracefully sidestepped him and pulled the trigger, sending a bullet into her enemy's face.

Point-blank.

"Didn't I warn you, Deputy! Deputy-pig!"

A single deadly shot aimed at the bridge of her enemy's nose. A bullet piercing the man's flesh, his bone, plowing into his brain in an instant. He had no time to cry out, to turn away or duck. He deserved no time to prepare himself. The towel wrapped around the gun had only partly muffled the sharp, cracking sound, but "Starr Bright" believed she was in no danger, no one would hear; God would protect her as He'd protected her all along. She stood over her fallen enemy, panting in triumph, "Didn't I warn you, Pig-Deputy! Mask of Satan! All of you!"

But Deputy Fenke had collapsed, was dying, or dead. So swiftly, it had to be a miracle. His eyes were opened in astonishment and his lustrous-glassy gaze was fixed to hers—then fading, failing like a dimming light. "Starr Bright" bent to peer closely. Where was the man's soul?—had it departed his body? Was it already gone? Gone—where?

Soft now and spineless as a creature pried out of its shell to die on dry land the man lay at her feet. Her bare feet. She stepped back, out of the flow of blood. Blood flowing darkly from the single wound to his broken face and soaking into the cheap nylon carpet of what unknown room he'd brought her to, to rape her; what unknown cheap hotel in this Sodom and Gomorrah of the desert that God might strike with lightning to annihilate should He wish at any time. "Starr Bright" was trembling, panting. Her thoughts blasted clean. *For these are the days of vengeance, that all things which are written may be fulfilled.*

THE CONTRIBUTORS

John Edward Ames

Ames is a full-time writer living in New Orleans. He has more than thirty novels to his credit, recent titles including *Soldier's Heart*, *The Unwritten Order*, and *The Asylum*. His short story credits include *Hottest Blood* and *Borderlands 3*. Of his latest *Hot Blood* story, Ames commented, "Novelist John Barth once said, 'The key to the treasure is the treasure.' My story is a warning: Take very good care of the key."

Mike W. Barr

A long-time comic book writer of such series as *Camelot 3000*, *The Maze Agency*, and *The Outsiders*, Mike W. Barr nonetheless feels as though he is returning to his prose "roots" with his contribution to *Hot Blood 9*, since his first professional sale was to *Ellery Queen's Mystery Magazine*. He is currently working on a fantasy novel, as well as other projects. He describes "A Real Woman" as "my first prose treatment of a theme that cycles its way in and out of my work from time to time. I'm told that writing about an idea is a way of expelling it, but in this case I rather hope not—I've done okay by it."

Lawrence Block

Lawrence Block's novels range from the urban noir of Matthew Scudder *(A Long Line of Dead Men)* to the urbane effervescence of Bernie Rhodenbarr *(The Burglar Who Thought He Was Bogart)*. His articles and short fiction have appeared in *American Heritage, Redbook, Playboy, GQ,* and *The New York Times,* and he has brought out three collections of short stories. He is a Mystery Writers of America Grand Master, and a multiple winner of the Edgar, Shamus, Maltese Falcon, and Societé 813 awards. He lives in New York's Greenwich Village.

Ramsey Campbell

Campbell has been a multiple-award-winning author of horror fiction for more than thirty years. His works include *Scared Stiff, The Long Lost,* and *The One Safe Place.* The English resident's latest novel is *Nazareth Hill,* a ghost story.

Michael Garrett

The co-editor and co-creator of *Hot Blood* is an Alabama author and instructor of independent writing workshops across the nation. "'The Trouble with Hitchhikers' is reflective of my personal reaction to growing older," says Garrett. "My mind hasn't aged at the same rate as my body. Physically, I'm middle-aged, but mentally, I'm still in my twenties."

Jeff Gelb

California's Gelb got a special kick out of injecting (what he hopes is read as) humor into his latest *Hot Blood* submission, which he calls "Seinfeld meets Dragnet in the Millennium." His recent credits include a *Hot Blood* screenplay for a proposed film and the script for *Bettie Page Comics*.

Brian Hodge

Hodge is the author of nine novels, most recently *Prototype*. He has also published more than sixty short stories and two collections of his works. Of "Madame Babylon," he offered, "I'm drawn to Jungian notions such as the collective unconscious, and the idea of assigning a consciousness to a particular geography. That's been done since prehistory with the wild, untamed places of the earth, but I like doing it with cities and the quantum effects of all those people crammed inside."

Greg Kihn

After a series of successful rock recordings in the eighties, including "The Breakup Song" and "Jeopardy," rock star Greg Kihn turned to his love of horror fiction and decided to pursue his lifelong dream and become a novelist. *Horror Show* was published to excellent reviews in 1996, accompanied by Kihn's latest CD, also called *Horror Show*. His second novel, *Song of the Banshee*, was just published. When not writing or performing, Kihn can be heard on the morning show at KFOX in San Jose. A survivor of the early San Francisco rock scene, Kihn said his *Hot Blood* story was inspired by his early days on the streets. "It's Haight Ashbury 1967, and anything can happen. . . ."

Brian Lumley

Brian Lumley is the British author of the internationally best-selling *Necroscope* series, the tenth and final volume of which, *Resurgence,* was recently published by Tor Books. While the title of the current story might suggest otherwise, it has no connection with the series—though one of the characters might well have stepped right out of it! The story springs from a trip to Italy some years ago, where the opening incident was witnessed by the author. From there on, Lumley's imagination "just took over . . ." Or so he assures us. "Necros" has been bought for inclusion in an upcoming TV series here in the USA.

Joyce Carol Oates

Oates is the author of twenty-six novels and many volumes of short stories, poems, essays, and plays. Her recent novels include *Zombie* and *We Were the Mulvaneys.* She is the recipient of numerous national book awards. She lives in New Jersey, where she is the Roger S. Berlind Distinguished Professor in the Humanities at Princeton University.

Marthayn Pelegrimas

Pelegrimas's work has appeared in such anthologies as *Borderlands 3* and *Best of the Midwest II.* Two of her horror stories have been scripted and performed on the public radio program "Teknicolor Radio." She is currently editing *Hear the Fear,* an audio anthology of horror stories. Under a pseudonym, she also writes mysteries, including works for *Deadly Allies II, Lethal Ladies,* and *Vengeance Is Hers.* Her novel *Murder Is the Deal of the Day* is forthcoming in 1998.

Tom Piccirilli

New York's Piccirilli states that his third *Hot Blood* contribution was inspired by "wondering what it would be like if you were trapped with an old lover and a new, as the stress of leftover lust, rage, and bad blood rose to its own climax." Most of his seventy stories and six novels share the same fervent, emotional unease, including his latest mystery *The Dead Past* and collection *Inside the Works.*

Robert J. Randisi

Randisi has had twenty-six books published under his own name as well as some 270 others written under fourteen different pseudonyms. He has written in multiple genres, is the author of the Nick Delvecchio and Miles Jacoby private eye series, is the founder and executive director of the Private Eye Writers of America, the creator of the Shamus Award, and the co-founder of *Mystery Scene* magazine. He has edited sixteen anthologies, including several for audio treatment. His novel *In the Shadow of the Arch* will see print in 1997, along with its prequel, *Alone with the Dead.*

Stephen Solomita

Solomita is the author of ten novels of crime fiction, including the acclaimed Stanley Moodrow series. His next thriller, *Trick Me Twice,* will be published in early 1998.

Melanie Tem

Among Tem's novel credits are *Revenant, Desmodus, Wilding, Witch-Light,* in collaboration with Nancy Holder, and *Tides.* Her short fiction has recently appeared in *Worlds of Fantasy and Horror, Dark Angels, Gargoyles, Snapshots,* and *Cemetery Dance.* She lives in Colorado with her husband, writer and editor Steve Rasnic Tem. They have four children and two granddaughters.